Praise

Just Remember to Breathe

"I cried, I laughed, and I cried a little more....This book is too good to pass up, and I beg of you, please read it." - Adriane Boyd

"Poignant and sometimes emotionally overwhelming" - C.M. Truxler, The Literary Review

"I felt like I suffered a broken heart right along with these amazing characters." - Chrystle, The Indie Bookshelf

"I fell in love with this book from the first page. The characters will make you fall in love with them, the plot is superbly done and the story line is amazing." - Stephenie, The Indie Bookshelf

"The theme of healing and wholeness is stronger than the wreckage of war, stronger than the havoc of family misunderstandings." - Crystal Reviews

"I enjoyed this book immensely!" - Kindlehooked

"Raw and Beautiful" - Goodreads Review

"My heart broke over and over again for Dylan and Alex" - Amazon Reviewer

Republic

"Charles Sheehan-Miles is an exceptional writer" - *Midwest Book Review*

"Sheehan-Miles, already a good writer, has improved his impressive style...he writes sparse, clean narrative sentences. . .You care about his characters. As mentioned above, the blogosphere has gone wild over this book already... Pay attention to this new book... A lot of thought went into it. It might scare you into doing something productive for the nation, and for your future." - *Niagara Falls Reporter*

"This novel of America's future may be prophetic... It will disturb you...It should." - Kenneth J. Bernstein, *DailyKos*

"...a cracking story...one of America's criminally neglected authors" - Robert P. Beveridge, *Amazon.com Top 100 Reviewer*

Prayer at Rumayla

"...Honest and unsparing account...A much needed corrective..." - Seymour Hersh, Winner of the National Book Critics Circle Award and the Pulitzer Prize

"Bleak and disturbing... dead-on-target ...This first novel is a work of pure psychological conflict." – Gannett Newspapers

JUST REMEMBER TO BREATHE

8-10-13

Maria,

So wonderful
to meet you!

♡

BOOKS BY
CHARLES SHEEHAN-MILES

Fiction

Republic

Insurgent

Just Remember to Breathe

Prayer at Rumayla
A Novel of the Gulf War

NON-FICTION

Saving the World on $30 a Day:
An Activist's Guide to Starting, Organizing and Running
A Non-Profit Organization

JUST REMEMBER TO BREATHE

Charles Sheehan-Miles

Cincinnatus Press

CINCINNATUS PRESS
BETHESDA, MARYLAND

If you enjoyed this book, please share it with a friend, write a review online, or send feedback to the author!

WWW.SHEEHANMILES.COM

Published by Cincinnatus Press
Bethesda, Maryland
United States of America

ISBN-13: 978-0988273603

Printed in the United States of America
Cincinnatus Press
www.cincinnatuspress.com

v10232012

Acknowledgements

I'd like to thank my editor Shakirah Dawud for catching my errors in the final version.

Thanks to my awesome, wonderful beta readers: Patrick "Deuce the Two Cats" Patriarca, Barrie Suddery, Bryan James and Jackie Trippier Holt.

Finally, I want to personally thank Adriane Boyd, Tiffany King, Leslie Fear, Stephenie Thomas and all the gals at the Indie Bookshelf. Because of your willingness to go out on a limb and read the book and urge others to read it, *Just Remember to Breathe* has been far more successful than any other book I've written in the past. That couldn't have happened without such wonderful people telling their friends. I owe all of you, big time.

CHAPTER ONE

Broken Hearts and Coffee Mugs (Alex)

From the moment I put my mom's car in drive, my coffee mug still on the roof, I could tell it was going to be a rough day. The mug, which had been a cute gift from Dylan, went flying off the car and smashed into a million pieces. I gasped as I saw it spinning in the rearview mirror, falling in what seemed like slow motion until it hit the street, splattering my coffee and tiny pieces of porcelain across the road.

My eyes pricked into painful tears. Even though it had been more than six months since we'd spoken, even though he'd broken my heart, even though he'd refused all contact and ignored my letters, it still hurt.

I pulled to the side and took a deep breath. Dylan bought the mug from a vendor in Jerusalem, who had printed it right on the spot from a digital photo: the two of us together, holding each other as we stood waist deep in the Mediterranean Sea. In the photo, I had an astonishingly vacant expression on my face as we gazed into each other's eyes. In retrospect, I looked, and felt, as if I was on drugs.

Of course, Kelly had been telling me for six months it was time to get rid of the mug. Time to move on. Time to forget about Dylan.

I took a deep breath. Kelly was right. Yes, we'd had some problems. Yes, I'd gotten drunk, and said some things I regretted. But nothing unforgivable. Nothing that warranted his disappearing off the face of the planet.

I looked in the mirror and quickly repaired the damage from my involuntary tears, then put the car into drive. In two days, I was flying back to New York and my second year in college, and I'd damned well get a new coffee mug. I would just add that to the lengthy, overly detailed to-do list my mother had oh-so-helpfully provided, which was now sitting on the passenger seat of the car. New coffee mug. One that didn't have my past stamped all over it. Kelly would be proud.

I started to put the car into drive, but my phone chose that instant to ring, and I'm not very good at ignoring it, so I left mom's car in park and answered the phone.

"Hello?"

"Is this Alexandra Thompson?"

"Yes, this is Alex," I said.

"Hello. This is Sandra Barnhardt from the financial aid office."

"Oh," I said, suddenly tense. Some people you don't want calls from the day before school starts, and the financial aid office was way up at the head of that list.

"Um... what can I do for you?"

"I'm afraid I've got some bad news. Professor Allan is going on leave of absence, so your work study assignment has been cancelled."

Indefinite leave of absence? My guess was Professor Allan was going into rehab. I was pretty sure she was a cokehead my first day working for her. Whatever.

"So, um… what exactly does that mean?"

"Well… the good news is, we've got you a new assignment."

I couldn't wait to hear this. No doubt I'd be scrubbing pots in one of the dining halls. I waited, and then waited some more. "Um… maybe you could tell me what the assignment is?"

Sandra Barnhardt from the financial office coughed, possibly a little embarrassed.

"This is all last minute, you understand. But our author-in-residence this year has requested two research assistants. You'll be working for him."

"Oh… I see. Well, at least that sounds interesting."

"I hope so," she said. "Are you already back on campus?"

"No, I'm in San Francisco; I fly back day after tomorrow."

"Oh. Well, then. Stop by when you get back, and I'll get you the information about the assignment."

"Great," I said. "See you in a couple days."

Okay. I'll admit. It really did sound interesting. Author-in-residence. What exactly did that mean, anyway? Whatever it was, it had to be more interesting than doing Professor Allan's filing.

Whatever. I'd better get moving, I thought, or the cops would be along to move me along. I'd been sitting in front of someone's driveway for nearly ten minutes.

I pulled the car out to finish my errands. Time to get supplied for the new year. Starting with a new coffee mug.

#

"*Alex!*"

Kelly's cry was somewhere around 125 decibels and somewhere in the upper reaches of pitch possible to the human voice. That was compounded by the fact that she was bouncing up and down, as if she had tiny pogo sticks, or possibly jackhammers, attached to her feet.

She bounced over to me and grabbed me in a huge hug.

"Oh. My. *God!*" she shouted. "The summer was so boring with you gone. We are going out for drink. Right. Now."

I blinked, then said, "Um… can I get my bags inside first?"

I'd gotten up at 5 a.m. to catch the first flight out of San Francisco. Going east meant I'd basically lost an entire day: the flight landed at 4 p.m. at JFK. Then the long wait to get my bags, wait for a taxi, and fight the ridiculous traffic. I'd let myself into the dorm at 7 p.m.

"Well, of course!" she said. "But we can't lose any time!"

"Kelly…"

"I so have to tell you what happened with Joel. Yesterday he showed up here with no shirt on, and—"

"Kelly."

"—he's got a new tattoo. Which would be fine, except…"

"*Kelly!*" I finally shouted.

She stopped, as if I'd stuffed a plug in her mouth.

"Please," I said. "I've been up and traveling since five this morning."

"You don't have to yell at me," she said.

"I'm sorry. It's just... can we go out tomorrow? Or at least let me get a nap first? I'm seriously exhausted, and I need a shower."

She grinned. "Gotcha, of course. Nap. Sure. But then we are *so* going out. You need to meet Bryan."

What?

"Who is Bryan?"

"Good God, Alex, weren't you listening to anything I said?"

She continued as I dragged my bags inside. I loved Kelly. And she would have fit in great with my tribe of sisters back home. But God, couldn't she just shut up for *one second*?

I finally dumped my bags on the floor, then navigated around her. My bed, stripped since I'd flown home at the beginning of summer, looked inviting. I collapsed, feeling the weight of my body sink in. Kelly kept talking, but I was having trouble making sense of her words. I tried to nod at the appropriate times, but the world slowly faded to black. The last thought I remember before losing consciousness was my regret that I'd lost that damned mug.

#

Kelly woke me up an hour later and hustled me into the shower.

"I refuse to take no for an answer," she shouted. "It's time we cured you of your asshole ex-boyfriend!"

God, it was like she had the volume stuck on max.

I don't want to give the wrong impression of Kelly. Yes, she talks way too much. She's a girly-girl, in ways I've never been. Her side of the room is disgustingly pink, decorated with Twilight and Hunger Games posters, and she acts as if she's had more experience with guys than one of the girls posing on the back pages of the *Village Voice*.

My side of the room is mostly stacked in books. The truth is, I'm sort of a geek, and proud of it.

Kelly, though, she's shy as hell, and overcompensates by being super gregarious. She charges into the center of parties, dances like a wild woman, and does everything she can to drag me out of my shell.

Problem is, sometimes I don't really want to come out.

Once I got out of the shower and changed into a pair of black skinny jeans and a long-sleeved tee, she led me out. There was a party somewhere, she said, and we were going to go find it.

A Bad Idea (Dylan)

Coming here was a bad idea.

If I could go back up the chain of "if-only's" back to the source, I suppose the reason I was starting as a student at Columbia University is because one day when I was twelve Billy Naughton gave me a beer. Billy was a year older than me, and might have been a bad influence if my parents hadn't been somewhat worse. As it was, the effects of alcohol held little mystery for me, at least as viewed from the outside.

Viewed from the inside, though… that was another thing.

One thing led to another, and one drink led to another, and on my sixteenth birthday I dropped out of high school. Of course, by that time, Dad had left, and Mom had cleaned up her act. She laid down the law. If I wasn't going to school, I could just get out. She wasn't going to have her child turn out like her husband.

I went couch surfing. I slept in the park a couple times. I got a job, lost it, got another one, lost that one, too. And the damnedest thing was, Mom was right. I went back and registered for school. Then I showed up on her doorstep, showed her my registration and schedule, and she wept and let me back in the apartment.

A lot of other things happened since, of course, including me getting blown up by some hajis in Afghanistan. But I don't talk about that stuff so much. If you want to know, just read the papers.

Screw that. The papers never covered it right anyway. If you really want to know what it was like, walk into your kitchen right now. Grab a handful of sand. Close your eyes, stick your hand in the garbage disposal, and turn it on. That should give you a pretty good idea of what Afghanistan is like.

Anyway, long story short, Columbia apparently has a soft spot for reformed dropouts and combat veterans. So here I was, and it was the first day of classes, and I was pent up, tense as all hell, because the one person in the world I didn't want to see, the one person I wanted to see the most, all at the same time, well, she was here.

Thankfully, University Housing got me in with a couple of graduate engineering students. I don't think I could have stood living in the dorms with a bunch of eighteen-year-old freshmen right out of high school. I was only two years older, but two years was a world of difference. Especially when I'd seen my best friend killed right before my eyes. *Especially* when it was my fault.

When I got in town, I met my new roommates: Aiden, a bookish twenty-four-year-old mechanical engineering PhD candidate, and Ron, who introduced himself as "Ron White. Chemical engineering," then disappeared back into his room.

Perfect.

So here I was, limping across the street like an old man, my cane helping me stay upright. Some asshole yuppie bumped into me, in a hurry to get to his business meeting or his mistress or whatever the fuck it was he was after. Whatever it was, it precluded any common courtesy.

"Watch where the fuck you're going, asshole!" I shouted after him.

I was barely halfway across the street when the light changed. Jesus. Talk about humiliating. Most of the cars waited patiently, but a cabbie who looked like the cousin of the guy who blew away Roberts kept honking his horn at me. I gave him the finger and kept going.

Finally. Somewhere on the third floor of this building was my destination.

I was early, but that was for the best. For one thing, I'd gotten lost several times already today, and was late to my first two classes. This, however, I could not be late for. Not if I wanted to be able to pay for college. Of course, the VA was footing most of the bill, but even with the GI Bill a college like Columbia cost a hell of a lot. It still didn't even seem real that I was here. Like I really even belonged in college, much less in an Ivy. But every time I heard my Dad's cheerful voice in my head saying I was a little shit who would never amount to anything, I pushed forward.

The elevator, made sometime in the nineteenth century, finally made its way to the ground floor and I boarded. Most of the other students in the building were using the stairs, but I had to take this route if I wanted to get there before sunset.

I patiently waited. First floor. Second floor. It seemed like the elevator took five minutes for each short trip. It finally stopped on the third floor, and I pushed my way between the other people crowded in the elevator.

Out in the hall, it was crowded. *Jesus.* It was going to take a lot of getting used to being here. I looked around, trying to spot room numbers. 324. 326. Oriented, I turned in the opposite direction, looking for room 301.

I finally found it, tucked into a dark corner at the opposite side of the building. The hall down here was dark, one of the fluorescents burnt out. I reached for the door.

Locked. I checked my phone. I was fifteen minutes early. I could live with that. Better than fifteen minutes late. Slowly, I slid my book bag to the floor, and tried to figure out how to get myself down there without ending up sideways or upside down or something. I inched my way down, leaving my gimp leg slack and in front of me. Halfway down, I felt a sharp pain and muttered a curse. I put my hands to my sides, palms flat, and let myself drop.

Seated. Now the only trick would be getting back up. Carefully, I kneaded the muscles above my right knee. The doctors at Walter Reed said it might be years before I regained full function. If ever. In the meantime, I went to physical therapy three times a week, took lots of painkillers, and kept going.

I sighed. It had been a long, stressful day. I kept wondering if I should have stayed home, waited another year before trying to venture out. Doctor Kyne had urged me to go.

You'll never recover if you stay locked in at home. He wasn't talking about the leg. Doctor Kyne was my psychiatrist at the VA in Atlanta.

I suppose he knew what he was talking about. In the meantime, just take it a day at a time, an hour at a time, one minute at a time. This moment. Just get through now. Then the next now. I took out a book, a beat-up, nearly shredded paperback Roberts loaned me before he got blown away. *The Stand* by Stephen King.

It's the best fucking book ever, Roberts had said.

I'm not so sure it was all that, but I had to agree it was pretty good. I was buried in the midst of reading about the outbreak of the super-flu when I heard footsteps coming up the hall. They were clicking. A girl, wearing heels or wedges or something. I forced myself not to look up. I didn't want to talk to anyone anyway. I wasn't feeling very friendly. And besides, my instinct was to watch everyone, to keep my eyes on pockets and loose clothes and mounds of trash beside the road and anything else that might represent danger. The challenge was to *not* look. The challenge was to live my life just like everyone else. And everyone else didn't look at approaching girls as a source of danger.

What can I say? I was wrong.

"Oh, my God," I heard a murmur. Something inside me recognized the tone and timbre of that voice, and I looked up, my face suddenly flushing as I felt my pulse in my forehead.

Forgetting about the gimp leg, I tried to jump to my feet. Instead, I ended getting halfway up, then the leg gave out. As if it was cut off, not there. I fell down, hard on my right side, and let out a shout when the sharp, tearing pain shot up my right leg, straight up my spine.

"Son of a bitch!" I muttered.

I pushed myself more or less upright, then put a hand to the wall and the other hand on my cane and tried to lift myself.

The girl of my nightmares darted forward and tried to help me get up.

"Don't touch me," I said.

She jerked back as if I'd slapped her.

Finally, I was in a standing position. The pain didn't go down, and I was sweating, hard. I didn't look at her. I couldn't.

"Dylan," she said, her voice quavering.

I grunted something. Not sure what, but it wasn't terribly civilized.

"What are you doing here?" she asked.

I finally looked up. Oh shit, that was a mistake. Her green eyes, which had always caught me like a fucking whirlpool, were huge, like pools. The faintest scent of strawberry drifted from her, making me lightheaded, and her body still arrested attention: petite, curved hips and breasts; as always, she was like a fantasy.

"I'm waiting for an appointment," I said.

"Here?" she asked.

I nodded. "Work-study assignment," I said.

She started to laugh, a bitter, sad laugh. I'd heard that laugh before. "You have got to be kidding me," she said.

Nothing significant at all (Alex)

*I*t was late when I got to the Arts and Sciences building, and I ran up the six flights of steps to the third floor, knowing the elevator would take forever. I checked my phone. It was three o'clock. I needed to get there right now.

I counted down the room numbers, finally reaching a dark hall. The light was out at the end of the hall, casting the area in not quite darkness. There it was, room 301. Next to the door, a student sat, his head resting on his fist, face turned away from me. He was reading a book.

I took a breath. His hair reminded me of Dylan's, but shorter, of course. That, and his arms were... well, very muscular, and he was tanned. This guy looked like someone out of a catalog. Not that I went fainting over guys with big biceps, but seriously, a girl can look, right?

As I approached though, I felt my heart begin to thump in my chest. Because the closer I got, the more he looked like Dylan. But what would *he* be doing *here?* Dylan, who had broken my heart, then disappeared as if he'd never existed, his email deleted, Facebook page closed, Skype account gone. Dylan, who had erased himself from my life all because of a stupid conversation that shouldn't have happened.

I slowed down. It couldn't be. It just... couldn't be.

He took a breath and shifted position slightly, and I gasped. Because sitting in front of me was the boy who'd broken my heart. Quietly, I said, "Oh, my God."

He jumped to his feet. Or rather tried to. He got about halfway up, and a look of excruciating pain swept across his face and he fell down, hard. I almost cried out, as he tried to force his way back up. I started forward to help, and he said his first words to me in six months: "Don't touch me."

Typical. I had to stuff down the hurt that threatened to burst to the surface.

He looked... different. Indefinably different. We hadn't seen each other face to face in almost two years, not since the summer before my senior year in high school. He'd filled out, of course. In all the right places. His arms, which I vividly remembered being held in, had doubled in size. The sleeves of his tee shirt looked like they were going to burst. I guess the Army does that for you. His eyes were still the same piercing blue. For a second I met them, then looked away. I didn't want to get trapped in those eyes. And damn it, he still smelled the same. A hint of smoke and fresh ground coffee. Sometimes when I walked into a coffee shop in New York, I'd get an overwhelming sensation that he was there, just from the smell. Sometimes memory sucks.

"Dylan," I said. "What are you doing here?"

"I'm waiting for an appointment."

"*Here?*" I asked. That was crazy.

He shrugged. "Work-study assignment."

No. No way.

"Wait a minute... are you saying you're in school here?"

He nodded.

"What happened to the Army?" I asked.

He shrugged, looked away, then gestured toward the cane.

"So of all the schools you could have chosen, you came here? To the same place as me?"

Anger swept over his face. "I didn't come here for you, Alex. I came here because it was the best school I could get in to. I came here for me."

"What, did you think you could just show up and sweep me back into your arms after ignoring me for the last six months? After erasing me from your life?"

He narrowed his eyes, looked at me directly. In a cold voice, he said, "Actually, I was hoping I just wouldn't run into you."

I stifled a sob. I was *not* going to let him get to me. I spat back, "Well, looks like we both had some bad luck. Because I'm here for my work-study assignment, too."

His eyes widened. "You're going to be working for Forrester?"

"Is he the so-called *author in residence?*"

He nodded.

"Oh, God," I said. "I'm going to be sick."

"Thanks. It's great to see you too, Alex."

I almost shouted at him, but a jovial voice down the hall called to us. "Hello! You two must be my new research assistants!"

A ridiculous looking man, trying way too hard to look like an *author* with a capital A, walked toward us. He wore a tweed jacket, with leather patches on the elbows, and corduroy pants. He couldn't have been much older than thirty-five, but he wore reading glasses perched halfway up his nose.

"Well, hello," he said. "I'm Max Forrester."

"Alex Thompson," I said. I glanced at Dylan. He was glaring at me.

"Dylan Paris," he said.

"Come in, Alex and Dylan. My apologies for being late. Sometimes I get lost in the throes of creation and forget the time."

Forrester's back was already to me as he unlocked his door. I rolled my eyes. Lost in the throes of creation, indeed. You could smell the whiskey on his breath from fifteen feet away. Smelled like he'd gotten lost in the nearest watering hole.

Dylan waved me ahead of him. He was leaning heavily on the cane. *What happened to him?* I walked in behind Forrester, and Dylan followed me, limping.

"Sit down, you two, sit down. Can I get you some tea? Water? Or something with a little more, um... life?"

"No thanks," Dylan said, grimacing as he eased himself into his seat. Once seated, he leaned his cane against the wall. His expression was unreadable.

"I'll take some water," I said, just to contradict *him.*

Forrester filled up a small glass with water at a tiny sink in the back of the office and brought it to me. My eyes narrowed a little when I got a look at the glass. It was filthy. Eww. And there was something oily floating on top of the water.

I pretended to take a sip, then set it on the edge of the desk.

"Well, let's get down to business," Forrester said. "Do you two know each other?"

"No," I said, forcefully, just as Dylan said, "Yes."

Forrester liked that. A smile lit up on his face, then he said, "I bet there's a story there."

"You'd be wrong," I replied. I glanced at Dylan, and said, "Nothing significant at all."

Dylan blinked, and he darted his eyes away from me.

Good. Part of me wanted to hurt him just as badly as he had hurt me.

Unfortunately, Forrester picked up on it. He said, very slowly, "I trust there won't be a problem."

"No, no problem," I said.

"No, sir," Dylan responded, his voice cool.

"Well then," Forrester said. "That's good. So, let me tell you what you'll be doing. I'm here for a year, and I'm working on a novel. Historical fiction, centered around the draft riots here in New York during the Civil War. Are you familiar with them?"

I shook my head, but Dylan said, "Yes. Sad story... some of it turned to lynch mobs."

Forrester nodded, enthusiastically. "That's right. Miss Thomas... the story is this. In July 1863, there was a series of riots here in the city. Mostly poor and working-class Irish, protesting because the rich could buy exemption from the draft. The protests turned ugly, then violent. A lot of people were killed."

"They burned down the orphanage," Dylan said. What a brownnoser.

"That's right, Dylan! The colored orphanage burned to the ground. A dozen or more black men were lynched during the riots."

"So..." I said. "What exactly will we be doing to help?"

"Well, you see, Columbia has a mass of historical material about the riots. Much of it primary sources. As I work on my outline and the actual manuscript, your job will be to help me with the details. The historical context, the source material, all of the information I'll need to get the story just right."

"That's... incredible," Dylan said. "No offense, Doctor Forrester, but this is way better than I expected as a work-study assignment."

Oh, God. This was going to be one long year.

CHAPTER TWO

I felt like an impostor (Dylan)

The last time I saw Alex... or at least her image on Skype... I took my laptop and smashed it. When that didn't do sufficient damage, I took it outside the tent, out to the edge of the camp, and fired a thirty-round magazine through it. Needless to say, that attracted some unwanted attention.

Sergeant Colton convinced the old man not to court-martial me. I did, however, get confined to the barracks for thirty days, a moot point since we were in the middle of the boonies in Afghanistan, and extra duty, which was most definitely not moot, since that mostly meant filling sandbags.

In any event, it didn't matter much, because the next day I was in the passenger seat of our hummer when we rode over a bomb, and I didn't need a computer much for a while after that. I got smashed up pretty bad, and got my best friend killed.

Point is, Alex always evoked, um, strong emotions, from the very first time I laid eyes on her.

We met almost three years ago: my senior year in high school and her junior year. And to be blunt: it changed my life, in ways I can't really measure.

But to understand that, you have to understand how we got there in the first place. For me, it's kind of a backup problem. As in, for each part of the story, you have to back up to an earlier part. I was at Columbia because I got blown up, and I got blown up because I volunteered for the Infantry when I enlisted in the Army, and that happened because of the first time she broke up with me, which was... you get the point. So to have this make any sense at all to you, I have to work my way back to high school.

I was a lousy student, but I'm not stupid. I can add, and when my mom kicked me out of the house, I had to add minimum wage to minimum wage, and it didn't come up to nearly enough to pay rent on an apartment, much less rent and something crazy like food. Plus, the guys I was hanging out with... let's just say, they weren't shining lights of humanity.

So I cleaned up my act. I quit drinking. Quit smoking dope. I still smoke cigarettes, but everybody's gotta have one vice. And I went back to high school. Problem was, I was behind, way behind. When I registered for school again, I went to see the principal of my high school and explained my situation.

The first question he asked me was, "Where are your parents?"

I sighed. "I'm sort of homeless at the moment," I replied. "But that's not permanent. Look... I don't want to involve them in me going back to school. I guess I need to prove to my mom that I can do this on my own. Maybe I need to prove it to myself, too."

He understood. And backed me, all the way. And much to my surprise (and my mother's) I got nearly straight *As*.

At the end of the year, he called me into his office.

"Listen," he said. "I want to tell you about a program we've got. Every year, the city sends half a dozen students as part of a national program to visit several other countries. Sort of an ambassador, exchange program. You've been nominated."

I was in shock. *Me?*

"Isn't that for the smart kids who didn't get in trouble?" I asked.

"You are one of the smart kids, Dylan."

I noted he didn't address the trouble part.

"Look, Dylan, all I'm saying is... it's a hell of an educational opportunity. I think you should apply."

"Okay," I said, not really believing it. "What do I do?"

"Write an essay. Here's the application packet. Explain in your essay why you should have the opportunity."

I took the packet home, and read over it. To be honest, I was terrified. Seriously. I came from a blue-collar family, with a drunk for a dad, a recovering drunk for a mom, and well... I was a screwup. I'd be competing with kids with 4.0 grade point averages, kids who were planning to go to Harvard and Yale and other places I couldn't dream of. But, I wrote the essay. I wrote about growing up with drunks, and becoming one myself. I wrote about putting myself back into school, and catching up with my class. I wrote about how important getting an education was, from the point of view of someone who'd worked the stupid no-skill minimum-wage jobs just to keep myself in food while I was in between homes.

And you know what? Somehow, I got accepted into the program. Next thing I knew, I'd been selected as one of half a dozen kids from Atlanta who would be traveling to Israel for two months.

And that is how I met Alex.

The first time I saw her was right before we left for Israel. I guess there were about forty of us, sitting in a big room at Hunter College on Staten Island. She was clear across the room from me, and that first sight of her is etched in my memory forever. Long brown hair, parted in the middle and flowing down her back. Green eyes that caught me from across the room. Slightly olive skin, full lips. I'm not exaggerating to say that she was the most beautiful woman I'd ever seen. She was so far out of my league that I didn't even bother to approach her. The fact was, all of these kids were out of my league. Some of them downright brilliant, all of them studious, hard-working kids who had busted their asses for the chance to take part in this program. Frankly, I felt like an impostor.

Not that that was going to stop me from going. When we got on the plane for Tel Aviv the next morning, by lucky chance that would change my life, I ended up seated next to the beautiful green -eyed girl I'd watched the night before.

"Hi," I said. "I'm Dylan."

"Alex," she responded.

Alex. I rolled the name around in my head. I liked it.

"Where are you from, Alex?"

"San Francisco," she said.

"Really? Wow. I'm from Atlanta, Georgia. Never been out west."

She smiled, and I did my best to remain nonchalant. Which was difficult. Really difficult, because her eyes were just... entrancing. It was like getting drunk, but the good kind, with no hangover.

"This was my first trip east, actually," she said.

"Tell me about yourself, Alex."

She sat back. "That's a pretty open-ended question."

"I guess. Let me start over. I'm Dylan, and I have lousy social skills. I'd like to get to know you by asking stupid questions. How's that?"

She giggled, and I almost died.

"Tell you what," she said. "I'll ask a question. Then you ask one. Then I'll ask one. Got it? They have to be specific. And you can't lie."

I tried my best to look wounded. "Do I look like someone who would lie?"

"Silly. Your questions are supposed to be about me."

This time I laughed. "All right. Hmm... you're from San Francisco... Do you ever ride on those silly street cars?"

"Never," she said. "Those are for tourists."

"Ahh," I said. "Figures. Your turn."

"Okay... Hmm... what's your favorite subject in school?"

I had to think about that one for a second. "Well ... it used to be drama, but I'm not taking any electives any more. I'd have to answer English. I love writing."

"Really? What do you write?"

"That's two questions. It's my turn."

"Oh," she said. She grinned. "Fair enough. Your turn."

I tried to think of a good question, but it was hard. For one thing, she kept looking at me, and those eyes! Plus, I kept smelling a hint of strawberry. Why the hell did she smell like strawberries? Was it her hair? Whatever it was, it was tantalizing. This girl scared the hell out of me.

"What's your favorite memory?"

She sat back and thought, then a beautiful, huge smile came across her face.

"Easy," she said. "When I was ten, we were living in Moscow. And my father let me go for the first time to an official function. It was... glamorous. All the men and women were in ball gowns and tuxedos, and my mom took me out and got me fitted for my own gown. When the dancing started, my father took me out and danced with me."

"Moscow? Holy shit! What were you doing there?"

"My dad was Foreign Service. And no fair, that's an extra question."

Her dad was in the Foreign Service, she said casually. Holy shit. Way out of my league.

"Oh, rats, sorry. Okay... you get two questions."

"All right... What scares you more than anything else in the world?"

You do, I almost said.

I took a deep breath, then I said, honestly, "Ending up like my dad. He was a drunk."

Her face took on a look of... sadness? Pity? I didn't want pity. She changed the subject.

"What's the best thing you've ever done?" she asked.

"The best thing? Hmm..." I had to think for a bit. I slowly mulled it over, then said, "I was homeless for a while. Dropped out of school. Anyway, sometimes I didn't know where I was going to sleep, or get something to eat. One night I was riding on MARTA... that's our subway... just back and forth, trying to get some sleep on the train before they shut down for the night. They shut down the train at 2 a.m., and I was stuck downtown, and I ran into a family. All of them were homeless, like me. Parents, two kids. The dad had lost his job. And I was working, and had a little bit of money. So I treated them to dinner at Waffle House. It wasn't much... maybe twenty dollars. But you could tell the kids hadn't been eating much at all. They were so... grateful."

I squeezed my eyes shut. Those kids were... overwhelming. Overwhelming in their need, and in their love for their parents, and... just overwhelming.

Alex looked at me like I was from Mars. "You were homeless?" she asked, very quietly.

"No, that was already two questions. My turn." I thought, then blurted out, "Why do you smell like strawberries?"

She blushed, a deep red. *Oh. My. God.* Why did I ask that? *Idiot!*

Finally, she spoke, a shy smile on her face. "It's um, my shampoo. I like strawberries. I wear strawberry lip gloss, too."

My turn to freak. Because the thought of her, and strawberry lip gloss, was too much to contemplate. Her lips were perfectly curved, the lower one slightly pouty. And, to be honest, every time I looked at her body it made me want to touch her. Anywhere. Everywhere.

"My turn," she said, turning toward me. She had a mischievous look on her face. "Do you have a girlfriend?"

Alarm bells were screeching in my head. I said, "Um... not exactly. I've been seeing a girl, but not sure where it's headed. If anywhere."

She smiled.

I smiled.

"What about you?" I asked. "Is there a boyfriend?"

"Sort of," she said. "I'm dating a guys named Mike. I don't know if it's serious or not, either."

I swallowed. She had a Mike back home. I had a Hailey back home. And this trip was only two months anyway. My brain was telling me, *Stay the hell away, Dylan!* But let's be honest. I've never been that smart anyway.

Crying: Not. Going. To. Happen. (Alex)

Okay, look, I'm not exactly an emotional basket case or anything. Not a drama queen. But Dylan had been a big part of my life for a long time. And sitting there next to him in Doctor Forrester's office was literally torture.

When the appointment was over we got up, awkwardly. Forrester shook our hands. I turned and left, without a word, while Dylan was still trying to figure out how to get out of his chair and collect himself.

I went straight to the Financial Aid office.

The office was packed, of course. Beginning of the school year, and people were trying to sort out their financial aid. Every single person who had a problem just had to choose that moment right then to go to Financial Aid to get it sorted out. So when I asked to see Sandra Barnhart, I was told to take a seat. And I waited. And waited. And waited.

She finally let me into her office. She was exhausted. Hair frazzled, her desk was stacked high with papers. When I entered the room she was fishing the last pills out of a bottle of Tylenol.

Not a good sign.

"Hi, there, what can I do for you."

"Hi... I'm Alex Thompson. We spoke on the phone the other day... my work-study assignment was being switched?"

"Alex, Alex... oh yes, I remember."

I shifted in my seat. "Um... I was wondering if it's too late to switch to something else. Anything else."

She frowned. "That might be difficult. Generally, the work-study assignments are made at the beginning of summer. To be honest, you were lucky to get this one. Doctor Forrester's contract wasn't confirmed until last week, which was why we had a last minute opening. What's the problem?"

Oh, God. I didn't really have a good reason. At least, not one I could explain. *I've been assigned next to my ex-boyfriend.* Yeah, that would go over well. I tried to think of something, and stupidly I just said, "I'm not sure it's a good fit."

She sighed. "I can tell you for sure, right now, that there aren't any other openings. You're actually the fifth student to come in and ask to be reassigned. It might be possible for you to switch with someone; you could always post something on the bulletin board outside. But I can't promise you anything. Although you can always check back in a couple weeks. We often drop a few students in the first two weeks. Something might come up."

I nodded. Disappointed. This was going to make for a very difficult year. I did *not* want to be stuck working with Dylan for the entire year. It would turn what had been a pretty wonderful college experience into misery.

"I'm sorry I couldn't be more helpful," she said.

Okay, I can take a hint. I was being dismissed. I thanked her, and got out of the office. I could survive a few weeks, and then I'd come back and get a job washing dishes or something equally entertaining.

Back on the street, I walked toward the dorm.

I was not going to cry. I refused.

Crying: Not. Going. To. Happen.

I remember being charmed and intrigued by Dylan. I'd never met anyone like him. My life was centered around academics. I worked, and worked damned hard. But I also had all kinds of support, from my parents, who hired tutors and piano teachers; to my sisters, who helped each other in subjects we had trouble with. We'd lived a block from Golden Gate Park in a wonderful old rowhouse ever since my dad retired from the Foreign Service.

Dylan was... so different. He'd been homeless, for God's sake. He didn't talk much about the difficult parts of his life... at least not when we first met. But it was clear we were from different worlds. But he was strong. He had to be, to come back from a drinking and drug problem, go back to school on his own, get the kind of grades he got.

I fell fast.

We spent the twelve hours of our flight to Tel Aviv talking while most of the rest of the students were asleep. I remember playing a stupid game of questions, until some of them got uncomfortable (*Do you have a girlfriend?*) and we changed the subject. To favorite books. Harry Potter. Hunger Games. Both of us hated Twilight, but loved Katniss Everdeen.

"I love a strong heroine," he told me with a grin. Oh, my God. How could someone so cute be so perfect?

But he was also a contradiction. He was passionate for Hemingway, and could get lost talking about his favorite book, *The Sun Also Rises.* He looked mystified by my attraction to Milan Kundera.

The exchange students spent the first two nights in Tel Aviv at the Youth Hostel. We attended a bunch of information sessions, then went to a big formal dinner. Dylan looked uncomfortable at the dinner. I don't think he was used to formal functions like that. Afterward, a bunch of us walked down to the Old City of Jaffa, which we'd seen during an official tour earlier in the day.

We sat on the pier, looking out at the Mediterranean Sea. He smoked, and we talked. I told him about my sisters (all five of them) and he talked about his friends.

"We just kind of fell in with each other," he said. "Bunch of drama geeks, mostly. All the kids who were mostly outcasts in middle school. But... you know how it goes. The wrong person sleeps with the other wrong person, and *drama*."

I laughed. I'd never slept with anyone, but I knew all about high school drama.

I kept stealing glances at him, and I knew he was doing the same. His blue eyes were incredible, and he had adorably long hair, growing into loose curls. At one point I found myself resisting the urge to run my fingers through them, which would not have been a very cool and collected thing to do. I carefully kept an inch of space between us, because if we'd touched I might have thrown myself on him. Oh, God, it was intense.

I wonder if that's why it was so painful when we split up? Because we'd fallen so hard, so fast. I lost myself in him.

One thing I knew for sure. I would not allow that to happen again.

When I got back to the room, Kelly was there. She was lying on her bed, staring at the ceiling. Absolutely still, eyes wide open.

I'm not sure I've ever seen Kelly stationary, except possibly while passed out.

"Kelly!" I asked. "Are you okay?"

She burst into tears.

"What's wrong?" I dropped my bag and rushed to her side.

"Joel," she said, then erupted in a new burst of weeping.

"Oh, honey," I said, sliding onto the bed next to her.

"He needs space. He wants to 'play the field,' whatever the hell that means."

"Son of a bitch," I said. "What an asshole."

She burst into a new round of tears. Was this what it was like living with me last spring? No wonder she got so impatient. I hugged her, not saying a word.

After a few minutes, she stopped sobbing, then said, "So, um, how was your day?" She giggled, but not a good giggle... more like she was going to go into hysterics.

"Well," I said carefully. "It turns out that Dylan Paris is out of the Army and going to Columbia. And we're assigned to the same work-study job."

She sat up suddenly. "Oh, my God, *what*? You have got to be shitting me." It's possible the neighbors three blocks down heard her screech.

I nodded my head, miserably.

"It was super awkward. And... hostile."

"What did he say?"

I squeezed my eyes shut, trying to stop myself from crying. "He said he'd hoped we wouldn't run into each other."

She reached out and grabbed my hand. "Oh my God. I didn't think it was possible to hate him even more, but I do. Let's go. Right now. And get drunk."

I nodded, because right that minute, it seemed like the best possible idea.

Ground Rules (Dylan)

"I think we need to set some ground rules," she said.

It was the third day of classes, and our first day actually working for Doctor Forrester. Forrester had a gigantic pile of information, books, files and source documents. It was a disorganized mess. Our first assignment was to begin organizing it and cross-referencing it. We divided up the work fairly easily: I set up a database, and she sorted the material and began feeding it to me.

Unfortunately, it was difficult to work together when we spent most of the time either glaring at each other or ignoring each other.

"What are you talking about?" I asked.

"Look... like it or not, we have to work together."

I nodded. I'd tried to get reassigned to a different work-study assignment, but there weren't any openings.

"So, let's go get a cup of coffee. And talk. And figure out how we can do this without being at each other's throats."

I felt a lump in my throat. It was one thing to sit here in Forrester's office with her. It was another thing entirely to go somewhere else with her, and sit, like normal people, and talk about anything. But she was right. If we were going to be doing this every other day, we had to set some ground rules, or we were both going to be miserable.

"Fine," I said. "When?"

"I'm finished with classes for the day. What about right now?"

I nodded. "All right."

I slowly stood. I was in a lot of pain. The day before I'd had my first physical therapy session at the Brooklyn VA hospital. Loads of fun. My physical therapist was a forty-five-year-old former Marine, and he was of the school of thought that pain was good for you. Problem was, it's hard to argue your point with someone missing a leg. Seriously, what sympathy was he going to give?

I never liked Marines anyway.

So I followed her to the coffee shop around the corner from Forrester's office. It was nice, a small place, with a few outdoor seats. I was incredibly self-conscious as we walked. She'd picked up a New Yorker's pace during her year in college here. I, on the other hand, moved at something like the pace of a turtle, thanks to the gimp leg and the cane.

She slowed down to keep pace with me. About halfway there, she finally said something.

"So... what happened to your leg?"

I shrugged, gave a terse answer. "Hajis thought I would look better without it, I guess. Roadside bomb."

She sighed. "I'm sorry."

"It's not so bad. I got to go to the hospital, and lived. That makes me lucky." What I didn't say: *unlike Roberts, who left that roadside in a bag.*

At the coffee shop, she said, "You grab a seat. I'll get us coffee. You still take yours loaded?"

I nodded, and muttered, "Thank you," then eased myself into a seat next to the sidewalk.

While I waited for her, I took out my phone and scanned through my email. Junk. More junk. Email from Mom. I'd answer that one later. She was naturally worried about me. Some things would never change. For the longest time I'd been angry with my mom over kicking me out when I quit school. Nowadays, I was grateful for it. It gave me a chance to get some hard knocks early. It gave me a chance to get my head on straight and figure out my priorities when

I was young enough the damage wouldn't be permanent. Tough love, they call it in the program. She was a believer. I'd have never guessed she'd have five years clean and sober, so something was working there.

When Alex returned to the table, bearing two gigantic cups of coffee, I put the phone away.

"Thank you," I said. I sipped the coffee. Oh, that was good.

She smiled, met my eyes, then looked away very quickly. The brief eye contact, which remarkably wasn't a glare, twisted at my stomach and made me look at the ground.

"Okay," I said. "Ground rules."

"Yes," she said.

We were silent. What, did she expect me to come up with them?

I shook my head, then said, "Okay, you start. It was your idea."

"Fair enough." She looked at me thoughtfully, then said, "All right. The first rule. We never, ever talk about Israel."

I closed my eyes, and nodded. Talking about it would hurt way too much. "Agreed," I muttered.

She looked relieved, which somehow broke my heart all over again.

I spoke. "We don't talk about what happened after, either. Not when I visited you in San Francisco. Or the year between. Or the year after."

"Especially not the year after," she said. Her eyes were glistening as she looked at the table.

We were silent again. This was just a barrel of laughs. I felt like I was attending a funeral.

"I don't know if I can do this," I said.

"Why not?" she replied.

"Because ... because, well, sometimes it hurts, Alex. A little. A lot. Jesus Christ."

She looked away, and damn if her eyes weren't beautiful. Her lashes were like a mile long.

"If we're going to get through this year, I think we have to move past that," she said.

"Yeah."

"It'll be like we're strangers."

I shrugged. "Okay." Like that could happen.

"We start over. We just met. You're some guy who just got out of the Army, and I'm a girl from San Francisco going to college here. We've got nothing in common. No connection. Not friends. Certainly not... what we were."

Not friends. Of course not. How in hell could we be friends, after what we'd been through?

I nodded, feeling miserable. Shit, it's not like I had any friends anyway, not anymore. I'd lost touch with the ones from Atlanta, who couldn't deal with what I'd become. And the ones in Afghanistan... except for Sherman and Roberts, I'd never gotten close to any of them. Roberts was dead, and Sherman was still out in the boonies.

"I don't know what we were, anyway. None of it ever made any sense."

She shrugged, and then hugged her arms across her chest, and I felt like crap for what I'd said.

"I'm sorry," I said.

"Why?" she asked, looking away from me, out at the street.

Her lower lip was trembling, and I wanted to hit myself in the head with a sharp pointy object.

"It's true, isn't it? We never did make any sense?"

"Oh, God. Let's not do this. Please."

"Okay."

Her face was twitching, and it was obvious she was holding back a tear.

"Look," I said. "This sucks. But we'll be okay, all right? It's only a few hours a week, anyway. What we had... it was another world. We were in a foreign country, being exposed to all kinds of amazing stuff. We weren't ourselves, our real selves. It was... it was fantasy. A beautiful fantasy, but fiction all the same, okay?"

She nodded, quickly, then wiped her eye with a fist, smearing her mascara.

"For what it's worth, I'm sorry."

"We're already breaking the rules," she said.

"No. We're not. No more talk about the past. From this point forward, we only talk about now. You're absolutely right. Any more rules?"

"I don't know."

I frowned, then said, "Fine. What do you think of Doctor Forrester, anyway?"

She shook her head. "He's a giant fake."

I raised my eyebrows. "Really?"

"Well, yeah. Just look at him. Tweed jacket! He wrote one novel fifteen years ago, won a National Book Award, and he's been coasting on that ever since."

I grinned. "That is one hell of a case of ... um...."

Oh shit, not now. I couldn't think. Sometimes this happens to me now. I forget words, phrases. I closed my eyes, trying to center, let my mind come at it from a different direction. I pictured a typewriter, an old manual one, and it popped in. "Writer's block."

She giggled. Still upset, but the change of subject helped. It was nice to see a little color on her cheeks. "Do you still write?" she asked.

I nodded. "Of course."

"What about?"

I shrugged. "The war right now. It's all … stream of consciousness, I guess. Not organized in any way. Just trying to get my thoughts down. My therapist down in Atlanta said it might help."

She turned and looked at me, really looked at me, for the first time, I think, since we'd run into each other three days before.

"Your therapist?"

I shrugged. "Along with the gimp leg, I'm technically diagnosed with Post Traumatic Stress Disorder. And traumatic brain injury. Got my brainpan rattled when the bomb went off, you know? It's all labels, anyway."

"What do you mean?"

I frowned. "I'm just… I'm not exactly the guy you knew, Alex. Sometimes things here… they don't seem as… as real. As it was over there. Maybe I've become an adrenaline junkie. Reality just isn't colorful enough for me."

She sighed. "I felt that way for the longest time after we got back from Israel."

"You're breaking your rules again."

"Oh, right."

She paused, then spoke again. "But I really did. It was so intense, and interesting and colorful. Then all of the sudden things were mundane, and grey, and it was get up and go to school and do homework and none of it seemed to matter as much."

"Yeah," I said. "Anyway, I think working with Doctor Forrester will be interesting, at least. I thought for sure my work-study would be slinging dishes or mopping floors or something."

"Yeah, this is a lot better," she replied. "And just think, you get to see a *real* writer in action." When she said the word 'real' she held her hands up and made little quotes. I laughed.

"Okay, you're probably right. Let's see if he produces anything this year. At least we can make sure the research is all lined up."

She grinned. "We should make a little wager on it."

I raised my eyebrows. "Feeling a little competitive?"

"I say he produces absolutely nothing. Twenty dollars."

"Fair enough. What's the threshold. Fifty pages? A hundred? Two?"

"He has to finish at least a first draft."

"Deal." I reached across to shake her hand. She took it, and though the action felt natural, it felt *too* natural. Taking her hand. I let go quickly, feeling as if I'd been burned. Touching her... it was just too intense.

We were both silent again. Awkward. As. Hell.

"I should get going," I said, at the exact same time she said, "Well, I've got somewhere to..."

We looked at each other and both of us burst out laughing.

"Okay," I said. "Yeah, this is awkward. Are we really going to be able to do this?"

She shrugged, and gave a smile I knew was fake as a three-dollar bill. "Of course, Dylan. It can't be that hard."

I started to gather my bags, then took three dollars out of my wallet. "For the coffee," I said.

"Keep it. You buy next time."

I paused, then put the money back in my wallet. *Next time?* Was this going to be a regular occurrence? Probably not a good idea. Not a good idea at all.

CHAPTER THREE

Strawberries (Alex)

When he finally got himself standing, he leaned close and said, "I think we need one more rule."

"Yeah?"

He took a deep breath through his nose, and said, "Yeah. Um, yeah... you need to get different shampoo."

What. The. *Hell?*

"What are you talking about?" I asked, suddenly very uncomfortable.

"You still smell like strawberries, and it's breaking my heart," he said, his voice a low growl. With that, he turned, slung his bag over his impossibly broad shoulder, and began to walk away.

He was twenty feet away before I could even think again. Without thought, without regard for consequences, I shouted as loud as I could, "You can't do that! That's breaking the first rule! Do you hear me, Dylan?"

I was attracting stares. He waved over his shoulder and kept walking.

Bastard.

I gathered my bag and turned to go in the other direction, back to the dorm. Oh God, I was a mess. I was a mess because of his impossibly blue eyes, because of how his arms and chest had become... so developed. He smelled the same as always, and being around him was impossible. Sometimes when he was close to me I couldn't even breathe. How in hell was I supposed to stay detached and professional when he set off every single nerve in my body?

Why did he have to say that?

I still remembered. I remembered him asking me on the plane a million years ago, during our questions and answers game, *"Why do you smell like strawberries?"*

Damn it.

It's not like we even really knew each other. I was a different person in Israel. Free. At home, and here in college, I was ... well, I was kind of a bitch. I focused, one hundred percent, on my studying, on success. I was driven. I didn't have room for the crazy sensations and emotions I'd experienced during our trip.

As I walked, I remembered. His smell. His touch.

Three days after we arrived in Israel, we'd gone to our first set of host families, in Ramat Gan, a suburb of Tel Aviv. Somehow, because of a stupid mixup, I ended up being the only female student assigned to a male host. Ariel was nothing but a giant ball of hormones and glands, a hyper-masculine dickhead who was absolutely certain he was going to sleep with me some time during my ten-day stay in his home. By the end of the second day I was exhausted from fending off his advances, and went to our advisor. She got me placed with a different family, thank God. That night, our host families held a party for all of us.

I remember watching Dylan at the party. All of the kids were drinking. Some, like me, kept it to a minimum, but some, like Rami, the host of the party, were really packing it away.

Everyone except Dylan. He spent the night nursing a coke, and relaxing in a corner. At one point he took out his guitar and played some songs, and had several of the drunken students singing along with him. I watched, and smiled, thinking to myself how beautiful his eyes were. When he played the guitar, his face went through exaggerated facial expressions, his lips pursing sometimes, his eyes closing. He kept looking at me.

Later that night, he approached me and asked, "Can we talk for a minute?"

I shifted a little. *Oh. God.* What was this? Was he going to ask me out? I wanted him to. So badly. We went to Rami's room in the back of the apartment and sat next to each other on the bed.

"Listen," he said. "I know we're only here for a few weeks. And that's it. Nothing could ever work between us. But... I'm really, really attracted to you. And I'd like to know if you feel the same."

I was drawing in low, shallow breaths. I couldn't believe this was happening. Finally, I nodded, quickly. "Yes. I do," I replied.

"Maybe... maybe we can just see what happens then?"

I smiled. "Okay," I said.

The last two years would have been a lot less painful if I'd just told him, then and there, to go to hell. But maybe I was a little book-smart and not enough life-smart, because I fell for him. I fell off a cliff. And I still haven't recovered.

Two hours after Dylan walked away from me oh-so-casually at the coffee shop, Kelly gasped when I told her what he'd said.

"He said what?"

I sighed. "He told me he wanted to change my shampoo. Because the smell of strawberries was breaking his heart."

She looked at me, her eyes wide, and said, "That's so romantic."

"Oh God, Kelly, that's no help at all!"

She nodded. "I know."

"I thought you hated him."

"Only because he hurt you. But it's obvious you still have a huge thing for this guy. Maybe you should just jump his bones and get it out of your system."

"That is *enough!* The only thing I'm going to do with him is survive the year working for Forrester. He hurt me, Kelly. Worse than I could have imagined possible."

"I know," she said, quietly. "But maybe there's more to the story than you know. I mean... I'm just saying, it's possible."

"No. It's completely impossible. Me and Dylan? Never again."

She sighed, and leaned back in her bed.

"What's going on with Joel, anyway?" I said, trying to change the subject.

She shrugged. "He's still an asshole."

"There's a shock," I replied.

"Was I too clingy? I don't understand it."

"No," I said. "There were times last year you couldn't have separated you two with the Jaws of Life. Something else going on there."

"Oh, God. You don't think he was cheating on me while we were dating, do you?"

I shook my head. "I'd have given odds that couldn't happen. Maybe he's just ... I don't know. Scared?"

Kelly frowned. "What does he have to be scared of?"

I gave a sad, sort of bitter laugh. "Maybe he's scared of getting his heart broken. It happens."

She looked me in the eyes. "Could be," she said.

Our job was to go out and draw fire (Dylan)

O kay, so I shouldn't have said what I said about the strawberry scent.

Two days later, she showed up in Forrester's office reeking of strawberries. She gave me a defiant look and sat down and started working.

I didn't know whether to fly into a rage or break down crying, so I did the next best thing. I laughed. Long and hard, until tears were nearly running down my face.

"Are you all right?" she asked.

That just set me off again, and she gave me a wry look. But finally, I settled down, started working, and began to feel optimistic. Maybe this could work after all.

At this point we were falling into a routine. Occasionally we would stop to discuss a particular item: journal articles, personal accounts, newspaper articles, whatever, and discuss precisely how to categorize and cross-reference them. Sometimes, when she was busy poring over some obscure document, I'd casually... not so much... glance over and let my eyes rest on her.

I knew it was stupid to do it. I knew it. But I couldn't stop myself. Because she was just as beautiful as ever. She wore faded blue jeans and calf-high boots that emphasized the curve of her legs, a grey t-shirt with a band logo on it (I didn't recognize the band, but a Google search later would fix that), a thin white sweater. The t-shirt hugged her upper body, emphasizing her breasts and waist in a way that grabbed my attention and held it. Her hair was down, falling lush on her shoulders and halfway down her back. I kept wanting to reach out and run my fingers through her hair. I found myself remembering: leaning in, kissing her neck, feeling her hair tent around me, and just breathing her scent.

"What are you doing?"

I shook my head, embarrassed. "Sorry," I said.

"You were looking at me."

Now I looked up at her eyes, then away. "Well, shoot me, then."

I turned back to the computer, keyed in the information on the latest piece, the priceless diary of a banker who had witnessed the beginning of the riots.

I could hear her breathing as I typed in the information. The monitor of the computer just barely reflected her. *She* was staring at *me* now. Damn it. Back to business.

"You know what I don't hear?" she asked.

"What's that?"

"I don't hear any typing from his office."

I snickered. "Maybe he only writes at night?"

"Or on alternate decades?"

"Smart-ass."

She giggled.

"He might surprise us both," I said.

"Anything's possible," she said. "But I think he's a fraud."

I exhaled suddenly, then said, "Maybe. But I was thinking about it last night. Imagine hitting the peak of your career at twenty-two years old. He was still a senior in college when he won the National Book Award. Twenty-two, and you've got a major bestseller, the top award in your field. Who wouldn't be intimidated? How do you follow up something like that?"

"Huh," she said. "You're right. I hadn't thought of it that way."

I grinned. "I love hearing those words from you."

"What words?"

"*You're right.*"

She gave me a grin, then threw a pencil at me. "Some things never change," she said.

"Yeah, well, it's hard to improve on near-perfection."

She shook her head. "It's five o'clock. Let's wrap it up."

"Okay," I said. Then my stupid, stupid, stupid mouth ran ahead of my brain. "You want to grab a cup of coffee?"

She gave me an odd look, eyes a little narrowed and head slightly tilted, and said, "Okay."

I carefully stood, hands at the edge of the desk, and grabbed my cane. A few steps to the door of Forrester's office. I didn't hear any sound inside at all. Jesus, I hoped he was alive. I quietly opened the office door and looked inside.

Forrester was passed out at his desk, a little bit of drool pooling on the papers under his face.

Guess we didn't need to ask if we could go. I closed the door and turned back to him.

"Is he writing?" she asked.

"Yeah," I said.

She looked surprised. "Really?"

"No. He's passed out."

"Oh. My. God."

I shrugged.

Depending on your point of view, experience, and attitude, we made our way to the coffee shop in either a companionable silence or an oppressive, awkward one. I'd prefer to think it was the former, but the pessimist in me says it was definitely the latter. About two thirds of the way there, she said, "You seem to be doing better today." She nodded toward the cane.

"Yeah," I said. "New physical therapist."

"Oh yeah?"

"He moonlights, I think, as a dom. Advertises on the back pages of the *Village Voice*."

She threw her head back and laughed out loud. "You're crazy," she said.

"No," I said, shaking my head. "I'm dead serious. I think I caught sight of leather straps hanging out of his desk yesterday. I'm going to have to give you my emergency contact information, in case I ever disappear after one of my appointments."

"How often do you have to go?"

"Twice a week. And I'm supposed to walk at least a mile every morning. I think he's going to make me start running soon."

"What exactly happened?" she asked.

By this time we were at the coffee shop, so I said, "Let me get our drinks, then I'll tell you the whole story."

Five minutes later we were both seated out front, coffee in hand, and I said, "It happened back in late February. We were out on a patrol. Basically, our job was to go out and draw fire. Drive around until someone shoots at us, then the quick reaction force dives in and gets the bad guys. Or at least that's the theory."

She nodded, encouraging me to go on. "Anyway, that particular day we'd been in a small village, about three miles from the FOB."

"The FOB?" she asked.

"Sorry. Forward operating base. Remember Fort Apache? It's basically where you take a small part of the army, plant them on a small target in the middle of hostile territory, and hang them out to dry."

She leaned back, looking shocked. Probably more at my bitter tone than the words I'd used.

"Anyway, the village was about three miles away, and we went through there all the time. It was supposed to be friendly territory, but that's all relative. Friendly means we didn't get blown up there every day, just maybe once a week. The kids could get candy from us, and we were pretty sure they wouldn't be killed for it, and that they wouldn't be secretly holding grenades or whatever."

A sad expression passed across her face. Almost a pitying expression.

I didn't need her fucking pity. I leaned forward and said, "Listen, whatever you do, don't ever give me pity. I don't want to see that expression on your face, all right? I walked out of there alive. That makes me a fucking lottery winner, okay?"

Her eyes widened, and she nodded.

"Anyway... We got held up that day. One of the shopkeepers... okay, that's a stretch. This guy ran what was basically a cart beside the road, selling stuff to us, or to truck drivers who came through. Probably made fifty cents a day. I think he realized he could make a lot more working for the Taliban, because he held us up that day, telling some bullshit story about insurgents leaving the area, and he knew where they were going to be moving to, and so on. We finally finished with him, which gave the bad guys enough time to set up an ambush along the road back to the FOB."

"So... what happened?"

"I don't remember much. We were about halfway back when my Humvee ran over the bomb. My friend Roberts was driving, and it hit mostly on his side. Everything went white, very suddenly. I couldn't see anything, couldn't hear anything, and then it was all gone. I woke up in Germany three days later, very lucky to be alive. Shrapnel had cut most of the way through my thigh and calf muscles. I got some permanent ringing in my ears, though the docs say that night go away in a few years. And... well, I spent a long time in the hospital. First in Germany, then after they stabilized me, they moved me to Walter Reed Army Hospital in Washington."

"And your friends?"

I grimaced. "I basically had two friends in the Army. Sherman was in the humvee behind us. Got out without a scratch. He's still over there in the boonies. And... well, Roberts didn't make it."

Her eyes dropped to the table, and she said, "I'm sorry."

I shrugged, trying to look casual, knowing that it was a lie as I said the next words.

"It happens, Alex. People die. Roberts wouldn't want me to spend my life all screwed up over what happened, any more than I would if our positions were reversed. He's up there somewhere right now urging me to go get drunk and get laid, probably."

She chuckled. "And are you following his advice?"

"Not yet," I said, "But there's always tomorrow."

Not the smartest thing to say, I guess. Her gaze slipped away from me, out to the street. Finally, very slowly, she asked, "Why didn't you contact me? After you were injured?"

I didn't like the expression on her face, which was full of ... grief? Longing? Sadness?

I couldn't answer that question out loud. Because you ripped my heart out, I wanted to say. Because I couldn't talk to you without hating you.

Because I loved you too much to put you through my bitterness and rage. Because I didn't deserve to have you.

I shook my head, and said, in a light tone of voice, "It would be breaking the rules to answer that one, Alex."

No pepper spray in the bar (Alex)

"I don't know, Kelly. I'm not sure I'm up for it."

Kelly rolled her eyes at me while she was shimmying herself into a sheer halter that would take a can-opener to remove, then said, "Alex. It's the first Friday back in school. We are going out. What's gotten into you?"

"What's gotten into me is I need to study. I need to focus."

Kelly stopped what she was doing and walked straight at me. She put her hands on either side of my face, looked me in the eye, and said, "I call bullshit."

"What?"

"You heard me, Alex. You've been crazy all week. It's not your need to be Super-Geek Girl; you'll be just fine with a night off from that. This is about Dylan."

Oh, go to hell.

I stopped myself. The surge of anger was a surprise. Maybe she was right. I mean... I was over him. I thought. Okay, that's not true. But... I didn't think my behavior was different.

"Helloooo?" she said, shaking her head as she dragged out the word.

"Um... I haven't really been crazy all week, have I?"

"Oh, for God's sake, Alex, get dressed! We are going out, right now! And just wait and see... some amazingly hot guy is going to come around and swoop you up, and it will be way too late for soldier boy. He'll never know what hit him."

She turned around and went back to her mirror, then started applying her mascara.

I started looking for something to wear. I wanted attractive, but... not too attractive. I hadn't forgotten last spring. There. Jeans, with a medallion belt. Tight long-sleeved tee with a vest. Maybe not exactly bar-hopping attire, but Kelly was showing enough skin for both of us. And much as she talked about it, I didn't really want some guy to swoop down on me. To be honest, the thought made my skin crawl, and that worried me, too. I dug through my bureau and got out my knee-high black suede boots, with their two-inch heels.

An hour later we were standing at the 1020 Bar, trying to spot a place to sit in the packed bar. The bouncer took a second glance at my ID when we walked in, but let me and Kelly through anyway. Maybe he was hoping her tank would burst.

Okay, yeah. I was being bitchy.

A crowd surrounded the bar on our left, three or four rows deep. All of the booths were taken, of course, but we slowly worked our way to the bar. Kelly was in rare form, chatting up every guy we passed. I was feeling a bit more reserved, and frankly hated the crowd gathering in on me like that. This had never been my favorite place to hang out, mainly because of the crowds on the weekends. But somehow Kelly and I ended up here at least once a week.

We finally squeezed ourselves onto stools side by side at the end of the bar closest to the pool tables. A group of twenty or so guys were crowded up against the bar to our left, chanting as they threw back shots. The band was setting up at the tiny stage near the pool tables, and the general volume of the place had grown louder and louder in the thirty minutes we'd been there.

That's when I saw Randy Brewer, and felt a sudden twist in my stomach. I literally felt my heart lurch into gear, the pulse making the arteries in my neck throb. I grabbed Kelly's wrist, gripping it hard.

"What's wrong?" she shouted in my ear. "Is it Dylan?"

I shook my head, unable to speak, even to tell her that Dylan didn't drink.

Randy saw me, and leaned against the bar, leering at me. Slowly a grin broke out on his face, and he winked at me.

"That fucker," Kelly said.

I turned my back on him, toward her, and blurted out, "Let's go somewhere else."

The guy she'd been talking to leaned in and said, "What's wrong baby? I'm not boring you am I?"

Kelly smiled sweetly, and I don't think he saw the daggers headed his way.

"Yeah, you are," she said. "You should go find something more exciting to talk about, then come back, okay?"

"Bitch," he said, then let out a loud belch and wandered off.

Kelly met my eyes, her smile genuine, and we both burst into laughter.

"You really know how to pick 'em, Kels."

"Oh, my God," she said, still laughing. "Am I boring you, *baby?* Wow." She giggled.

"Hey, did you hear from Joel?"

Her tone was still light, but she said, "Jesus, Alex, way to kill the mood."

"Oops, sorry."

"Yeah, I heard from him this morning. He wanted to go out tonight. What the hell? I'm breaking up with you, because being in love is too much, so let's just date casual while I screw other people? What the hell is wrong with him? What the hell is wrong with all guys?"

I shrugged. "I don't know. I hope it's not contagious."

She grinned, then said, "Only sexually."

I groaned, laughing, then jerked when I felt a hand close around my upper arm, then a voice thick with lust in my ear.

"Hey, Alex. I've been looking for you, how 'ya been?"

Randy. I jerked away, but he didn't let go.

"Let go of me, Randy. Get away from me."

"What the hell? I just wanted to say hi."

He looked offended, but didn't let go. He started rubbing my arm with his thumb. "Come on, Alex, I made a mistake last spring. But it wasn't that bad."

I looked him in the eyes, and said furiously, "Get your hand off of me, *now.*"

"Babe, I just want to talk to you, okay?"

"I don't want to talk to *you!*"

Some of the people around us were starting to shift positions, sensing the tension and anger. Some guy tentatively said, "I think she wants you to leave her alone."

"Alex, listen to me. Look... I admit I screwed up. I had too much to drink, and I shouldn't have pushed so hard..."

I saw a flash of movement to my left as Kelly stood up, reached in her purse, pulled out a bottle of something and lifted it up to his eye level. His words transformed into a scream, and he backed away suddenly, hands at his eyes.

"Fucking bitch!" he screamed.

"Stay away from her, asshole!" Kelly screamed back.

Seconds later a bouncer waded through the crowd. "What the fuck is going on here?" he shouted.

I was frozen in place.

"I pepper-sprayed his ass. He sexually assaulted my friend last year, and he wouldn't let go of her just now."

Someone else in the crowd said something to the bouncer and pointed at me. The bouncer's eyes landed on me. He was huge, at least six five, maybe two hundred-fifty pounds of muscle. He walked over to me and said, "That true? The guy wouldn't let go of you? And you told him to?"

I nodded.

"All right. Next time you fucking call for me. I'm Wade. You don't pepper spray people in the bar, got it?"

I nodded, quickly.

"All right."

He turned away, then grabbed Randy by the arm. "Come on, asshole. You're done for the night."

He lifted, and half-dragged Randy through the crowd and away from us.

I turned back to Kelly, my eyes wide. "Oh. My. God. You didn't just do that."

She grinned.

I grabbed her by the shoulders and hugged her. "Kelly, you are the best friend ever! I love you!"

But my eyes darted back toward the door, where Wade the bouncer was dragging Randy. For the thousandth time I found myself wishing I'd reported him when it happened.

I don't really know why I didn't.

I'd briefly dated Randy last spring, after Dylan and I had our last fight. It was a stupid fight. I was drunk, and had been agonizing over the danger he'd been in. I said some things, things I regret. That I was afraid it wasn't working any more, that the distance and danger was ruining us. I mean, it had been a long time since we'd seen each other. A long time. And so much had happened.

Dylan's eyes went cold without any warning. I can't even describe what his look did to me without breaking into tears. It was a look of incredible sadness, and worse, of contempt and disgust. He disconnected the Skype connection without a word. No warning, no word, no nothing.

I tried to call him back, but there was no answer.

The next day, I tried again. His Skype account was gone. So was his Facebook account. He didn't just de-friend me... he deleted the account entirely. He didn't answer my emails or letters, and until this week it was like he had just ... disappeared off the face of the earth.

After a month of pure devastation, Kelly started urging me to date again. And I tried. I really did. I went out a couple times with Randy. Then one night, Randy and I were having drinks, and then we had a couple too many. And somehow I found myself back in his room, and he tried to make out with me. I wasn't ready. Not by a long shot. But the next thing I knew, Randy had shoved me down on the bed and was trying to rip off my shirt. I tried to fight him off, but I could barely move.

I screamed, and it was pure luck that his roommates were coming back in right at that moment. They pulled him off me, and I stumbled out, crying.

It would never have happened if Dylan hadn't cut me off so suddenly.

It would never have happened if I hadn't drunk too much.

"You okay?" Kelly asked.

I looked over at her and nodded.

"I was just thinking about Dylan, and ... and everything."

"Oh, shit," Kelly said. "You're still head-over-heels for him, aren't you?"

"No," I said, at the same time I nodded.

Kelly grinned. "Try that again."

"Oh, shit, Kelly. I still love him."

"You know he was a complete asshole to cut you off like that."

"I know."

"He didn't give you a chance to explain. It was just stupid. He let his stupid male pride kill the best thing he ever had."

I nodded. This wasn't helping. Not. One. Bit.

"You're going to try to get him back, aren't you?"

"No," I said.

"I don't believe you. You're lying to me, Alex."

"No. Not a chance. He blew it, Kelly. He broke my heart. I can't go back there. Never. Not a chance."

"Sure, Alex, sure. Whatever."

She went back to her drink, and I looked in the mirror over the bar. Was I lying to her? To myself?

I didn't know the answer to that.

CHAPTER FOUR

Bring it, jarhead (Dylan)

Eight a.m. Monday morning. It was time for my torture session at the VA.

When I was first injured, they evac'd me to the hospital in Bagram, a sprawling affair hidden behind blast walls and littered with shipping containers and temporary facilities. I saw it briefly from the doors of the hospital, still somewhat conscious. I remember watching the hospital flying by below me, and realizing that I was probably going home.

I remember being wheeled into the ER, but nothing after that until I woke up in Germany. There, the doctors told me there was still a significant risk of losing my leg: the muscle and deep tissue damage was pretty bad. I spent almost thirty days in Germany, then they shipped me to Washington, DC, where I stayed until my discharge from the Army in the middle of May. They'd saved my leg, but at that point I was still in a wheelchair.

It was at Walter Reed that I met the outreach coordinator from Columbia University, who urged me to apply. I was doubtful. Beyond doubtful. I didn't think I'd be able to succeed in college, must less at a top-rated college like Columbia.

My mother, though, pushed me to do it. She pushed me to get out of the wheelchair, to follow through with my physical therapy, to do everything the doctors said and more. She worked with the guy from Columbia, who smoothed the path ahead of me, including the fact that I'd long since missed the application deadline. And so here I was.

Look, I get it. I'm a pretty lucky guy. Roberts is pushing up flowers in a cemetary in Birmingham, Alabama. I met his family back in August. I'd finally gotten free of the wheelchair, and I went out there to have a beer with his dad, hug his mom, and cry. Of course, I didn't tell them it was my fault Roberts was dead. Sometimes I wish he'd been the one who lived. I mean, it was just chance. Why did it kill him and leave me alive? I don't know.

The flip side of being a lucky guy is, sometimes I'm not the same guy I was. I want to draw a picture in your mind. Just imagine a brain... a big gray blob, connected to your body through the brain stem and spinal cord, floating and cushioned by fluid and protected by my big thick skull. Now take a sledgehammer and hit it, hard.

That's pretty much what happened. It's been tough to accept, to be honest with you. I may not have been the best student in the world, but I was pretty damned smart. Used to be, anyway. Now... I have some problems. Can't remember things sometimes. Like where I'm supposed to be, or what day it is, or how to add and subtract. It's much worse when I'm tired, but you can see evidence pretty frequently, when I forget words. I'll just be talking up a storm, then all of the sudden I'll forget simple words—like blue, or sky, or my own name. It'll be right there on the tip of my tongue, but I just can't get it out.

In any event, when I got accepted to Columbia, the Atlanta VA made arrangements for me to continue my physical therapy here in New York. Three times a week I'm down at the VA on East 23rd to get poked and prodded, stretched and pulled.

"Morning," I said when I was called and walked slowly, without the cane, to Jerry Weinstein's office.

Jerry's a big guy. A monster. A fortyish Marine who lost a leg in Iraq back in 2004, he's got zero sympathy for any bullshit from me. Strangely, I like him. But God if he doesn't love to cause me pain.

"What's up, Paris? Why are you so cheerful? It's Monday morning."

I looked at him, tried to keep a straight face, and said, "I can't think of any place I'd rather spend my Monday mornings than with a washed up Marine with a cruelty fetish."

He guffawed. "You're gonna get extra work for that, dogface."

"Bring it, jarhead."

He stood with a grin, asked, "All right, how's the leg?"

"Better. I've been off the cane for a few days. I carry it around just in case. Still moving slow as hell, though."

"What about the noggin?" he asked, tapping the side of his head.

I shrugged. "Struggling some, especially with math. I used to be really good at math."

"Hmm," he said, nodding. "Any light sensitivity?"

I tapped my sunglasses. "Yeah, always."

"Headaches?"

"Might be better, I'm not sure."

"All right. When was your last CAT scan?"

I thought about it. Then shook my head. "I don't know. It was in Atlanta... three weeks ago? A month ago?"

He nodded, slowly, then said, "All right, time to get another. I'm going to set you up for an appointment with the brain docs for next week. Let's see that leg."

He did an examination of my right leg. It hurt. The muscles in my thigh and calf were still extremely weak: you could visibly see that my right leg was way smaller than the left.

"Coming along," he said. "I think it's time you got back to running."

"*Running?* I can barely walk!"

"Yeah. Time to quit stalling, Paris. Just make sure you have a friend with you, in case you fall over and can't get up." He flashed a grin at me. "But I want you up and running, Tuesday, Thursday, Saturday. Start out short distance, but get out there and do it. You hear me?"

I nodded grimly, then said, "I don't have any friends."

"Yeah, well, hire someone, then. But get out there and do it."

"Yes, sir."

"You only say that because you love me."

"Sure, Jerry."

"All right, asshole. Time for your workout."

Grimly, I nodded and stood. I kept thinking. Who could I ask to spot me when I was running? There was no one. Or, there was one person, but... could I ask her? Was it crazy to even think so? I didn't want her taking pity on me. I didn't want her doing it because she knew I was friendless and alone. I didn't want her doing it because of our past, which was against the rules to talk about anyway. And the hell of it was, no matter what I did, I couldn't stop thinking about her. I couldn't stop imagining her scent, I couldn't stop thinking of how wonderful it once felt to hold her in my arms.

A little hair of the dog (Alex)

*D*ylan and I had settled into a bit of a routine. We were both on the same schedule, work-study with Doctor Forrester on Monday, Wednesday, Friday from 3 p.m. until 6. We were making a lot of progress, and had categorized most of Forrester's library within the first two weeks. Once, maybe twice a week, we'd go get some coffee afterward, and talk.

Dylan was different. I'd known that since we first encountered each other again, but sometimes I could see it in conversation. Yeah, he was physically different, of course. But he was also quieter. When we knew each other in Israel, he always had a goofy smile, made silly jokes. Now, not so much. Occasionally I had to prod a little to get him to talk at all. It was disconcerting.

This day was different. I'd been delayed in class, and I got to Doctor Forrester's office a few minutes late.

When I walked in the door, Dylan looked like... I don't know. Like he was sick. His face was pale, and he was staring out the window, not actually doing anything, and he was breathing really quickly.

"Hey," I said. "Are you okay?"

He looked at me, startled. He was wearing sunglasses in the office, something he did pretty frequently, now that I thought about it. Almost like he was hung over. But Dylan didn't drink. At least he didn't used to.

"Yeah," he said. "I'm all right, just a rough morning."

"You want to talk about it?"

"No," he said.

Well, that wasn't ambiguous.

We went to work, sorting through the last of Forrester's collection. Next time we'd be moving over to the library of rare books and manuscripts to start searching for additional materials. I dreaded the change. Not because there was anything horrible about it, but mostly because I'd come to really enjoy our sessions in Forrester's office.

Speak of the devil. The door opened, and Forrester stumbled in.

His eyes went to Dylan, and when he saw his pale face and sunglasses he grinned. "Good afternoon, you two. The morning after is always a little rough, isn't it Dylan?"

Dylan sort of grunted, didn't really answer.

"A little hair of the dog?"

"No thank you, sir."

That was the first time I came close to really disliking Forrester.

An hour later we were sitting in the coffee shop. He was looking worse, his face even paler than before. I said, "Dylan, I'm worried about you. You sure you're okay?"

He took off his sunglasses and rubbed his hands against his eyes. His hands trembled.

"Hey," I said. I leaned forward when he put his hands down, and took one of them in my own. "I know we've got our... um... history. But if you need to talk, I'm here."

He looked almost as startled as I was when I took his hand. He looked at me, and swallowed. I let go, and you know, it kind of hurt to do that.

He shook his head, quickly, then muttered, "Brain injury. I'm not sure I'm going to make it through school. I'm not..."

He tried to say something else, then just stopped. I'd seen him do this several times over the last couple weeks. He'd be saying something, then just clam up. He closed his eyes, emphasizing the dark circles under them, and took a couple of breaths. Then he said, "I'm not... smart. Not like I used to be. Can't remember things."

Oh, Dylan. I had to blink back tears.

"Maybe I can help," I said, very quietly. *Please, just say yes.* Okay, Kelly was right. I still loved him, and seeing him like this, on a bad day, made me want to go quietly somewhere and cry. *Please,* I thought, *let this man heal. And God, please protect my heart, because I can't take breaking it again.*

He shook his head. "I don't know."

"Well," I said, sadly. "Think about it."

"There is one thing," he said in a husky whisper.

"What?"

"My doc says... I have to start running again. And... well... you've seen how I walk. I need a spotter. Basically someone to follow me and call the ambulance when I fall over."

"You want me to... run with you?"

He nodded. His eyes darted away from me, as if he was looking for an escape route, then back. "Look, I shouldn't have asked. I just don't really know anyone here."

My heart might have stopped. "I'd be happy to go running with you, Dylan. When?"

"Tomorrow? At six?"

"In the morning?"

"Is that too early?"

Yes.

"No. That's fine."

Good God. What was I doing?

My mouth ran off with me again. "Let me get your number, in case something comes up."

So, for the first time since we broke up last February, we exchanged phone numbers.

After we split up, I walked back to the dorm. And I was afraid. Oh, God I was afraid. Afraid I was going to ruin it. Even more afraid that he would. That I'd let myself get close to him again, and that I'd let him break my heart again.

Last February... it was a nightmare. I'd cried myself to sleep every night. Tortured myself really.

I was a mess.

I got back to the dorm and let myself in, then sat down on my bed, my eyes turning to the bottom drawer of my bureau. *Don't do it,* I thought. I'd packed everything away, when six weeks had gone by with no word from him, no response from him.

Feeling like I was going to cry, feeling like a robot with no control over my own actions, I leaned forward and slid open the drawer.

To a casual examination—for example a nosy-as-hell room-mate—there were folded sweaters in the drawer.

Underneath, however, was a box. I slid the box out of the drawer, sat it on the bed next to me, and opened it.

On top was an eight-by-ten photo of me and Dylan. He was leaning on the grass on his side, head propped on his right arm. He wore a black trenchcoat and a white turtleneck, and he was smiling. I was curled up against his legs, facing him. In the photo our eyes are locked, faces close together, huge smiles on both of our faces.

A tear ran down my face, looking at it. Angrily, I swiped it away, then set the photo to the side.

Underneath the picture was a thick leather photo album.

Inside was our own love story.

There we were, together in Tel Aviv. Holding hands as we walked on the pier in Jaffa. Standing waist deep in the Mediterranean Sea, arms around each other.

Sitting together on the tour bus. He was wearing the ridiculous kuffiyah he'd bought in Nazareth. I was wearing a light brown sweater, hair loose around my shoulders. Because he liked it down. His arm was around my shoulder.

A whole series of the youth hostel in Ein Gedi near the Dead Sea... where we'd kissed for the first time.

Someone took a picture of us together standing on the Golan Heights, the Sea of Galilee to our backs. He was standing behind me, arms around my waist, my head thrown back in a giant laugh.

A series of greying photos taken in the photo booth at the bus station in San Francisco. He'd taken a Greyhound all the way from Atlanta to see me, the summer after his senior year. In the photos he was wearing a leather jacket and fedora, and we were kissing.

Dried roses. They'd come on my nineteenth birthday, last fall, not long after he left for Afghanistan. It was the last thing I'd ever expected, to have flowers delivered from halfway around the world on my birthday.

When Kelly walked in the room, I was curled up on my bed crying, surrounded by all the evidence of my stupid inability to let go.

She got one look and said, "Oh, no. Alex, hun. You've got it bad."

"Oh, shit, I'm sorry Kelly."

"It's okay, babe. Slide over."

I did, and she climbed into bed beside me and hugged me while I cried my eyes out.

CHAPTER FIVE

Just remember to breathe (Alex)

The alarm started ringing at an ungodly hour. As in before six in the morning. I hadn't seen that early in the morning since high school, and I'd been perfectly happy that way.

Kelly, across the room from me, muttered, "Oh my God, what the hell is that?" then started snoring again.

At first, I rolled over and hit the snooze button. I closed my eyes, thinking I should just go back to sleep. My mind drifted, half unconscious, to a semi-dream.

I was holding hands with Dylan, and it was the summer before my senior year of high school. I could feel the calluses on the tips of his fingers from guitar playing. We'd walked a quarter of the way out on the Golden Gate Bridge, staying close the entire time, and were looking down at the bay. His eyes were wide, dreamy, and we talked about our dreams of the future.

We were struggling, because our dreams were... different. He was going to travel, and write. I was going to college, probably in

New York. He was finished with high school, and planned on leaving the country within months. I had another year in San Francisco. We'd turned to each other, there on the bridge, and as the wind blew through our hair he gently kissed me.

Dylan.

Dylan.

My eyes popped open. It was 5:56, and I was going to be late.

I jerked out of bed, stumbled, and fell flat, catching myself at the last second. Heart beating rapidly, I threw open my top drawer and started throwing clothes, trying to find something to wear.

"What are you doing?"

Kelly asked, her voice slurred with sleep.

"I'm late. To go running with Dylan."

"Oh. I must be dreaming. It sounded like you said you're going running. I'll talk to you later."

Her words faded into a mumble, and I finally found some shorts, a sports bra and a halter top. Where the hell were my sneakers? I searched for them, and finally stumbled over them and nearly hit my head. Oh, God. I was being such a spaz.

At 6:05 I sent Dylan a quick text message:

Running Late. There vry soon.

Then I ran out the door. I hoped he'd get the text. I hoped he'd wait for me. I hoped he wouldn't hate me. Oh, God, why was I putting myself through this?

It was ten after six when I finally ran across 114th Street, past the Butler Library and onto the field. At this time of the morning, the campus was virtually deserted, though there were a few early risers out there running in the darkness.

I came up short when I saw him, my breath caught in my throat.

Dylan wore grey cotton shorts and a t-shirt with the word ARMY emblazoned on it in large black letters, and he was in the middle of doing pushups when I saw him. His broad shoulders and thick biceps were clearly used to this form of exercise. The muscles in his neck and shoulders were tense, bulging as he worked himself up and down.

"I'll just be a minute," he said to me. He was hardly winded.

That's when I realized I'd just been standing there, staring. For how long? I didn't know. Quite a while. Was my tongue hanging out?

Stop that, I thought. *Bad Alex.*

I looked away, because that was the only possible thing I could do, then looked back. Tearing my eyes away from those arms, I could see the damage the bomb did to his right leg. Thick, ropy scars covered his entire calf. Another ugly looking red welt, sewn back closed and healed like a dark red zipper, ran from below his knee right up his thigh and under his shorts. More jagged scars covered his entire right thigh. His right leg was noticeably less bulky than his left: the left was well defined, with powerful calf muscles.

"Got your text," he said, as he finally stopped doing pushups. He pivoted on his butt, pulling one leg in close and stretching out the other. He leaned forward, reaching for and grabbing his left foot. "Sorry I didn't answer. Limbering up. Last thing I want to do is get out there running and freeze up."

I'd carry you home if you did. Right up to my room.

Oh, for God's sake, I thought, *get a grip.* He's your ex-boyfriend. The asshole who left you to grieve, not knowing if he was alive or not. The guy who broke your heart, without any warning, without any explanation.

"It's okay," I said.

I wasn't exactly an athlete any more than he had been before the Army, but I did understand the importance of stretching. I sat down across from him and tried to mirror his actions, stretching out as far as I could, taking hold of my left foot, then switching to the right.

"So, um... I don't do this often. Or rather, I never do this."

"What's that?" he asked.

"Go running," I answered.

"You might find you enjoy it. I used to run with the boxing team in our battalion sometimes... they'd go out for fifteen, twenty miles every morning."

I gaped. Then noticed the pack of cigarettes rolled up in his left shirt sleeve.

"You did that and smoked?"

"Yeah, well, everybody gets some vice, I guess."

I didn't know how to answer that. I put both my feet directly in front of me, facing him, and stretched forward as far as I could.

I literally heard him stop breathing, and I sat up quickly. He averted his eyes, and then I realized, holy shit, Dylan was looking down my shirt!

I felt the heat rise on my face, so I averted my eyes and stood up.

"I'm all stretched out, I think," I said.

He chuckled, then said, "Um... I'm sorry. That was... totally uncalled for. And... unintentional. And... I better shut up while I'm ahead."

"You're an ass, Dylan."

He nodded, frankly, with just the hint of a smile curling up on the left side of his mouth. "It's true."

Okay, he thought it was funny. He really was an ass. I frowned, said, "It's not funny. I'm going home."

His face instantly dropped the joking expression. "Wait... please don't go."

He looked so wounded, I stopped in place, and he said, "I'm sorry. Sometimes I forget, that's all. I know about the rules and all that, but you're still the..."

He trailed off, and turned away. "Sorry. This was a bad idea."

I wanted to know what he was going to say before he trailed off. But somehow I had the feeling that the answer would be breaking one of my rules, and damn it, that made me want to start crying. And hadn't I done just about enough of that lately?

I closed my eyes, then said, "Dylan. You're right. I'm too sensitive. And, to be fair... maybe I was checking you out, too. Let's go."

He turned back at me, took a deep breath, and nodded, carefully avoiding what I'd said.

He started out slow, so I was able to keep up. But I won't lie. My legs aren't used to running, and I can't even imagine what planet he came from that he came to enjoy running 15 or 20 miles on a regular basis. The Army put him on drugs, I'm sure of it now.

"So, um, how far are we going?" I asked.

"Not far," he replied. "I haven't been running since... well, before. I don't want to push it too far."

"Do you always go this early?"

"Yeah," he said. "It's... long standing habit, really. Plus, it's not really muggy yet. You wouldn't want to be running anywhere in noon heat, know what I mean?"

He had a point.

And, after a few minutes, I realized something else. Even though I was breathing heavily, and my legs were starting to hurt, I was enjoying myself. Maybe too much.

I could tell Dylan was really working at it now. He was loping along, every time his right foot came into contact with the sidewalk he lurched just slightly to the right. His lips were set in a grim line, face staring straight ahead.

"You okay?" I asked.

He nodded. "Yeah. Just got to remember to breathe. Two more blocks, and I think we walk back?"

"Okay," I said, really winded now.

"Are you okay?"

"Yeah, just not used to this."

"We can slow down," he said.

"No, keep going."

We ran two more very painfully long blocks, then slowed to a walk.

"You want to keep walking at a pretty decent pace," he said. "Don't come to a sudden stop. Helps your heart rate come back down to normal."

"Okay," I said, feeling a little inadequate that I was having difficulty keeping up with someone who'd nearly lost his right leg just a few months ago. And, looking at his chest and arms, tight inside that t-shirt, I thought it would take a lot more than a short walk to bring my heart rate down.

"You look kind of flushed," he said, eyeing me closely.

Jesus. I felt more heat run to my already overheated cheeks. Then it suddenly hit me. Dylan Paris was flirting with me. I snapped back immediately. "Yeah, well, chasing after guys does that to me."

His eyes widened a little bit, and then he smirked.

I blushed a little more, as if that were possible.

A few seconds later, he pointed. We were approaching Tom's Restaurant, a diner just off campus.

"Stop for breakfast?" he said. "It's on me. Least I can do for you keeping me company."

Did I really want to let Dylan buy me breakfast? Where was this leading? Normally, all my caution signals would be up and blaring, but for some reason I just gave in without an argument.

"Sure, thanks."

Two minutes later we were sitting at a table in the garish, fifties styled diner. With bright red chairs, stainless steel equipment, and black and white checks everywhere, it was frightful to the eye. But also kind of comfortable. Not the diner. What was comfortable was being there with Dylan.

A tired waitress who looked as if she'd been working all night came over and took our order. Me: a single scrambled egg, wheat toast with tomato slices and a glass of orange juice. Dylan ordered a ham and cheese omelet, pancakes, bacon, biscuits with gravy, coffee and hashbrowns. I don't know where on the table they were even going to fit all that food.

I couldn't help it.

"Eat much?" I asked.

He chuckled. "You get an appetite in the Army. I can put away some food these days."

While we waited for the wagon train to pull up with his breakfast, I asked him, "So, um... I know this is weird, but other than Doctor Forrester's work, I don't really know much about what you're doing these days."

He leaned back and looked me in the eyes, an odd smile on his face. "That's a pretty open-ended question," he replied.

Oh, wow. That was exactly what I'd said to him on an airplane a lifetime ago. "You remember that?"

"I'd answer that, but I don't want to break the rules."

"Very funny," I said, wrinkling my nose at him.

He grinned, and said, "All right, fair enough. You go first."

"What?"

"I won't say whether I remember it. But you get to ask the first question."

I laughed and shook my head. "All right. I guess I let myself in for that one. Why exactly did you pick Columbia University of all places?"

He shrugged. "Believe it or not, Columbia has really active outreach to vets. One of the recruitment guys found me in a hospital room at Walter Reed back in March. The rest is history."

At this point he was leaning back in his chair, one arm resting on the empty seat next to him. I leaned back in mine as well, stretching my feet across underneath the table and letting them sit on the empty chair.

"Your turn," I said.

He looked at me, and I blushed a little, looked down at the table.

"So, last winter you were trying to decide what to write for your final paper. What did you end up settling on?"

I took a deep breath, and looked up at him. "I can't believe you remember that. I mean... you were in the middle of a war, and getting shot at and blown up and hospitalized, and you remember me agonizing over my paper?"

A sideways smile, and he replied, "I'm the one asking the question right now."

I rolled my eyes. "Okay. I ended up doing a paper on the legal defenses for rape in the nineteenth century in the United States."

"Wow," he said. "That's fantastic. I'd love to read it sometime. I probably wouldn't understand word one of the legal stuff, but I'm interested anyway."

"Don't knock yourself, Dylan. You may come from a different background than me, but you're a smart guy."

"Not anymore," he said, grimacing and tapping on his forehead.

I grimaced, thinking with regret that I wished he'd stop beating up on himself, and said, "My turn?"

He nodded.

I thought. There was so much I wanted to know. And most of it skirted too close to the topics we avoided, too much of it broke the rules, too much of it simply led to heartache. Finally, I said, "What was the best thing you saw in Afghanistan? I know there was horror, and war. But were there moments of ... I don't know... grace?"

He swallowed, and nodded once. I was astonished to see his eyes start to water.

"I'm sorry, I didn't mean to —"

He held up a hand, saying stop. "It's okay." He took a deep breath, then said, "Okay. So, we're out there in the boonies. And I mean... way out there. Little village in the middle of nowhere called Dega Payan. It's way up in the mountains, and until a couple years ago, there wasn't even much of a road to connect them to anything. It was like a five hour drive to get anywhere."

"So, one day we're there. Helping distribute food, there's UN workers, and we're trying to make a nice impression and all that. And there's this little girl, standing there watching us. I guess she was... about twelve, maybe? I could picture her in middle school, if they allowed her to go to school, which they probably don't. Anyway, she was smiling, and joking around. Kowalski... he was from Nevada. Also from the middle of nowhere, go figure. Kowalski gives her a candy bar, and she hugs him. And then he turns to come back to us, and we hear a clink sound. Everybody panics, and I look down, and see the grenade. Someone threw it from the crowd, and it landed right at the little girl's feet."

Oh, my God. All I could think was, this was his moment of grace? His good thing that happened?

His eyes were really red now, and his face twisted a little as he said, "So, anyway, Kowalski... he threw himself on the grenade. He hugged it, with his back to the little girl. And it went off, and ... he was just... shredded. Killed instantly. And you know... that little girl... she didn't get touched. Not even a drop of blood. He saw that little girl, and just... threw his life away to save her."

I shook my head, and even though he couldn't cry, I started to. I couldn't help myself. Because when he was telling that story, it was like I could see into his soul, and oh, God, did that hurt.

"I'm so sorry," I said. "I'm sorry I asked. I'm so sorry that happened."

"No," he said, shaking his head. "Don't be. Don't you get it? Can you imagine the... the heroism? That's what grace is all about. He didn't even think for one second about himself. All he thought about was that little girl, and saving her life."

I sniffled. "Okay, new rule. If I'm about to ask you something that will make me start crying when I hear the answer, um, can you veto the question?"

He smiled, gently, and said, "If you want."

"Your turn, then."

The waitress showed up then, and brought us our food. And... let me tell you. I had actually underestimated how much he ordered. She had to bring two trays. Seriously. He tried to reorganize the plates a little, and ended up taking three quarters of the table. Pulling the pancakes toward him, he poured about ten thousand calories worth of syrup and butter on them, then started eating.

After swallowing he said, "Okay. What's your favorite thing to do now that you're in New York?"

I took a small bite of toast while I thought. Then I frowned. What was my favorite thing? I had things I liked to do, for sure. Kelly and I going out together. Going to the Butler Library. Picnicking in Riverside Park. What else? It's not that I hadn't enjoyed my freshman year in college, I really did. It's just that... nothing stuck out that I could tag as a favorite thing. Except one. And that was sitting in Doctor Forrester's office. With Dylan.

I frowned, then said, "I can't answer that one."

He widened his eyes and grinned. "You're kidding me. That's not in the rules."

"Screw the rules," I said. "The only answer I can give is a lie."

"Why?"

"Pick some other question, soldier boy."

"I'll get an answer one way or another. You can't tell me you've been in New York for a year and you still haven't come up with anything you love doing."

"I can tell you anything I want."

"You set the rules of this game, Alex. Not allowed to lie."

"Nothing says I have to answer, though."

He shook his head, then laughed. "I'm going to be obsessed with this."

"Why?"

"Because in all the time I've known you, I have never seen you change the rules of anything mid-game. This is just... mind-blowing."

I wanted to growl at him. Instead I ate a bite of my eggs, then said, "If I answer, you have to promise to just forget I said it."

He was thoroughly enjoying this. *God.*

"All right," he said. "My short term memory sucks anyway."

I stifled a laugh, then said, "Okay. Then the truth is, the time we've been working together in Doctor Forrester's. That's the answer."

He blinked, the smile slipping for a fraction. I couldn't figure out what his expression meant, because if I'd seen a picture of it,

I would have guessed abject terror. But that only lasted a moment, and then he said, "I don't remember any question or answer, so I get another one, right?"

"Dylan! That's not fair!"

Now he was really grinning.

"Fine," I said, trying not to burst out laughing. He looked so happy.

"Okay," he said. "Now I'm finally getting somewhere."

I chuckled. I couldn't help it.

"Let's see… Kelly's still your roommate here, I'm thinking. Tell me all about the last time you two went out. I want to know about your life here. What did you guys do?"

Jesus. He had a knack for asking heavy questions, didn't he? But I found myself telling him the story. Of our night out, and how Randy had grabbed my arm, and she pepper sprayed him. I left out all discussion of Dylan, of course. I also left out the background between me and Randy, including the fact that I'd known him since middle school, and especially the fact that he'd tried to rape me.

"Okay, wait a minute, I don't understand. I get it that the guy was coming on too strong, but why did she pepper spray him?"

Suddenly I was blinking back tears again.

"Oh, shit," he said. "I'm sorry. Whatever it is, you don't have to talk about it if you don't want to."

I bit my lower lip, then whispered, "He tried to rape me last spring."

Everything about Dylan's demeanor changed in an instant. He went from relaxed, enjoying himself, then concerned, but after the word "rape" came out of my mouth, he was sitting up straight in his chair. His face had gone cold, rage in his eyes like I'd never seen before. He was shaking.

"What did you say his name was?" he asked, his voice very low.

"It doesn't matter," I said.

"Yes. It does."

"Why?"

"Because if I ever see him, I'm going to put him in a fucking hospital. For a long time."

He was serious. Really serious. I had no doubt that if Randy Brewer was in front of us right now, Randy would end up in the hospital. And Dylan... would end up in jail.

"You really have changed a lot," I whispered.

"What?" he asked.

"I've known you... in a lot of different ways. But the one thing I've never thought about you was that you might be dangerous. Except to me."

He blinked. "Alex. Listen... whatever our history is, doesn't change the way I feel about you. The way I've always felt about you. I'd do anything to..."

He stopped. Was he struggling over a word again? Or holding back? Or was there a difference? And he didn't even say a word about me telling him he was dangerous for me. Because really, he knew that, didn't he? That we were dangerous for each other. Where was the big surprise in me saying that? I turned back to his stall.

"You'd do anything to what?"

He almost growled in frustration. "To... go back... go back and prevent that from happening to you. To protect you."

Was he about to say, to go back and change things? To go back and not hang up on me that night? To not disappear like he did?

"Listen to me, Dylan. This is important."

He was still staring at me, his eyes crazy intense. He nodded. "Okay."

"Forget about it. It's past. Okay? We don't need that. We don't need... this. Eat your breakfast. All right? Time for a change of subject."

He looked at me, calm, his gaze cool. Concentrating. I felt a bead of sweat in my hair, and took a deep breath.

"All right," he said. His voice had fallen back into that low growl that used to drive me insane. "It's your turn."

"My turn for what?"

"Your game."

I closed my eyes. This was playful four years ago. Now it was... frightening. Time to turn to something more cheerful.

"I'm not sure I want to play any more."

He practically collapsed in his seat, no longer intense, no longer staring. He closed his eyes, and took a deep breath, and said, "I'm sorry. Christ, I'm sorry. Alex, I've got some... let's just say, anger issues."

"I can see that," I said, desperately trying to regain the light tone we'd had before.

"So ask me a question," he said. "But try to pick something not so intense, and I'll do the same."

I shook my head, then said, "All right. Your favorite memory, ever."

He smiled bitterly. "I can't answer that. It's against the rules."

"Oh, screw the rules. Tell me."

He took a deep, shuddering breath. "My favorite memory, was sleeping with you in my arms in the Tel Aviv hostel the night before we left. It was... bittersweet, but wonderful. I didn't actually sleep that night. I just watched you. All that night, and then again, all the way home on the plane. We only had a few hours left, and I didn't want to lose a second of it sleeping. I was up about forty-eight hours I think, finally crashed hard on the plane back to Atlanta from New York."

I gave him a small, tentative smile. "Mine is the night we first kissed."

"Near the Dead Sea," he replied.

"It was dark, and the wind was blowing," I said, "and it was cool, and we were alone."

"You said, 'This could get complicated.'"

I suddenly laughed out loud, trying to hold back tears at the same time. I remembered saying that. I'd never been more right in my life. "It sure did."

"Yeah," he said. "It did."

"Where did we go wrong?"

He shrugged. "I don't know if it's because we couldn't let go, or because we let go too much."

I shook my head. "I don't either."

He looked at the table, and didn't reply.

Finally, I said in a near whisper, "Dylan… do you ever think…" I couldn't finish the question.

He kept looking at the table, and then replied, so quietly I almost couldn't hear him. "Always," he said.

I swallowed. "We should go."

"Yeah," he replied.

Run Away Fast (Dylan)

O kay, I'll be the first to admit that we'd crossed a line here, and I didn't know how to go back. Both of us had more or less admitted that we still loved each other. Both of us were so screwed up I hardly knew what to think or say.

I went to class in a fog. On Tuesdays I take college algebra at nine a.m. I'm already struggling with it, to be honest. It drives me nuts, because it ought to be an easy A. I took calculus in high school for God's sake; this was practically high school freshman stuff for me, and when I was in high school, I was really good at math. Now, sometimes I stare at the problems, and I can feel the headache building behind my forehead, and the formulas just swim in front of my eyes, letters and numbers everywhere, like they're swimming around in a damn whirlpool.

Three weeks into it, and I was already failing the class. And the thing is, I was on the GI Bill. I couldn't afford to be failing classes. So I broke down that day, and at the end of class that day I walked to Professor Wheeler's desk from my own in the front row and said, "Professor Wheeler, can we talk a minute?"

He looked up from his papers and said, "My office hours are Thursdays at 10 a.m."

"This won't take but a couple minutes, sir."

He frowned, deep creases forming in his face below his beard, and said, "What can I do for you, Mr. Paris?"

I took a deep breath, and said, "I'm failing your class."

He nodded. "You are."

"Listen, sir... I'm wondering... is there tutoring available that you know about?"

"Perhaps, Mr. Paris, algebra is simply beyond you. Have you considered taking 'Math for Liberal Arts Majors' or something similar?"

For a brief second I wanted to punch him, to wipe that smug smile off his face. He'd made no secret of his antipathy for soldiers since I'd walked into his class. I took a deep breath, and counted to ten, and then I laid it out. That math had been one of my real talents in high school. The bomb, and what it had done, scrambling my brain so I couldn't remember things.

"Sir... I know you don't like me. But... I'm asking you for help here. I'm doing everything I can to rebuild my life. I need to get this. Do you understand?"

He tugged at his beard with his thumb and forefinger, staring at me. Finally, he said, "I can put you in touch with a couple of tutors."

I breathed a sigh of relief. He wrote down the contact information, and passed me the sheet.

"Understand, I expect you to perform," he said. "Just because you were a soldier doesn't mean you get any kind of a pass from me, Paris. If you're going to stay in my class, you'll earn the grade that you earn. Am I clear?"

I nodded. "That's all I ask."

From there I moved on to my Ancient Western Civilization Class, which I was having a much easier time with. That night, I sent off an email to the tutors he had suggested.

I had trouble sleeping that night. And I should be clear: I never have trouble sleeping. The Army taught me to sleep at any opportunity I have. Got a fifteen-minute ride in the back of a two-ton truck going down a dusty road in the middle of nowhere? Sack time. For the last two years, I've been able to close my eyes and sleep without preparation, thought or warning. But the night after Alex went running with me, my mind kept turning back to the things I'd said—the things she'd said.

She didn't have to say it for me to realize it. If I hadn't been such an asshole, deleting my Skype and Facebook and refusing to answer her emails, she wouldn't have been out trying to date last spring. And that guy wouldn't have tried to rape her.

It was my fault. I'd left her unprotected. I'd put the woman I loved more than life itself at risk.

That wasn't going to happen again. It was too late for Alex and I as a couple, but I'd damned sure be her friend as long as she would have me.

I'd be whatever she wanted.

But my traitor of a mind turned to other things. It wasn't the first time we'd broken up, not by a long shot. In fact, when we returned home from Israel, both of us said it was over. What we had was beautiful, magical... and temporary. She was going back to dating Mike in San Francisco, and I was going back to Hailey in Atlanta.

But I broke up with Hailey four days after my return to Atlanta. And she did the same with Mike.

Neither of us said anything, really. It was just what happened. We weren't dating, we weren't exclusive, we weren't anything at all. Which was why I found myself in bed with Cyndi Harris on New Year's Eve, which was fun but... also sad. All the time we were rolling around in bed, I kept thinking of Alex, and how much I wished it were her. It made me... incredibly sad. And Cyndi knew it.

At one point she turned away from me, then said, "What's her name?"

"Who?" I asked.

"The girl you're in love with."

So, what could have been a fun roll in the hay on New Years Eve turned into me breaking down and crying, telling her how much I missed Alex. Cyndi was cool about it. She hugged me, and said all the right things, and we parted as friends.

I didn't date again for a while. Alex and I talked on the phone almost every day, anyway. We wrote emails to each other, and sent texts constantly, and prodded and poked each other on Facebook. We were four thousand miles away from each other, and I Facebook stalked her, checking out the photos she posted, trying to figure out what her status meant every time it changed.

Honestly, it was crazy. There I was, a senior in high school. The girl I loved was fully across the country from me. One week we were on, the next we were off. Neither of us could figure out what made the most sense to do. I planned going to visit her in March during spring break, but in early January, business was slow at the restaurant where I waited tables, and they let me go. No money meant no trips all the way across the country. So we missed each other in March, and one night during spring break she called me. Drunk.

The words that came out of her mouth stunned me. "I wish I could make love to you."

It stopped my heart.

So, I scrounged. I kept looking for a job, but no luck. It was 2009. Jobs waiting tables or washing dishes were going to guys with Masters degrees. An eighteen-year-old high school student didn't have a chance. I pawned my iPod, my mom and I held a yard sale, and I managed to scrounge up the sum total of one hundred and twenty dollars. And that was enough for a round trip Greyhound ride from Atlanta to San Francisco and back. I left the day after I graduated high school.

Anyway. Not much point in talking about the visit. It was... poignant... painful... pathetic. We kissed in Golden Gate Park. We made out in a photo booth at the Greyhound station before I left. We fell in love all over again, even though it was impossible. A week after I returned home, we had our first really nasty fight over the phone.

I did what I sometimes do best. I ran away fast. The morning after our fight, I enlisted in the US Army.

Is it any wonder that lying here in my bed at Columbia two years later, I wasn't able to get to sleep?

Instead of sleeping, I thought of holding her in my arms.

I thought of the literally hundreds of emails we'd sent back and forth.

I thought of the hundreds of hours we'd spent on the phone, talking about our lives, our dreams.

After running with her in the early morning it was hard to forget how much I loved her, and I needed to forget. Because the one thing I couldn't forget, or forgive for that matter, was the last conversation we had. Kowalski had been killed that morning, and we'd returned to base, shaken, horrified by his death. It was the low point in our deployment for most of us, and certainly for me. I desperately needed to talk. I needed her. Worse than I ever had before. And when I got her on Skype, she was fucking drunk. That much was obvious.

I tried to tell her what was going on, but she brushed me off. She started telling me it wasn't working, that we couldn't be together. And then, I saw the one thing I never expected to see. A guy, walking past her in her room, with his shirt off. As he passed her, his hand briefly touched her shoulder.

Even thinking about it makes me want to vomit. It makes me want to scream with rage. I'm not over it. I don't think I'll over get over it. And while I can spend all day long thinking about how much I love her, I can't forget that moment. I couldn't think. I couldn't say anything. I reached out and closed the connection. I logged on to Facebook and disabled my profile. I deleted my Skype account. I erased my digital identity. Then I took the laptop and smashed it.

The next morning we went back out into the field.

It was weeks before I got a chance to get to my email again. For reasons I'll never understand, my mother brought me a used laptop when I was at Walter Reed.

I had about twenty messages from her. For one aching moment, I almost read them. I couldn't do it. But I couldn't delete them either. So I stuck them in an archive folder where I wouldn't have to see them. And I tried to forget.

Like a lot of other things in my life, I did a pretty crappy job of forgetting.

CHAPTER SIX

I don't understand either one of you (Alex)

"Alex, I need your help," Kelly said the moment I walkedinto the room.

"Hey there. What's up?" I asked, setting my bag down next to the bed. I settled in on the bed, curling around one of my pillow.

She looked at me, then said, "Okay, so ... I think Joel may be coming around."

I rolled my eyes. "Oh come on, Kelly. He just wants to be out there, getting laid."

"You don't know that."

"What makes you think differently?"

She leaned back, her back against the wall, her legs hanging off the side of her bed. It looked extremely uncomfortable.

"Well," she replied. "I told you he asked me out on Friday. I turned him down again. So he sends me a poem."

"Oh, no, he didn't."

She nodded, grinning. "It was awful. But really sweet, too."

"I didn't know he wrote poetry."

"Well... don't tell him I said this, but he really shouldn't."

I burst out laughing.

"So... this morning I was in Doctor Abernathy's office." Kelly was also on work-study, and spent two mornings a week as a receptionist at Columbia University Medical Center. "And a courier comes in. With a bouquet of hollyhock."

"A bouquet of *what?*"

"Come on, Alex. It's only my favorite flower. Point is, he remembered. He didn't send me a dozen roses, which would be nice, but unoriginal. Instead, he sent me something he knew I would love."

"Okay, that's really sweet, I'll admit it."

"Okay, so he wants to go out Saturday. And I really want to. But... not alone. Not the first time. I need my best friend along."

"Won't that be awkward?"

"Not if you bring a date."

"Um... no."

"*Alex!* Come on!"

"Seriously, no. There's no one I'm even remotely interested in dating."

Now she rolled her eyes. "Oh yeah, right. I see. Let me think. I'm trying to think of a guy you can ask."

"Good luck with that," I replied.

"Oh, I know," she said, her voice sarcastic. "Let me think... I bet there's someone you see every other day at work-study. And spend hours with. And then on the other days you get up at a nightmare hour to go running with. Eww. Seriously."

"Kelly, stop. It's not like that."

She sat up straight and threw a pillow at me. "Come on, Alex! You're my friend. I need you on this. And it's not like you don't spend six days a week with him anyway!"

"Yeah, but those aren't dates!"

I was telling the truth. Even though he hadn't asked me to come again, I'd been showing up at six a.m. every other day. We ran together, sometimes in silence. This morning, in fact, we'd gone almost three miles. To be honest, I was secretly pleased I'd been able to keep up. And at least once or twice a week we had breakfast. Or coffee, after leaving the rare manuscripts library. But we weren't dating. And, by and large, we'd avoided the kind of talk that had gotten us into trouble a couple weeks ago. We were following the rules, and it was working, and I didn't want to ruin it.

I held my breath, thinking, hard. I really didn't want to ruin it.

I swallowed, then said, "All right. But it won't be a date."

"Whatever, Alex."

I smiled at Kelly.

She said, "Thanks."

"Don't be surprised if he turns me down."

"I don't understand either one of you."

I sighed. "I don't either."

Flowers from Afghanistan (Dylan)

Bad idea, I thought. Really bad idea. First of all, it was a Saturday night, and I was walking to Alex's dorm room to meet her and pick her up for our non-date. Or our non-date date? Undate? Whatever. We were going to a bar, where people would be drinking, and loud, and obnoxious, and my only tenuous connection to reality would be the one person I could not reach out to.

This was a really fucking bad idea.

I checked my phone. Ten after ten already. I was late. I quickly sent her a text.

BE THERE IN A MOMENT SORRY LATE

She wrote back damn near instantly.

Ok. Hugs. :)

Oh, come on. Seriously? Hugs? That was the absolute last thing either one of us needed to be doing.

After our way-too-open morning run and breakfast, I'd worked hard to reestablish normality. It was necessary. But we were still spending a huge amount of time together. The next Thursday morning, at six am, she'd shown up on the green without a word, in running shoes, and a significantly less revealing outfit than the first day. That was a relief. If she'd only known how my breath had caught when I'd caught sight of her that first day.

Better she didn't.

So, not only did I follow her rules, I made up my own.

No flirting.

No excessive eye contact.

Above all, nothing that could be misconstrued as a date.

I was protecting myself, but I was also protecting her. And then, Friday afternoon, after we left the library, she approached me about tonight.

"It's for Kelly," she said. Kelly and her boyfriend, whatever his name is, are on the verge of getting back together. This is the first time they're going out since they broke up, and Kelly needs a buffer, something to keep them from getting into a huge fight or something. But three is a crowd, and going as two couples wouldn't be so painfully awkward, she said.

Yeah, sure it wouldn't.

I found the building and hit the buzzer for her room.

She buzzed me in.

Damn. I'd hoped she'd just meet me down here. Seeing her room was going to be awkward in its own way. Somehow we'd managed to avoid that level of intimacy. And I desperately needed to keep my distance.

Whatever.

So I worked my way up the stairs to the fourth floor. This had been my own personal challenge for the past week. Never take an elevator when there were stairs. In two weeks of running, more strength had returned to my right leg than I'd felt in a long time. I was a long way from whole, but I was even further away from where I'd been seven months ago, when they were debating whether or not to cut off my leg.

On the fourth floor, I followed the room numbers to hers, then knocked. A cute chalk-board was attached to the door, saying simply *Kelly and Alex*.

"Be right there!" I heard her call. She opened the door, and I caught my breath.

Oh, my God.

Her hair was in some kind of complicated bun on the back of her head, with long tresses hanging down over her shoulders in a very loose curl. She wore a dark green sleeveless dress, cut just above the knee, that hugged her form perfectly. I took a shallow breath. She'd done something with her makeup. Her deep green eyes looked huge.

Color flew to her cheeks when she looked at me. Both of us averted our eyes.

"Come on in, I'll be ready in just a second," she said.

Nervous as hell, I followed her into the room.

It was obvious which side was Alex's.

Kelly's side of the room was swathed in pink, movie and band posters, huge fluff pillows.

Alex's was subdued. A world map hung over her desk, and a stack of books was loosely arranged on one side of the desk.

A picture frame contained pressed and dried flowers. A date was written on the backing of the frame, just below the flowers. *November 19th, 2011.*

Those were the flowers I sent her when I was in Afghanistan, last year.

On the bureau was a picture that nearly ripped my heart out. It was the two of us, curled up together. I remembered when it was taken. We were in Haifa, at a park near the Central Carmel. I'd been playing guitar most of the night, and when I stopped, we curled up together, laughing and talking. I had a copy of the same photo.

I averted my eyes, trying to keep my breathing calm.

"I'm ready," she said, coming out of the restroom. She looked at me, then her eyes darted to the picture, the flowers, and her cheeks colored. We avoided each other's eyes as we left the room.

She headed for the stairs, even in her heels, which looked impossible to walk in, and also impossibly sexy. That dress complimented by a tiny wrap over her shoulders, hugged her body in a way that made my pulse rush in my temples. I shook my head. This was Alex trying to take care of me, because she knew I'd sworn off elevators. I couldn't help but scan her entire body with my eyes as she walked ahead of me a few steps. Holy shit, but she was beautiful. This is going to sound crazy obnoxious, but I wanted nothing more at that moment to lay her down, take her legs in my hands and lick her calves.

This was going to be a long, long night.

"We can take the elevator," I said.

"They're just heels, it's fine."

I shrugged.

When we got to the street, I said, "So, I got an email from my friend Sherman."

"Oh yeah?"

I nodded. "He's coming home next week, and said he wants to come to New York for a couple weeks. I think he's thinking about college up here."

"Oh wow, that's exciting!"

"It'll be strange. That part of my life and this part of my life... they don't really connect. It's hard to imagine having him here."

"We'll show him the town," she said. "It'll be good for you to have a friend here."

I took a sharp shallow breath at her use of the word *we*. Every moment I spent with this girl was a show of restraint. Hard to imagine as it was, I'd had a lot of sleepless nights lately. She was busy making plans for "us" and I was trying my hardest to keep my distance. Maintaining that distance was killing me. I loved her, but honestly, part of me hated her too.

I tensed up as we approached the 1020 Bar. A small crowd of people stood out front smoking. Inside it looked like a madhouse. Extremely loud music, people packed in like it was a Japanese subway. Screaming and shouting. It sounded like a band was playing inside.

Unconsciously I slowed to a stop as we approached the door.

"You okay?" she asked. "You look a little pale."

"Sorry," I said. "I don't do well with crowded places any more."

"I'll stay close," she said.

That ought to help me relax. *Yeah, right.*

She took my arm, curling herself close to me, and we walked into. She was scanning the crowd, looking for Kelly and boyfriend, whose name I couldn't recall.

After a few minutes pushing our way through the crowd, we found them, sitting at a tall round table with four stools around it.

I froze when I saw the boyfriend.

"Dylan, this is Kelly and Joel. Kelly and Joel, this is Dylan."

Kelly smiled, a huge grin, and said, "Wow. Dylan, it is so cool to finally get to meet you."

Joel held out his hand to shake, and said, "Hey man, yeah, it's good to finally meet you. I've heard so much."

I stared into the face of the man I'd seen in the Skype video. The shirtless guy who had been in Alex's room the night I broke it off with her for good. I couldn't breath, and my eyes darted to Alex, who was starting to look concerned, then I looked back at him and muttered, "Motherfucker."

I shook my arm free from Alex, turned and pushed my way through the crowd back to the exit.

Um, yeah. I better see a doctor (Alex)

"What the hell?" Kelly asked when Dylan pushed away from us and almost ran for the door.

"I don't know!" I said, my voice rising into a near wail. What was wrong? What had I done?

"Go after him, Alex. Don't let him go without an explanation. Not again!"

I was shaking, and breathing fast, shallow breaths. Freaking out. A vision of all those weeks I'd spent in February and March, mostly curled up in my bed crying.

That son of a bitch was not doing that to me again.

I turned and ran for the door, not caring if they followed.

He was halfway down the block. I ran after him, shouting, "Dylan! Wait!"

I saw his shoulders tense up when he heard me. He stopped walking, his back straight, still turned away from me.

"Dylan! What the hell?" I screamed. "Why did you do that? Why did you walk out like that?"

He turned toward me, and it felt like I'd been punched. His eyes were red and watering, eyebrows scrunched together, making a line down the center of his forehead.

He pointed his finger back at the bar, and shouted, "You know how I feel about you. How the fuck can you bring me here, knowing he was going to be here?"

I flinched at the shout. Never in all the time we'd known each other had he done that. And the question. *What?* It didn't make any sense at all. He didn't even know Joel.

"I don't know what the hell you're talking about, Dylan!"

He shook his head, his face etched in grief. "I thought you were... something else, Alex. I... oh, fucking Christ, I never even imagined this."

"Imagined *what?* I don't understand you at all!"

"*Him!* He was in your room that night. Don't bother to deny it, I saw him! You're on fucking Skype, breaking up with me on what was already the worst day of my life, and then that fucker comes over, his fat ass shirtless, and puts his hand on you as he walks by. Did you guys laugh it up when you planned the breakup? Were you fucking before you called me?"

It felt like he'd punched me. I backed away two or three steps, then said, "Dylan... that's Joel. He's Kelly's boyfriend."

"Then why the hell was he there?"

Now I screamed back. "Because he's her boyfriend, you asshole. He was over all the time, those two are attached at the hip! Are you telling me you broke it off with me because of that? You broke my heart because of a stupid misunderstanding? Because you thought you saw a guy in my room?"

He shook his head.

"He was with Kelly?" he said in a ragged whisper. His face was twisting in grief and anger. Anger with himself? I didn't understand.

Suddenly he screamed, "Fuck!" and slammed his fist into the metal grating of the store we stood next too. He let out a howl, a real, literal howl, and slammed his fist into the metal grate again. Then he did it again, and again, shouting, "Fuck!" every time he slammed his fist into the wall.

The rage just left me, because the last time he hit the wall, blood splattered against it. I started crying, really hard, because he was hurting himself, he was really hurting himself.

"Dylan," I whispered. "Stop."

He didn't even hear me. So I did the only thing I could think of. I put my arms around him, right around his chest, and buried my face against his back, and I cried out, as loud as I could, "Dylan, please stop! Please don't hurt yourself! I love you!"

He stopped, and stiffened in my arms. I sobbed against his back. Abruptly he turned in my arms, and wrapped me in his, his muscles holding me so tight I almost couldn't breath.

Both of us were crying, and I started to say, "I'm sorry," and he said, "I didn't know. Oh, my God, I'm so sorry, Alex."

He started to sob, real howls of pain, and he somehow punched out the words, "That was the day Kowalski threw himself on the grenade, Alex. I was crazy out of my mind when I called you." His voice dropped to a whisper, and he said, "You were drunk, and I needed you so bad."

I cried even harder, and tried to curl against him even tighter, and said, "I'm so sorry, Dylan. I didn't know. I didn't know."

"I never stopped loving you," he whispered. "Not even for a second. Even when I hated you."

I whispered, "I love you, too, Dylan."

It had been more than two years since the last time we held each other like this, the morning he left San Francisco to go back home. Both of us had changed, but for the first time in two years, I felt whole with his arms wrapped around me.

The moment would have been perfect, but I heard Kelly's voice behind us. "Um... I hate to interrupt this incredibly touching scene, but um... he needs to go the hospital. Like, right now."

Dylan and I both jerked. We pulled slightly apart, and I took his arm in my hand.

Oh, shit.

His hand was... mangled. Knuckles split, blood dropping to the ground in great big splatters. I felt my breath speed up suddenly, and realized that I could see the *bone* of one of his fingers.

"Jesus Christ, Dylan, look what you did to your hand!"

He looked down at his hand, a lost expression on his face. He shook his head, and said, "Um, yeah. I better see a doctor."

He closed his eyes and swayed a little.

"We're coming with you," Joel said.

Kelly nodded.

So I took my wrap off, and wound it around his injured hand, and we waved down a cab.

CHAPTER SEVEN

Worth fighting for (Dylan)

So, next thing I knew the four of us were crammed into the backseat of a taxi, on our way to the VA hospital all the way down on the Lower East Side. I was all the way over on the left side of the seat, with Alex somehow wrapped around me, my right hand resting palm up in her lap, wrapped in her silk wrap, which wasn't going to be much good for wearing after tonight. She leaned against me, and as much pain as my hand was in—which was a lot —most of my focus was on her.

Neither of us spoke, I think because this moment was just too big to get words around it.

Kelly and Joel pretty much took care of that for us. Kelly was sitting in the middle of the back seat, and she muttered to Joel, "You never mangled your hand for me. What kind of boyfriend were you, anyway?"

"Are you fucking kidding me?" Joel answered.

"I'm just saying. I don't think you're really serious. If you were, you'd find a way to show it. Like completely fucking up your hand or something."

Alex shook with laughter against me. I turned my head, looked down at her, resting her head on my shoulder.

"It's not that I don't take you seriously, Kelly. Or that I'm not serious. I'm just not fucking crazy like this guy obviously is." He looked across the car at me. "No personal offense meant, Dylan."

I grimaced. Oh, Christ, that hurt like a motherfucker.

"None taken," I croaked.

"Look, Kelly," he said. "I need you to hear me on this."

Kelly was sitting as far from Joel as she could get, which meant that she was jammed hip to hip against Alex. Her back was straight and she was staring straight forward, her arms crossed over her chest.

"I think I just got scared, okay? What are we, nineteen? It's a big fucking commitment! Neither of us dated anyone else since we started college, and… I was afraid."

"That's not true," Kelly said. "You've been busy *playing the field* since school started this year. If I do ever let you near me again, you're getting tested for STDs first."

"Oh, for God's sake."

"Seriously, what the hell does playing the field mean anyway? Am I like some sports metaphor for you? You made it to home base, so now it's time to go to the Superbowl or whatever?"

He shook his head. "Superbowl is football hun, home base is baseball."

"Oh. My. *God!*"

"Aww, shit. Look, I screwed up, Kels. I love you! I don't want anyone but you!"

"Well, now you're back in Little League, buster, and they don't have bases. Or field goals. Or... whatever. You're so going to have to convince me."

"I got you those weird flowers you like."

Alex started to shake, hard, suppressing laughter. I looked back down at her, and our eyes met. She smiled, and I wanted to lean over and kiss her more than anything else in the world, except that would have moved my damned hand.

She stretched up, putting her lips next to my ear, and whispered, "She's a goalie now, isn't she?"

I couldn't help it. I burst into laughter.

"*Weird* flowers? You are so far from convincing me, you have no idea."

"What do I have to do to convince you, babe?" he said.

"Send me more *weird* things that I like."

"Done."

"You're going to have to grovel. Maybe forever."

"Jesus Christ, lady," the taxi driver said. "Give the guy a break!"

I couldn't hold it in any longer. I guffawed, shaking with it, and Alex joined me.

Kelly looked over at us, and said, "Well, you two are no help at all!"

Oh, God! I laughed even harder, tears running down my cheeks. I wiped them away with my good hand, and said, "Kelly, I'm so glad I finally met you."

She gave a loud "*Hmmmph,*" then said, "Only because it looks like you and hormone girl are back together."

I was lightheaded, and gave her a big smile. Were we? Back together? I don't know. But whatever we were, it was better than being heartbroken.

Kelly and Joel bickered the entire way to the hospital. At one point I leaned down and whispered to Alex, "I thought she wanted to get back together with him."

She whispered back, "Don't worry, this is normal for them."

Jesus Christ. If this was normal, I didn't want to see what they were like when she was upset.

Then again, it seemed a lot less painful than what Alex and I had been doing all these months.

And that was when the weight of it hit me again. She might be all curled up against me now, when I was injured, but could she really forgive me? I got it, finally. Because it was nothing more than a misunderstanding. It hadn't been *some guy* in her room. It was just her roommate's boyfriend, being friendly. I'd so totally screwed this up that I was afraid there was no going back. The significance of the photo on her nightstand, the dried roses framed on her wall, didn't escape me. We'd loved each other, and I'd hurt her. Hurt her badly. Did I even have a right to be forgiven?

Right then and there, I promised myself we'd talk the moment we were alone. We would hash this out. We'd break every rule either one of us had, until we really understood each other, and what happened, and whether or not we could move forward.

Because, for the first time since that hideous week when Kowalski and Roberts died, for the first time since I landed in the hospital, I began to feel some hope. Hope, because of the woman curled up against my side. And that was something worth fighting for.

The cab pulled up to the emergency room, and I started to stretch around, trying to get at my wallet with the wrong hand.

"Don't be an idiot," Alex said, fishing in her purse. She passed a twenty to the cab driver, and we got out of the cab. I staggered a little, and she wrapped her arms around my side.

"Sorry I ruined your night," I said to Kelly and Joel.

"Don't worry about it, man," Joel said. "Watching you guys fight was way more entertaining than sitting at 1020 anyway. Besides, I'm glad we sorted it out. If we'd met alone somewhere, you might have been hitting *me* instead of a wall. And that would have been kind of upsetting."

Kelly rolled her eyes and slapped Joel on the shoulder. It was a possessive slap, and I was pretty sure she was giving in.

"Yeah," I said, my voice cracking a little. "Misunderstanding, okay?"

"Yeah, we kinda heard the whole thing," he said. "Don't stress it."

At the desk in the emergency room, we did paperwork. And I bled a little on the desk, then apologized. A few minutes later a physician's assistant came over and did triage, decided that as bad as it looked, my hand wasn't life threatening, then said someone would be with us eventually.

"This might take a while," I said.

"We've got all the time in the world," Alex murmured. She still hadn't let go of me.

So we waited. After a little while, Joel and Kelly stopped bickering, and started making out. They were getting a lot of interested looks from the other people in the waiting room, until finally an elderly lady sitting two seats down from them tapped Joel on the shoulder with her cane.

"You two are indecent," she said. "Why don't you take it somewhere else."

"Oh God," Kelly said. "I'm so sorry."

"Yeah, sorry," Joel mumbled.

"Maybe you two should get going," Alex said. "We'll be fine here."

"You're sure?" Kelly asked.

By this time Joel was standing, tugging on her hand.

"Yes," Alex said, nodding. "Go!"

Kelly leaned in close to Alex and whispered, "I probably won't be home tonight."

Alex grinned. "See you tomorrow, then."

Joel looked over at me, said, "Later, Dylan. Nice to meet you." He stuck his hand out to shake, and I automatically did the same, then gasped in pain. We did *not* shake hands.

I nodded to him. The two of them hurried out of the emergency room, hand in hand.

"They're funny," I said.

She grinned. "Yeah. But they love each other."

She leaned in a little closer to me as she set it.

I took a deep breath, trying to ignore the pain in my hand, and said, "What about us? What are we exactly, now?"

She looked at me, her eyes stealing away my breath, and said, "Do we have to figure that out right now?"

I said, "Not right this second. But soon. Before... before we get our hearts broken all over again."

She winced. "Good point, I guess." She looked away, and I could see her lower lip quivering.

"Alex," I said. "Listen to me."

She turned back toward me.

"I want to talk about what happened. Between us."

She nodded, then said, "Why?"

"I think we need to clear the air. Alex... we've been dancing around this for weeks. Sometimes flirting, sometimes not. Remembering, but not. Playing by rules that seemed to make sense, but maybe they don't really. I think it's time to be honest about what's going on with us."

She blinked, and took a deep breath. Her expression radiated anxiety.

"Talk to me, Alex. Why are you afraid of this?"

Her mouth twitched at the edges into a smile. She whispered, "Because I'm happier right now than I've been in a long time. I don't want to screw it up."

I took a deep, shuddering breath. It was clear she really meant it. She was happier right now than she'd been in a long time, *because she was with me.*

All the more reason to be honest, about everything.

"Neither do I," I said. "And I'm afraid if we don't talk, I'll have assumptions, or you'll have assumptions, that the other doesn't share. And we'll screw up again. And that... I don't think I could take it."

"Just answer me one thing," she said.

I nodded.

"Do you love me? Really? Still?"

I pulled her closer, and said, quietly, "More than life itself."

She wrapped her arms around me and leaned against my chest. "Okay. Then I'll talk about whatever you want to talk about."

So, now that you've mentioned the pill (Alex)

"Okay," I said. "Then I'll talk about whatever you want to talk about."

I couldn't seem to stop holding Dylan. My hands were wrapped around his waist, and I could feel the hard muscle of his abdominal muscles under them.

There was no question Dylan was not the same boy I'd fallen in love with. He'd grown, matured in ways I couldn't have foreseen four years ago. Sometimes I could look at him and see the hardened soldier he'd had to become: occasionally grim faced, chest and arms built like a boxer, short cropped hair, and especially his eyes; eyes that sometimes stared off into the distance as if he were a million light years away. That was the Dylan it was hard to get used to: the one who could get so angry he would slam his fist over and over again into a wall until he broke bones. I sort of understood what had happened to the man, but it was difficult to match up the reality with the boy I'd known and fallen in love with.

The Dylan I'd fallen in love with was gentle, and kind. Thoughtful. Funny. He was still all of those things, but had an edge to him that was new and, to be honest, frightening. This was a guy who'd carried weapons in a war for most of last year. This was a man who had killed, who had seen his friends killed in battle. There were depths to him that were all new, and scary as hell.

"So..." I said, my voice dropping to a whisper. "Where do we start?"

He smiled brilliantly, but I could tell he was in a tremendous amount of pain.

"I have no idea," he said.

I leaned my head back, letting out a low chuckle. Finally I said, "Let's take our time. Here's what I'll promise. I promise to give it a chance."

He nodded. "Me too," he said.

"In some ways, you know, we hardly know each other."

"It's true. I mean... we were seventeen the last time we spent any time together."

"I was sixteen. And yes... that's a long time."

"Plus," he said, "It wasn't exactly a normal environment. As much as the Middle East sucks in my mind, there's no denying the incredible romance of it all."

I looked up at him, meeting his gaze again, and he said, "You know what?"

"What?"

"There's a side benefit to this. We get to learn about each other, get to know each other, all over again." His voice dropped to a husky near whisper, and he leaned close and said next to my ear, "We get to fall in love all over again, for the second time. How cool is that?"

I smiled so wide it hurt my cheeks, and put my lips next to his ear and whispered, "I'd say you're worth falling in love with twice."

The old lady who had run off Kelly and Joel cleared her throat, then began grumbling. I rolled my eyes a little, but pulled back all the same. It was just as well, because a few moments later Dylan's name was called.

I stood and walked with him, holding his uninjured hand. In a curtained-off examination room, a young doctor, probably a medical student, took a look at Dylan's hand, and said, "Holy mother, what did you do?"

Dylan grimaced. "I kind of punched a wall. Pretty hard."

The doctor shook his head. "That's one hell of a punch. We're going to need to get ex-rays. This is going to hurt like hell, I've got to clean the wound or it will go septic. Couple questions... any previous hospitalizations?"

"Um, yeah," Dylan said. I knew he had answered this on the intake form. "Roadside bomb, in February. Screwed up my leg pretty bad. TBI."

"How's the leg doing?" the doctor asked.

"I walked in here. The other guys from my hummer are dead. I'm doing okay."

I shivered at the matter of fact way he said it.

The doctor looked over his glasses at Dylan, then said, "You taking any medications?"

Dylan hesitated, looked at me as if considering something, then answered. "Oxycodone. We've been tapering the dosage down for a few months. Paxil. And trileptal."

I swallowed. He was taking a boatload of drugs. I had no idea.

"Trileptal," the doctor said. "For seizures?"

"Yeah, I've had them occasionally. My primary care doc in Atlanta has been reducing the dosage of everything, but when we tried to stop the anticonvulsants, well... I had seizures. It wasn't pretty."

The reality of his war injuries was hitting me hard. Dylan Paris, the guy I knew when we were teenagers... he was a disabled veteran with severe injuries.

"Hmm... I think just continue the oxy for the pain. We'll get some X-rays done, then decide what to do about the hand. It's going to be a long night for you, Mr. Paris. Wait here, I'll be right back with you."

Dylan sighed, then closed his eyes. I held his left hand, and he said, "You don't have to stay. This is going to take all night."

I leaned over and kissed him on his eyelid. "Dylan, there's nowhere I'd rather be than here with you."

"You're crazy," he said.

"Crazy for you."

He let out a short, bark-like laugh, then kissed my forehead. "You didn't know I was on all that stuff."

I shook my head.

"The oxy we've taken down to very little in the last couple months. It's awesome stuff when you have big gaping holes in you. They started me out on morphine, believe it or not. Holy cow, that stuff is dreamy. I've been trying to get them to keep it to an absolute minimum. A little pain won't kill me, but drug addiction will."

I nodded, just listening.

"The uh... Paxil... Well, you know. I told you I've got some uh, anger issues. Post-traumatic stress. Depression. All that fun stuff."

He sounded almost ashamed of himself.

"It's okay, Dylan. That's perfectly normal. Half the people I know are taking Paxil or something like it."

He shook his head. "Yeah, well, I'm not a big fan of drugs of any kind."

"Except your cigarettes."

He shrugged, then smirked at me. "That's different. Think they'd notice if I had one in here?"

"Yeah, I do."

He frowned. "Bummer."

We sat in silence for a few moments. Then he said, "It doesn't bother you? The anticonvulsants and all that shit? I'm like taking half the pharmacy. I could break down and have a seizure any time;

it still happens sometimes, even with the pills. I can't even get a driver's license because of it."

I frowned. "Does it bother you that I'm on birth control pills?"

Dylan nearly choked, and I got to see something I hadn't seen in years. He blushed.

I started to giggle, then broke into real laughter.

"Okay. You made your point," he said.

I still snickered a little, so he decided to turn the tables on me.

"So, now that you've mentioned the pill..." he said.

"No. Not ready yet." I shook my head, a little theatrically.

He raised his eyebrows, grinning.

"Stop that."

"Stop what?"

"Stop eying me like I'm a piece of meat."

He grinned. "I was thinking more along the lines of... hmm... strawberry shortcake?"

"Oh, no. You are *so* not going there. I am not short. And you are ridiculous."

"That's why you love me."

We heard a loud cough and throat-clearing behind us, and the doctor whisked the privacy curtain to the side. "This way, please, Mr. Paris."

Screw the rules (Dylan)

efore the long, long night at the emergency room was over, I tried twice more to send Alex home. She refused to go. Instead, during the hours I was waiting for treatment, she lay curled up on the chair next to me, her head resting in my lap as she slept.

The last time we'd been like this, her sleeping next to me, was on a plane a thousand years ago.

It was four in the morning before we finally got out of there. By that time, my hand was wrapped in a heavy cast, immobilizing the fingers. Two of my finger bones had been fractured, the skin torn open on all of them. At one point, when Alex was out of the room, the doctor had suggested I come back to see a psychiatrist and possibly seek out some anger management classes.

"Look," he said. "We see a lot of guys in your situation. You've been in combat. I'm guessing you've lost friends."

I nodded.

"It's not unusual to have long-term emotional responses to this stuff. Combined with the brain injury, it could be a real problem for you."

I sighed. "I was seeing a therapist at the VA in Atlanta, before I came up here for college."

"I think you need to consider setting up an appointment here."

"I already spend three mornings a week at the VA for physical therapy."

"So one more won't hurt."

I nodded. "I suppose. I'll do it."

"Good," he said.

A moment later Alex returned, carrying two large cups of coffee, and the doctor changed the subject.

In the cab, after leaving the hospital, she said in a sleepy voice, "Just come back to my place for the night?"

I swallowed and took a deep breath, a flash of anxiety running through me.

"Are you sure?" I asked.

She nodded. She was leaning against me, arms wrapped around my waist, as the cab cruised up the dark, nearly empty early-morning streets.

"Yes," she murmured. "I don't want you alone." She breathed for a couple minutes, then said, "I don't want to be alone."

So the cab let us off in front of her dorm. She unlocked the door, and we took the stairs up. At the door to the room she shared with Kelly, she turned back to me and put her arms around me. "Just sleep, okay? I meant what I said, I'm not ready for... you know."

"Of course," I said.

"It's all too new, and different, and confusing," she said.

"Sleep is good," I said. I was pretty fucking groggy at that point.

She smirked, then turned around and unlocked the door. She took my hand and pulled me in. We tiptoed, in case Kelly was there, but as promised, she hadn't come back to the room. *Good for her and Joel,* I thought.

I took a deep breath, looking at her. She looked back, her eyes wide and green and beautiful, and I said the first thing that came to mind.

"Is kissing you against the rules?"

"Screw the rules," she said. She stepped closer to me, and I put my arms around her, holding the heavy damned cast slightly away from her body. Oh, God, it felt good to touch her. She was breathing quietly as she tilted her head back, and I leaned close, and our lips touched.

My eyes closed, and all my attention focused on where our lips touched, warm, welcoming. Hungry. Her arms came up around me, pressing hard against my back, and suddenly she was pressing her entire body against me. I could feel her breasts against my chest, her hips against mine, and I nearly gasped at the intensity of it. Her mouth opened, and our tongues touched, and she let out a soft moan.

I let my knees bend, then gripped her hard around the waist with my right arm and behind the knees with my left. Our lips never lost contact as I lifted her up and carried her toward the bed. Slowly, I sat down with her still in my arms. She twisted, then wrapped her legs around me.

My right hand trailed down her back and side to her thighs, then back up, and I breathed deeply, drinking her scent in. The smooth skin, the curve of her thigh, the sweet smell of her hair and face.

"Oh, my God, I've missed you, Dylan," she said.

I shifted, bringing my mouth to her neck. She tilted her head back, exposing her entire neckline, and I slowly moved my lips along her jawline to just below her ear.

I whispered, "I love you."

At that, she put both hands to my chest and pushed, tilting me back onto the bed. I kicked off my shoes, and she straddled me, laying her chest against mine. She brought her lips to my neck, and I could feel her incredible hair against my lips. I felt her hands against my shirt buttons.

She let out a low chuckle.

"What?" I said.

"You know," she said, her voice almost a growl, "With this cast, you're going to be practically helpless. I've finally got you under my control."

"I can live with that," I said, shivering.

She kept unbuttoning my shirt, working her way down slowly, licking my chest as she moved. I closed my eyes, arching my back a little, pushing closer to her. I gasped as she lightly bit one of my nipples, then let out a low groan as her tongue worked its way down my chest. My right hand lay uselessly at my side, encased in its cast, as the left one slowly traced the line of her back, her butt, her legs. I was lightheaded; this was better than any drug I'd ever known.

We were both breathing heavily as I said, "I don't ever want to be the voice of reason. But is this leading further than you intended?"

She nodded, her hair running across my chest, then she whispered, "I don't care."

I looked down my chest, then reached out with my left hand, taking her underneath her armpit and pulling her up to me until we were face to face. There was no way she didn't know just how aroused I was, not in that thin little dress, with her legs wrapped around me.

I took a deep breath, and said, "You wanted to wait. I don't want to fuck this up by going too fast. Alex… you mean too much to me for that."

She kissed me, her lips slow and deliberate, her tongue just touching my upper lip, then whispered, "Dylan, make love to me. It's been at least twenty minutes since we got here. I've waited long enough, damn it."

I chuckled, and then she laughed, and got up on her knees and slowly pulled her dress up over her head.

I won't lie. I'd been fantasizing about this moment for three years. In our time in Israel, we'd done a lot of making out. A lot of breathless moments. But I'd never seen her without her clothes, and right at that moment, there was nothing in the world I would have traded for it. She had a fantastic body, curved, her breasts hidden behind a black lace bra that took my breath away. My heart was pounding. From excitement, from fear.

"You'll have to do all the hard work," I murmured. "You know, my hand...."

She grinned. "I think you're taking advantage."

I nodded. "Yes."

She whispered, "I'm... not... um..."

Her face flushed red, and she leaned close to me. Oh, God. The feel of her skin against mine set me on fire.

"You're not what?" I asked.

She buried her face against my neck. "I've never done this," she whispered.

I took a deep breath.

I'd suspected. She'd been a virgin when we met, of course, and if she'd had any lovers since, she'd kept them secret. Letting out my breath, I said, "We don't have to do this if you aren't ready."

My body so disagreed with what I had just said. I would be in a lot of pain if we stopped now, but pain was something I knew intimately anyway.

She whispered, "Are you sure?"

"Yes," I said. I looked her in the eyes. And her eyes were frightened, there was no question. "Alex... I love you. I'll go where you lead me. I won't ask for more."

A tear ran down her face, and she said, "I don't know what I did to deserve you."

I gave her a half smile and said, "You've got that backwards, Alex. I'm the one who... who is undeserving."

"Don't ever say that," she said.

"Why not? It's the truth."

She shook her head. "You're wrong, Dylan Paris. About this, you are so wrong. We were made for each other."

I leaned close and kissed her forehead, and she curled up next to me. Before long, she'd fallen asleep, curled up against my left side, her head resting on my chest.

After she'd fallen asleep, I lay there a few more minutes. A tear ran down my own face. One, then another. I took a deep shuddering breath, knowing that somehow life had given me another chance. Somehow *she* had given me another chance. This time I couldn't blow it. Awkwardly, with my cast hand, I pulled a blanket over us, and soon fell asleep.

CHAPTER EIGHT

We call him Weed (Alex)

When the alarm went off on Saturday morning, I groaned and rolled over, rubbing my palm across Dylan's bare chest, feeling the bunched muscles. I slowly opened my eyes, just in time to see him reaching out with his right hand, which was still bound in a heavy cast, and hit the alarm clock with it. The clock went flying and then cut off.

I lay my face down on his chest. I could hear his heart beating, and his breathing had already gone from the slow, deep breath of sleep to normal respiration. I closed my eyes, and murmured, "Let's skip running this morning."

He was wide awake, the bastard. I'd never known someone who just popped their eyes open in the morning, bright and chirpy.

"Can't do it, babe. I've got a not-so-sexy former Marine breathing down my neck. If I don't run, he'll find out about it somehow."

I chuckled. He'd spoken often of Jerry Weinstein, his physical therapist. Usually in disparaging terms. I could tell Dylan really liked the guy.

"You can stay and sleep if you want, hon. I'll be back soon."

"No," I said. "I'm coming."

I rolled out of his bed, checked to make sure the huge T-shirt of his I was wearing covered everything, then stepped out of the bedroom and into the apartment he shared with two graduate students. A quick run down the hall and back, and I'd brushed my teeth and changed.

By the time I got back to the room, he'd changed into his grey Army tee and shorts. It would be chilly out this morning, but we'd warm up soon enough. Still, I wasn't crazy enough to go out in November cold in shorts. I wore pink sweats I'd picked up a couple weeks earlier.

It had been two weeks since the night he went to the hospital. Two weeks since we'd slept in each other's arms for the first time as adults.

To be perfectly honest: they were the two happiest weeks I'd ever had in my life, at least since that trip to Israel, junior year of high school.

Much to Kelly's disgust, Dylan and I had spent almost every waking moment together, and I'd slept here in his apartment on the weekend. Three mornings a week we still went running. Now, after eight weeks, he wasn't kidding around any more. No more three-block runs: instead, we went down Broadway to 110th, cut across to Central Park West, then ran the entire length of the park and back. It was about seven miles, and I was in better shape than I'd ever been in my life.

I probably wouldn't go much further, but I had the feeling that he was just getting started. He'd been talking for the last week about possibly competing in a marathon.

As we tiptoed to the door, trying not to awaken his mysterious roommates, who I had as yet to actually meet, I could see that his right leg was noticeably more fit than it had been our first morning running together two months ago. His legs still didn't quite match, but they were close. And despite the extensive scarring, they were still sexy as hell.

As always, we started out with warmups, then slowly running. As we hit 110th, he picked up the pace.

"What time does your sister's... um... um... shit. Can't remember the word."

"Flight?"

"Yeah. What time does her flight get in?"

"Three. I told her I'd meet her at the airport."

"Okay."

We ran in silence for a little while. He did that occasionally. Just blanked out on perfectly common words. Dylan said it was a side effect from the traumatic brain injury he'd suffered when the bomb blast killed his best friend. He didn't talk about it easily, but he was talking about it, and that was progress.

That afternoon, one of my older sisters, Carrie, was flying into New York. She graduated from Columbia two years ago, so this was sort of a homecoming. She said it was just to visit, but I had the uncomfortable feeling that she was being sent to check up on me. Because, well, I have that sort of family.

That's okay. Even though there was a six-year gap in our ages, Carrie and I had always gotten along well. Having five sisters is sometimes a blessing, but often a curse.

She'd freak if she saw me running seven miles in the morning. It was hardly in character, considering my past aversion to sports and anything resembling them. And that cheered me. As crazy as it was, I was getting a rush from the running. We didn't really talk, just ran side by side, and usually stopped and showered, then went and got breakfast.

Kelly said that Dylan had cursed me. Last year the earliest I ever got up was 10 a.m.

We got back to his tiny apartment at about 7:30 a.m. And a guy was sitting on the front step. Crew cut, jeans and T-shirt, head was leaning back against the door, mouth hanging open, asleep.

"Holy shit," Dylan muttered. Then he ran up to the guy.

I was astonished at what happened next. Slowly, he reached out and squeezed his nostrils shut, then leaned forward and shouted, "Wake up, Weed!"

The guy jerked to a standing position instantly, saw Dylan, and shouted, "Holy shit! It's the Studmaster!" then grabbed Dylan in a bear hug.

They *growled* at each other, teeth bared, then Sherman, who was at least five years older and a head taller than Dylan, lifted Dylan off the ground and twirled him around. Like a ballerina, but with growling and laughing.

"Oh, man, what are you doing here?" Dylan said when Sherman put him down.

"Terminal leave, baby! And I'm gonna get so drunk I'll be blind! Those New York girls better watch out, because: I. Am. *Here!*"

Dylan shook his head, laughing, then said, "Alex, this is my so-called friend, Ray Sherman. Sherman, this is Alex Thompson."

I gave him a smile and approached. His eyes widened a little bit, and he said in an aside to Dylan, "*The* Alex?"

Dylan nodded, a smile curling up on one side of his mouth.

He turned to me and said, "Wow. I'm so glad to finally meet you, Alex. Dylan's been talking about you nonstop the entire time I've known him, but... wow. He actually understated how beautiful you are."

I smiled a little as my cheeks went red hot. "It's nice to meet you, too. Dylan's talked quite a bit about you too."

He shook his head. "Don't believe anything this guy says about me. It's all lies."

"I'm sure that's not true," I said.

"Huh. You obviously don't know Paris as well as you think. I bet he didn't tell you how awesome and super masculine I am."

I shrugged and grinned. "He did say you were kinda cute."

Sherman burst into loud laughter, doubling over. "Oh man, she got *both* of us, Dylan. I love this girl! Where did you find her again?"

Dylan smiled at me and said, "We ran into each other on an airplane."

"Man. I gotta fly more. So what's on the agenda?"

Dylan chuckled. "I wasn't expecting you this soon. Um... We're going to pick up Alex's sister this afternoon, she's visiting New York for a few days. Alex is dragging me to a party tonight. You should come, so I'll have someone to talk with. Right now, we're going to grab a shower and go get some breakfast. You coming?"

"Food! Hell, yeah. Alex, you gonna introduce me to your sister?"

"Of course," I said.

"Awesome. Let's get going then."

"Promise to keep quiet in the apartment," Dylan said. "My roommates aren't even alive this early in the morning."

"What the fuck is quiet?" Sherman asked loudly.

Dylan gave him a look, and Sherman smiled, then mimed locking his lips.

We entered the apartment, and Dylan showed Sherman where he could stow his bags. I went to get a shower first, and Dylan stopped me in the hall and whispered, "Is this okay? I know your sister's coming; I wasn't expecting Sherman until next week."

I kissed him on the cheek. "Of course it's okay."

He grinned. "You'll love Sherman. He's a great guy."

"I think I already do."

Almost an hour later we were eating breakfast in a booth at the back of Tom's Diner. I sat to Dylan's right, and Sherman was across from us.

"So," Sherman said, "If you don't want to tell me anything, you don't have to. But after two years of hearing about your story of love and woe, I'm really curious. Last I heard, you two had broken up, and Dylan was busy attaching explosives to his laptop. How'd you get back together?"

"I'll answer, but you'll have to tell me why you call him … what was it? *Studmaster?*" I grinned when I asked the question.

He burst into laughter. "Deal," he said.

"Oh, no," Dylan said. "Not going to happen."

"Too late, dude. I already promised the lady, and I never break a promise."

Dylan rolled his eyes and drank his coffee.

"Well," I said. "My second day of classes this year, I was walking down the hall to my work-study assignment, and there was this surly looking guy lurking in the dark. And the first words he said were something like 'Don't touch me.' And it was Dylan, the love of my life. One thing led to another and here we are."

"There's gotta be more to it than that."

I laughed. "A little bit. I did have to take him to the hospital one night after he punched a wall."

He raised an eyebrow. "Now that sounds like Dylan."

I asked, "What was that about his laptop?"

He chuckled. "I don't know if I should tell this story."

"You shouldn't," Dylan said.

"Now you have to," I countered.

Sherman put his hands out to his side in a shrug. "Sorry, Paris. I'm powerless before the lady's requests."

He turned to me and grinned. "Paris here has been known to be a little um, dramatic. The day you guys broke up, he was sitting there calmly on his laptop. After he finished doing whatever it was he was doing, he calmly closed it. Then he stood up, lifted the laptop and slammed it down on the table. I actually almost got a Purple Heart for flying shrapnel from the cracked case."

"You did not, you idiot," Dylan said. He was shifting in his seat, clearly uncomfortable.

"So anyway," Sherman said. "He hadn't done enough damage yet. So he picks up his laptop in one hand, and his rifle in the other. Then he says, calm as ever, 'I'm going for a walk, guys.' Obviously we were pretty curious, so we followed him. He goes out to the wire, and leans the laptop against a metal post. Then backs up 20 yards, raises his rifle, and empties a thirty round magazine *into the laptop.* Of course, shots are being fired, and we're in the middle of the boonies, so by the time he's done, the whole base is going nuts. Everybody's on red alert, running to their emergency stations, getting down in the bunkers, freaking out. And there's Dylan, blasting away at that laptop like it's an entire riot of hajis."

Oh, wow. I found myself wishing Sherman hadn't told me the story. It might make a good story, but it also made light of the very real pain he'd been in. Pain I'd caused, because I was drunk, and doubting our relationship. I put my hand on his thigh and squeezed. He leaned against me, just slightly, and I think it was okay.

"That's one story too many, Sherman," he said.

"But I haven't heard about the *Studmaster,*" I said, smiling at him. "I want to know all your secrets."

Sherman chuckled. "You know this clown and I went through basic training together, right? Well, he had several pictures of you taped up inside his wall locker."

Oh... I didn't know that. We'd been very much on the outs when he enlisted in the Army.

"Anyway, one day Drill Sergeant Powers is conducting an inspection, and he looks in the locker, and he says, 'Paris, is this your girlfriend?' And Paris here, he responds, 'She was, Drill Sergeant. I'm gonna get her back. I plan to marry her.'"

I froze in place, suddenly breathing shallow rapid breaths. He'd told his sergeant he wanted to marry me? *Oh. My. God.* I didn't know if Sherman noticed my sudden paralysis, because he kept talking, but Dylan sure did, because I accidentally squeezed his leg so hard it probably bruised him.

Sherman went on. "So, Sergeant Powers asks, 'Have you slept with her yet?' And Paris says no, that you're a good Catholic girl, or some bullshit like that."

I started to giggle, horribly embarrassed. I could definitely feel heat rising to my cheeks.

"Sergeant Powers says, 'Paris. You don't buy a car before you take it out for a test drive. You're not going to marry this girl before you try her on for size. Huh. I saw these pictures of this hot girl, and thought you were some kind of studmaster. But you're not, you're a pudmaster.' Ever since then, Paris was called the Studmaster."

I snickered, then started to giggle hard, almost spewing my coffee all over the table.

"That's terrible," I said.

"You're in so much trouble," Dylan said. I wasn't sure if he meant me or Sherman. But I did know that here we were, years later, and we *still* hadn't made love.

And just like that, I decided that I was ready. When the party was over tonight, when we got home, it was going to happen. To-night. No question. I gave Dylan a secret smile. He didn't know what it was about but he smiled back. By the time we went to bed, his smile was going to be a whole lot bigger; I was going to see to it.

I tried to divert my thoughts from the carnal direction they'd taken, which was hard, because I was still touching his leg. Well, thigh. Inner thigh. Whatever.

I looked over to Sherman, consciously distracting myself.

"So, do you have a nickname too?"

"Of course not," he said.

"We call him Weed. Because he's so short."

I shook my head, a grin forming on my face. Sherman wouldn't have looked out of place in an NBA lineup. I already liked him, a lot. He was cheerful, outgoing, and obviously cared about Dylan. And that mattered more than anything.

As usual, the hajis didn't cooperate (Dylan)

When we finished breakfast, Alex said, "I think I want to let you guys go off and play together, and I'm going to pick my sister up."

I looked at her, curiously, and said, "You're sure?"

She smiled and leaned close, then said, "Go have fun with Sherman. You guys haven't seen each other in a long time. Besides, I want to talk with Carrie. Girl stuff." She winked at me.

As always, her proximity took my breath away. We paid our bill and headed out. In front of the restaurant, she turned and grabbed me in a deep hug, then whispered in my ear, "I've got plans for you tonight, Studmaster. You might want to think about getting some rest."

Jesus Christ. My body instantly responded to her, even if she was using that hideously embarrassing nickname. She kissed me, then waved and started walking toward her dorm.

I just stood there watching her walk away, until Sherman said, "You still awake over there, Paris?"

I shook my head, a grin forming on my face, and said, "I don't know. I might be dreaming."

He gave a short laugh. "I'm happy you got back together with her, man. You're a very lucky guy."

"Yeah, more than you know."

So we hung out, playing on the XBox back at my place, talking occasionally about the other guys from our platoon.

I'd been in the hospital when they held the memorial for Kowalski and Roberts, out there in the middle of the Afghan boonies. Sherman told me a little bit about it, but I'd already seen pictures, and read emails from some of the guys.

"How's Sergeant Colton?" I asked.

"He's getting out," Sherman said.

"You're shitting me. I figured him for a lifer."

Sherman shook his head. "No. He's all done. Three tours in Iraq and Afghanistan was two times too many, he started saying, not long after you got hit."

"He was kind of like a dad to me, you know."

"You should call him sometime, let him know how you're doing."

I nodded. "Yeah, I will."

"So what's up with this party?"

I shrugged. "Some friend of Alex's."

"There going to be girls there?"

I chuckled. "Yeah, probably. It's going to be all college kids. Some grad students I think. I don't really know many of her friends."

"You want to hear something crazy?"

"Sure."

"I'm hoping it's not going to be like... I don't know, the movie college parties you see. Big crowd, lots of people drunk. I don't think I could take a crowd. I wanted to chew my own arm off in the airport."

I snickered. "Know what you mean, man. I don't do crowds any more. But I don't think so, this is mostly an older crowd than that, from what Alex said."

"You seem happy, man. Happier than I've ever seen you."

I thought about that for a minute, then said, "I am, dude. School is good, and Alex... Well... Shit, I got a second chance, you know? That's a big deal."

He nodded, then yawned. "Listen, I'm gonna get some *Z*s then, before the party. You mind?"

"Sure, that's fine. Crash in my room, let me just get my laptop."

"All right. You better have clean sheets, you fucker."

"You better not have brought back any funky Afghan parasites."

So I got my laptop, and he went to sleep, and I popped online for a little while, then did some homework.

And then I did something different.

See, when I was in the hospital, still trying to figure out if I was going to live or die, or if they were going to cut off my leg, or if I was going to end up addicted to the morphine they'd given me, the last thing I was ready to do was read her emails. Because, well: failure. I'm no stranger to it. Alex was everything to me. But she also had a future. And I didn't, really. All I had was some serious fucking brain damage, a leg that might go into sepsis and be cut off any moment, and the last thing I was going to do was drag myself back into her life and fuck things up for her, too. Like I fucked up everything.

So I buried her emails. Stuck them in a folder and never looked at them.

Now, with Sherman sleeping in my room, and Alex off to pick up her sister, I finally decided it was time.

I'll admit, I had some anxiety about this. I knew I'd hurt her. I'd hurt her bad. What had she said?

I was about to find out, and that scared the hell out of me.

February 10, 2012; 01:45 AM
TO: DYLANPARIS81@GMAIL.COM
FROM: alexlovesstrawberries@yahoo.com
Dear Dylan,
I'm sorry about what happened. I'm a little drunk, and feeling down in the dumps, and just frustrated as hell about our sometimes crazy long distance relationship. Forgive me? I know I upset you, and I'm so sorry. If you can get to skype, I'll be online in the morning and tomorrow night. Or email me. Or something.
Please don't forget I love you very much!
Hugs and kisses!
Alex

I stared at the email, feeling… staggered. She must have written the email minutes after I disconnected our Skype session. I was busy disabling my Facebook account right then.

February 10, 2012; 09:45 AM
TO: DYLANPARIS81@GMAIL.COM
FROM: ALEXLOVESSTRAWBERRIES@YAHOO.COM
Dylan,
I tried to message you on Facebook, but couldn't find you. Really? Did you defriend me? Talk to me, Dylan, what's going on? Please?
Hugs,
Alex

Reading the second email, I found myself breathing heavily. It was written ten hours after I'd hung up on her. Right after I shot up my old laptop, Sergeant Colton had dragged me in to see the Old Man. Captain Wilson was a fair guy; I never had anything bad to say about him. He, on the other hand, had plenty bad to say about me, and pretty much got all of it off his chest right then and there. I gave the only answer there was: I had no excuse.

After he dressed me down, he sent me outside to wait, and he and Sergeant Colton talked. Then they called me back in.

"Paris, personally I'm of the view that we should court-martial your ass. But Sergeant Colton here says you aren't completely worthless, and reluctant as I am, I have to agree. So we've agreed on a suitable non-judicial punishment. Are you ready to hear the terms?"

"Yes, sir," I replied, still numb and in shock from seeing the guy—*Joel*— in her room.

"This is a company-grade Article 15. The maximum sentence for a company-grade Article 15 is reduction in grade by one rank, forfeiture of seven days pay, plus fourteen days extra duty and restriction.

"Due to the seriousness of what you did, I intend to levy the maximum sentence. You'll be reduced in grade to Private First Class. Restriction doesn't mean a hell of a lot here, but the fourteen days extra duty will. Do you understand the terms of the punishment?"

"Yes, sir."

"You're entitled to demand a court-martial instead of this non-judicial punishment. Do you wish to demand a court-martial?"

I shook my head, and said, "No, sir. I did what I did. I'm guilty, sir."

He nodded. "All right. We'll take care of the paperwork later. For now, to underscore the seriousness of this, I'm changing up the rotation. Your squad is out on patrol tonight."

Oh, God, I thought. The guys were going to hate me. We'd just got back from a patrol that morning. Kowalski'd been killed out there, and everyone was reeling. The vision of him throwing himself on the grenade to save that little girl was burned on my eyes.

"Is there a problem, Paris?"

I looked at the floor. "Sir, if I demand a court-martial, will the other guys still get punished? It's not their fault. And... after Kowalski... everybody's pretty screwed up."

"Yes. The rotation change stands. I've already discussed this with Sergeant Colton. Do we agree, Sergeant, that if your squad was being properly supervised, your soldiers wouldn't be out shooting up electronics on the edge of the base camp?"

Colton winced. "Yes, sir."

And that was it. That night we headed out on patrol

A patrol we wouldn't have gone on, if I hadn't been such a fucking idiot. But, as I've pointed out now, I've got a history of fucking things up.

She sent another email. I guess about an hour after we were out in the boonies on the road, on a night patrol into the mountains, a night patrol that would last until well into the next day. Roberts and I rode together in one Humvee, and he was pretty good natured about it, ribbing me about being busted back to PFC.

February 10, 2012; 11:32 PM
TO: DYLANPARIS81@GMAIL.COM
FROM: ALEXLOVESSTRAWBERRIES@YAHOO.COM

I don't understand the silence. I don't understand what I did that was so wrong. I'm hoping you're just too busy to get my messages. I'm hoping you aren't ignoring me deliberately, because it kind of hurts, Dylan. Don't you think I deserve some kind of explanation?
A

I did. I'd give just about anything to go back and change it now. I'd give anything in the world to not have hurt her like that. And I'd literally give my life to be able to go back and erase the stupid, idiotic actions that brought down punishment on my entire platoon.

The patrol lasted all night. We were basically just a moving target, driving around, in a crazy attempt to draw fire from the Taliban insurgents that still operated heavily in our area. But as usual, the hajis didn't cooperate. It was a quiet night, very quiet. By sunrise, we were all tired and ready for some sack time. Sergeant Colton ordered the column to head back to base. We passed through a tiny village, and the guy who ran the road-side shop waved us down. The patrol came to a stop, and Roberts and I passed the time scanning the village for bad guys.

This was just weird. We *never* went out on patrol without getting shot at. It just didn't happen. I mean, the villagers here were pretty friendly ... at least they didn't try to kill us often. But the bad guys were always live in this area. I was tense, and I knew Roberts was, too. We all were.

We were tied up in the village for about forty-five minutes. And during that forty-five minutes, the bad guys were out there. They were setting up a roadside bomb and ambush on the direct route between the village and our base camp.

Sometimes I have dreams about starting out for the base camp from that shit village. I can tell what's going to happen, I know it's coming, and I want to just scream at Sergeant Colton, at Sherman or Roberts or even myself, and tell them we're about to get hammered. I try to stop it from happening, but no matter what happens we keep going down that road. We keep going down the road until the explosion hits, and my closest friend in the world is shredded, his blood literally *coating* the inside of the smoking humvee, my own leg torn to shit by shrapnel, then the bullets flying as I fell out of the Humvee onto the ground.

I don't remember if I screamed, I don't remember if I just sat there hoping to die because it was my fault we'd been hit—it was my fault we were out on that patrol in the first place.

I wanted to die. Because if it hadn't been for me and my stupid impulsiveness, Roberts would be alive. If it hadn't been for me, his parents back in Alabama wouldn't have had to plant their only son six feet under the ground because of some stupid war in a country halfway around the world.

It was my fault.

Alex wrote to me, again and again. Every day for the first week and a half or so, eleven daily emails that she sent to me while I was getting in trouble, getting my best friend killed, then being transported to Baghram and later Germany in a mostly unconscious haze with a torn-up leg.

By the tenth day she'd lost whatever patience she might have had.

February 20, 2012; 04:20 AM
TO: DYLANPARIS81@GMAIL.COM
FROM: ALEXLOVESSTRAWBERRIES@YAHOO.COM
Dylan,

I've been up all night crying, and Kelly has told me it's time to let you go. You're breaking my heart. Of all the things I've ever believed about you, I never believed cruelty was part of who you are. But I was wrong. You are cruel and heartless. If only you had any idea what you've done. I'm done crying over you. I'm done wondering where you are. Every day I've obsessively checked newspapers, looking for news that you've been hurt. I've checked casualty lists, terrified that you were killed over there. I've done everything I can.

I hope you find some way to live with yourself. But don't expect me to forgive you.

Alex

Oh, Alex. I didn't. I don't. How could I expect her to forgive me, when I couldn't forgive myself? I didn't fucking *deserve* forgiveness. I broke her heart. I killed Roberts, and broke his parents. When I went to see them this summer, I couldn't tell them the truth. I told them what a great friend he was, about all the good times we had together. I told them all the funny stories. I shared a beer with his dad, and we cried together. But I didn't tell them the truth. I didn't tell them that it was my fault their son was dead.

My life is all planned out (Alex)

As always, JFK airport was crowded beyond belief. Standing just outside security, I waited for Carrie, feeling alternately excited to see her and suspicious of her motives. Why suspicious? Because three days before, I had let slip in a conversation with my mom that I was seeing Dylan.

"Dylan? Isn't he the boy who came to visit you? The one who went off and joined the Army of all things?"

"Yes, mom. He was injured in Afghanistan, and he's going to Columbia now."

That was followed by a long, uncomfortable pause. Then she said, "Are you sure that's a good idea?"

"Yes," I replied, simply. I wasn't going to get in a drawn-out argument about Dylan. We'd had enough of those over the last three years.

"I just think you need to focus on your school work, Alexandra. Not on boys. Especially that one. He hurt you, honey. And your grades suffered because of it."

My grades suffered because of it. Of course that's what she cared about. I got a *B* last spring in my Comparative Religions course. It was the first *B* I'd had, well... ever. You would think I had murdered someone for all the conflict it caused at home. When my parents saw my final grades, they grounded me. I'm nineteen years old, and was home from college, and my parents somehow thought it was appropriate to ground me. Can we say overcontrolling?

But then, that's who they are.

I managed to bring the conversation with Mom to a graceful end, but the next day I got a text from Carrie.

> Coming into New York Saturday! Can we get together?

I should have seen that one coming a mile away. For one thing, Carrie was in graduate school, and just as dependent on the dole from Dad as I was. Where did she get the money to fly from Houston to New York on a last-minute trip? Dad. Which meant she'd been sent on a mission to spy on me and find out how serious I was about Dylan.

If they had any idea I was planning to sleep with him tonight, they'd go into full scale red-alert. I had a wild thought I should tell Carrie, just to provoke a reaction.

And there she was, coming off the plane, carrying a sizable carry-on. As always, she looked runway-model perfect. Long brown hair like mine, but always better cut and styled just so. Instead of the casual clothes you might expect on an airplane, she was wearing a chic flowered dress that probably cost upwards of two grand, and fantastic black leather ankle-high boots with three-inch heels. To say I was occasionally jealous of my sister Carrie would be like saying that the ocean is an oversized pond. When I was around her,

I felt inadequate, a little sister who could never live up to her big sister's accomplishments, beauty or charisma.

She smiled and waved enthusiastically when she saw me. I returned the smile and wave, and when she came through the gate we hugged. She was at least six inches taller than me, and that combined with the heels made me feel like I was still twelve years old.

"Oh, Alexandra, it's so good to see you! I've missed you so much!"

"I've missed you, too, Carrie."

"We've got so much to talk about; I'm so happy I got to come visit!"

I smiled, still uncomfortable. "Are you hungry? Should we go get some lunch?"

She nodded. "Yes, let's do that. I'm traveling light today, we don't need to pick up any bags."

"Great," I said. "We can get a cab back to the university and eat at Tom's?"

She grinned, nodding happily. "I'd love that, I haven't been there since I graduated! I had a lot of good late nights there."

I smiled back at her. "Yeah, me too."

So, into the cab we went. On the way into the city, we chattered about inconsequential things. Classes. She was working on her PhD. in behavioral ecology, or something like that. Carrie had always been a bit of a science fanatic. Given that the rest of us were heavy in the humanities, it made her a little bit of a freak in the family, but I'd always thought it was in a good way. She and Dad had a blowout when she selected her major. He'd intended her to follow him into the Foreign Service.

I was proud of her for defying him. Having one ambassador in the family was plenty, I thought, and sometimes I was sick of him and Mom trying to control our entire lives. The only one of us free was Julia. She'd finished her Bachelor's degree at Harvard, then basically gave Dad the finger and ran off with her boyfriend Crank.

Yes, really. Crank was a guitarist. In a punk rock band. They'd been happily touring the country for the last five years, and always brought a level of entertainment to family get-togethers during the holidays. By comparison, Carrie's rebellion was rather minor.

Finally, we arrived at Tom's Restaurant and got a seat in the back. Our waitress, Cherry, came over and brightened when she saw me. "Alex! You're back again? That's twice in one day."

I laughed, just a little, and said, "This is my sister, Carrie. She went to school here, so it's kind of a homecoming for her."

Cherry nodded in acknowledgement, then said, "Well, we'll try to make your visit worth the trip! Do you guys know what you'd like to drink?"

We ordered, then sat back and looked at each other. For a second I had a mental image of two cats, fur puffed, tails twitching, getting ready to pounce.

I was the one to break the impasse.

"So Dad sent you to report back on me?"

She grinned, then sighed in relief. "Yes. Of course. I should have realized you'd figure that out pretty quick."

"It was pretty transparent," I replied.

"They're worried about you," she said.

"Because of Dylan."

She nodded.

"Well, you can report back that there is nothing to worry about. Dylan and I are in love; we always have been. But before now there was never... it was never a possibility. Not with us separated all the time. Now we're not separated, and I'm happier than I've ever been in my life. Dad can go take a flying leap if he thinks he's going to interfere."

Carrie's eyes widened. "Wow," she said. "Tell me how you really feel."

I chuckled. "Seriously, though. There's nothing to worry about."

"I know that," she said. "Except for Julia, you're probably the only one of us really grounded in who you are. I'm not worried at all; I just want to know all about it! It's so exciting that you two are finally together, isn't it?"

I smiled, feeling warm all over. "He makes me happy, Carrie. Really, truly happy."

"If I promise not to repeat a word to Dad except what you approve, will you tell me about it?"

I nodded, suddenly pleased. Carrie and I had never been close. The difference in our ages, and her ability to intimidate everyone around her, had always placed distance between us. And I wanted to be close. She was my sister.

So I told her the story. Some of it she knew, of course. Everyone in my family knew something significant had happened during the trip to Israel three years ago, because I'd come home devastated. I'd cried for almost three days, which was hardly the homecoming anyone else in the family had expected. Then I'd bought a package of photo paper and printed out all of my pictures from our trip. Dozens and dozens of pictures of us together. It didn't take a genius to figure out that I'd fallen in love.

What Carrie didn't know was how hard it had been, so I told her. About the doubts, the distance. Knowing that he was planning on going off after high school to gain experience and write novels. Knowing that we'd be separated. I broke it off with Mike as soon as I got back to San Francisco, but I'd been anchorless, my existence for those first few months revolving around phone calls, emails and Facebook exchanges with Dylan.

What she didn't know was he'd joined the Army the day after I broke up with him. Which meant that, in a big way, his subsequent injuries were my fault.

I told her about how we'd slowly re-tangled our lives after encountering each other outside Doctor Forrester's office in September. How his injuries had impacted him, and how we ran together every other morning.

"I can believe that. I've never seen you looking so... svelte," she said.

"Well, we run about seven miles. Lots of exercise together."

"Oh?" she asked coyly, eyebrows raised.

Heat rushed to my cheeks. "Oh, my God! I didn't mean that, Carrie!"

She smiled. "It's okay, Alexandra. I wouldn't tell Dad. You can talk to me."

I looked down at the table, embarrassed, then said, "I've sort of decided we're finally going to."

Her mouth formed a big O. "Really?" she said.

I nodded. "I love him, Carrie. More than you can imagine. I want to spend my life with him."

She sighed. "I'm envious."

I sat back in my seat, shocked.

"You're envious of *me?*"

She gave me a bittersweet smile. "My life is all planned out, Alex. I guess all of our lives are, except Julia's. There's been no room for men. And ... let's just say I've been regretting that. I'm so happy for you."

"You'll get to meet him at the party tonight. Oh, and speaking of men," I said, leaning forward and grinning at her. "I promised to introduce you to his friend. Ray Sherman. Sherman just got home from Afghanistan."

Carrie blinked. "Dad would have a conniption if I were to date a soldier. Look at how he treated you."

I laughed. "You'll like him," I said. "He's a nice guy. And … objectively, knowing I've got a boyfriend I am absolutely in love with… Sherman is still really hot."

Her eyes twinkled. "Well, in that case, I'm looking forward to meeting him!"

"You really mean it? You're not going to report all this back to Dad? I don't think I can take all the grilling over Thanksgiving. It's going to be bad enough as is."

"I promise, sis. Not a word. I'll tell him you're happy and to leave you alone."

"That ought to go well," I replied, and we laughed, but there was an edge to the laugh. We both knew it wouldn't go over well at all.

CHAPTER NINE

Whatever (Dylan)

O kay. Yeah, reading through her emails, and seeing the heartache that poured through them… it put me in a pretty craptastic mood. I'm not usually the best at expressing myself, and even though my new therapist down at the VA has told me repeatedly that I have to let go of the guilt for killing Roberts, the fact is, what the hell does she know? Why does the VA have some non-combat veteran twenty-something girl as a therapist anyway?

Whatever.

When Sherman woke up, he could tell my mood had soured, but he didn't intrude, just treated it as normal. It probably was. I've always been pretty damn moody, and with the on-again, off-again nature of my long-distance relationship, well… let's just say I had some down times over in Afghanistan.

Maybe I needed to talk about it. With Alex, or Sherman, or someone who gave a damn. I don't know. How do you say the words, "I'm sorry," and have them mean something? You hear that crap all the time, but it's not sufficient when it comes to heartbreak. And that's just about all I'd accomplished in the last year: grief and heartache for other people.

Whatever. I needed to stop dwelling on all that crap. Sherman was in town, and Alex's sister, and Alex apparently had special plans for us tonight, which she'd hinted at, and I needed to just get over it, and stop ruining everyone else's night with my own problems.

I dressed in the tight pair of jeans and black t-shirt Alex had shown her appreciation for a week earlier by sort of... throwing herself at me. At least I think it was a hint she liked it, when she chewed on my ear.

The cast made getting dressed awkward as hell, but that's what I got for punching a wall. The hardest part was lacing up my boots, but I'd been managing it okay.

My phone chimed. Text message from Alex.

Meet us on the green? Carrie wants to meet Sherman. *Hugs*

I messaged back:

Be there in ten. Love you.

"Come on, Weed! We got to get going. Her sister wants to meet you."

That was all the motivation Sherman needed to speed up. Thirty seconds later we were on our way, heading the two blocks to the green where Alex and I met every other morning.

A couple of ostriches (Alex)

I heard the intake of Carrie's breath before I saw them coming.

"You're right," she whispered. "He is hot. Jesus, so is Dylan. He doesn't look much like the kid you had pictures of from Israel."

Dylan and Sherman were walking toward us. Sherman was extremely tall, gangly, but strongly built, with powerful arms and legs. He had short-cropped hair and white teeth and would have looked damned good on a recruiting poster.

Next to him was Dylan, wearing that black, slightly too-tight t-shirt that made me just ache to rip it off. I wanted to growl. He looked at me across the field and smiled, and I felt myself blush.

"Um… yeah," I said. "Somewhere along the line he grew up."

"I guess you did, too, sis," she said, eyeing me.

Knowing that I was planning to seduce Dylan that night, I'd gone all out. I was wearing a short black dress that felt almost insubstantial, with strappy heels that added about four inches to my height. I'd spent a long time on my hair and makeup, and I hoped it would have the right effect.

I saw Dylan catch his breath. There was *no* question at that moment what he was thinking about. I smiled impishly at him, and he approached and kissed me roughly.

"Wow," he murmured. "What's the occasion?"

"You are," I whispered.

I stepped back, then introduced my sister to Sherman and Dylan.

"It's really nice to meet you both," she said. She was staring at Sherman. At six-two, she didn't meet many men her own height, much less taller than her, but he was taller than any of us. It was a little strange to see my sister overwhelmed by anything, but Sherman was pulling that off pretty well.

She might have been here to report back on Dylan and me, but it looked like she was getting more than she'd bargained for. For the first time in our lives, my sister looked uncomfortable in her own skin, her eyes darting everywhere, hands curled at her sides.

"So, um..." she said. *Wow.* Carrie did *not* say "um." Ever. She continued. "You were in the Army with Dylan?"

Sherman smiled at her, his white teeth gleaming. He said, "Yeah... I had to drop out of college in 09, and ended up enlisting."

"Oh? Where did you go?"

"Stony Brook," he said. "It's actually not all that far from here...."

He continued, but I missed it, because Dylan and I fell back a few feet behind them as they talked. I took Dylan's left hand in my right. He moved a little closer, and naturally, without thought, my arm went around his waist, his resting on my shoulder.

"Hey," he said.

"Hey to you," I said.

"They sure hit it off," he said quietly.

"Oh, my God. I've never seen my sister so off-balance. She's in absolute lust."

He chuckled. "I feel almost insulted. She's not interested in talking with me at all. I thought she was here to... um..." His face twisted in anger. "I can't remember the word," he muttered.

"Spy," I replied quickly, not wanting to see him so unhappy.

"Yeah. I thought she was here to spy on us."

I laughed. "She is. But I think plans just changed."

He nodded. His eyes were far away. I looked at him as we walked. Something was off. He was here, but not here. It wasn't just the passing aphasia. It was his entire demeanor. It was as if he was huddled in on himself, defensive. I hadn't seen him like this since the couple of weeks after we first ran into each other again.

I took a deep breath, leaned my head on his shoulder, and asked, "What's wrong?"

He tensed a little, so I stopped walking. He did, too. I turned toward him, putting my arms around his waist and resting my head against his chest, taking a deep breath.

"It's complicated," he said.

"That's nothing new," I replied. "You can talk about it."

He sighed and whispered, "I don't deserve you, Alex."

I frowned, then looked up into his eyes. "Don't say that, Dylan. Don't ever say that. I love you, and you love me, and that's all that matters."

He closed his eyes and pulled me into a deep hug, leaning against me. He inhaled deeply, as if taking a breath before going under water, his lips against my hair.

"If you want to skip the party, it's fine," I said. "If you're not up for it tonight."

"No, that's fine. I don't want to ruin your night with your sister."

I snickered. "I think she's fully occupied."

"Tell you what," he said. "Let's do exactly what we planned, okay? Let's go to the party."

"And then you get your surprise, after."

He raised his eyebrows. "Oh? A surprise?"

I bit my lower lip, then whispered in his ear, "Make sure you're up for a long night, Dylan. I've got plans for you." As I said it, I pressed the full length of my body against him, slowly rising on my toes.

He took a deep, sharp breath, and I could feel his body respond nearly instantly. My meaning was unquestionably clear to him.

"Are you sure?" he asked.

"Oh, I'm more sure than you can imagine, Dylan Paris." My voice dropped to a whisper. "I'm losing my virginity tonight."

He spoke, his voice deep and husky in my ear. "You told me you were waiting for the man you wanted to marry."

"I did, didn't I?"

Oh. God. I didn't just say that. I did. Was he going to freak? We'd never, ever gone that far, or even suggested that we might go that far.

Except that I remembered what Sherman had told me. *She was my girlfriend, Drill Sergeant. I'm gonna get her back. I plan to marry her.*

Suddenly I found I couldn't even breathe, but every nerve ending in my body was alive with excitement; the feel of his strong arms, his chest against mine, his very slight stubble against my cheek. Oh, dear God. He'd gone through basic training two full years ago. I couldn't believe he'd told his drill sergeant that, that he'd been thinking it, that he'd even fantasized about it that long ago. Of course I had. I'd indulged in so many fantasies… fantasies of us running off to a foreign country together, of us telling my parents to go to hell and setting off on our own. I didn't guess that he had shared them, and suddenly I regretted that.

"You didn't really say that, did you? I'm imagining that?" he asked.

"What if I did?" I asked, trying desperately to adopt a playful tone. It was belied, though, by the intense grip I held him in. I slid my right hand around his side, then up his chest between us, feeling his heartbeat.

"Then I might pick you up in my arms and carry you back to the apartment right this second."

I gasped and whispered, "Please don't tempt me; I wouldn't even consider resisting you."

I heard a cough, then a deep-voiced throat cleared.

Damn.

I pulled a fraction of an inch away from Dylan and felt my face go red hot. Sherman and Carrie were standing there, looking amused.

"We got to the street to wave down a cab, and realized you weren't with us," she said.

Sherman laughed, then said, "You guys got lost on the way?"

"Yes," Dylan said, sounding winded. "We did."

"Come on, lovebirds," Carrie said. "And by the way... wow."

Now I was really blushing.

I hid my face, and Dylan said, "Be nice."

Carrie got a sly grin on her face. "I think my sister is being more than nice enough for the both of us, don't you?"

Sherman burst into loud laughter, then she did, and then, the earth shifted in front of me, because she and Sherman high-fived each other.

"Okay," I said. "My world just got really weird."

Dylan chuckled. "You know, I always thought Sherman was an alien, like from Mars, he's so freakishly tall. But he looks good next to her. It's like they're a couple of ostriches."

I giggled, and we put our arms around each other and walked after them. It would be funny if Sherman and Carrie ended up hooking up, though very strange, considering her history. But the two of them were chattering as they walked along as if they'd known each other for years.

At Broadway we flagged down a cab. Kelly and Joel were planning to meet us at the party, and I couldn't wait to introduce them to Sherman and Carrie. It was strange: as if I had all these segmented, altogether different parts of my life. Me and Dylan. My family. Me and Kelly. And for the first time ever, they were all coming together in the same place. It felt strangely exhilarating.

It was close to midnight before we reached Robert Meyer's apartment on the Upper West Side. Robert was, to put it mildly, obscenely rich. His father and mine were friends, and I'd received more than one obnoxiously heavy-handed hint from my parents that I should throw myself at him. I liked Robert, sort of, as a friend. But to date? Oh, hell no. Probably riddled with STDs, Robert knew exactly how his money affected girls, and had used to it to lay an impressive trail of crying women across the city of New York. At twenty-seven, he had shown no signs at all of improving, either in his disposition or level of responsibility.

But you could be sure I'd hear more about how marvelous he was when I returned home for Thanksgiving. Sometimes my parents were so clueless.

That said, his apartment was fantastic. A penthouse apartment with a large rooftop deck on West 73rd Street, I'd never seen anything quite like it. Even with thirty-something people attending, it didn't feel crowded. When the four of us arrived, Robert hugged my sister, a huge smile on his face, while Sherman glowered.

"It's so good to see you again, Carrie. It's been a long time. How is the studying going for you?"

"I'm at Rice now," she said, "Working on my PhD."

He raised his eyebrows. "I did hear something like that. Good for you. And this must be your sister."

I nodded. "Alex," I said. "And this is my boyfriend, Dylan Paris."

Robert gave Dylan an insincere smile and said, "A pleasure to meet you, Mr. Paris. You're a lucky man, indeed."

"Thanks," Dylan muttered. It was obvious he was extremely uncomfortable.

"Come join the party," Robert said. Behind him, past the entryway, was a large living room. Several small groups of people were standing or sitting around, all of them in various states of inebriation. The crowd spilled out onto the roof, looking out at the skyline. Loud music was blasting from a stereo in the corner, and I could see more people down the hall.

"Make yourselves at home!" shouted Robert as we entered the living area.

I saw a few people I knew from school, as well as friends of both my family and Robert's. This was going to be an extraordinarily strange night.

I leaned closed to Dylan, put my lips to his ear, and said, "You okay?"

He nodded. "Yeah. Just... this place takes some getting used to. What the hell does a rooftop apartment in Manhattan cost?"

I shrugged. "No idea."

"I guess if you have to ask, you can't afford it, right?"

"Pretty much."

Carrie let out an exclamation, and then she was hugging someone—an old friend from school I supposed. She gave introductions, taking Sherman around the room and introducing him to people. They stood out, taller than anyone else in the room, both of them looking like rock stars.

We mingled, and talked with a lot of people, the two of us holding hands all night.

At one point, he said, "I've got to sit down, my leg is killing me."

He sat and wiped his forehead, and I could tell he was uncomfortable, both with the crowding and the loud music. I was going to get him out of here soon, Carrie or not. She was staying at a hotel on 108th Street, and we could always meet up for breakfast.

"Let me get you a glass of water," I said.

He nodded gratefully, and I made my way to the kitchen. Sherman was there.

"Hey," I said. "You and Carrie sure hit it off."

He grinned. "Yeah, I like her. A lot."

I returned the grin. "I'm so glad."

"Paris doing okay?" he asked.

"His head's hurting, I was going to get him a drink of water."

He nodded, suddenly looking serious.

"Can I ask you a question, Alex?"

"Of course," I said, grabbing a glass and running the faucet to fill it up.

"Are you serious about him?"

"What do you mean?" I asked, turning toward him.

He looked around the room, at pretty much everything but me, and then said, "Look. He's my friend. And... I don't know if you know how much into you he really is. I don't know if you know everything that happened over in Afghanistan, either. But... look, I'm worried about him, okay? He's been through the shit. And it wouldn't take much to knock him over the edge permanently. Guy needs some time to heal."

I nodded, seriously, then said, "I love him, Sherman."

He closed his eyes and nodded. "That's all I wanted to hear, Alex. I just... If you were just playing with him... I don't know. I don't know what I'm saying."

I put my hand on his arm, and said, "You're saying that you're a good friend, and you're looking out for him."

"Yeah," he said, shrugging.

"I won't ever do anything to hurt him if I can avoid it. Fair enough? I'd rather gouge my eyes out than cause him any more pain."

He looked relieved.

"Okay. We're good," he said. "Back to chasing your hot sister."

I giggled, embarrassed and amused at the same time. He stepped out of the kitchen, and I stood there for a moment, just thinking.

The last two weeks had changed so much. For the first time in my life, I saw a real chance to carve out my own life. A life I wanted, not the one my father had planned out for me. And that life would include Dylan, no matter what. Right then and there, I repeated the promise I'd just made to Ray Sherman, but I made it to myself. I'd never, ever do anything to hurt Dylan.

I was so spaced out, my thoughts so far away, I didn't even notice when Randy Brewer stepped into the kitchen. But when I heard his voice, my back nearly spasmed.

"You look so thoughtful, beautiful. Have you changed your mind about me?"

I spun around, my eyes widening, my heart rate suddenly increasing.

"Get away from me," I said.

"What's wrong, Alex? You used to like me."

"We went out exactly twice. And then you tried to rape me."

"Jesus, will you just get over it already? I was drunk. It was bad judgment, and I apologize. Besides, you would have liked it. You know that."

I started to back out of the kitchen through the other door, away from him. But also away from Dylan and my friends. I didn't know what was down this hall, but I needed some distance from Randy right now.

"You're kidding yourself," I said. "Just leave me alone."

"Give me what I want and I'll be happy to."

A flash of fear ran through my mind. If he tried to grab me, would they even hear me out there? The music was so damned loud. As I backed away, into a darkened hallway, he stepped closer, matching my steps.

"It won't be so bad," he said. "You could learn to love me as much as I love you."

What the hell was wrong with him? I'd known Randy for years. His family ran in the same circles as mine. He'd always been arrogant, but this was something different entirely. My heart was pounding as I tried to keep my distance from him.

"Just leave me alone, Randy. I don't want anything to do with you."

I took one more step backwards, and my foot tangled in something on the floor. As I lost my footing, I started to fall backwards. I let out a scream when he reached out and grabbed my arms.

Where did she go anyway? (Dylan)

"So, yeah," Joel was saying. "I thought he was going to kill me, to be honest. His eyes were pretty damn cold. But it was all a misunderstanding, and I'm glad they sorted it out. Not just because they're so happy... but my own safety."

Joel chuckled, but I didn't think he was terribly funny. I felt Sherman's eyes on me briefly, as he put Joel's story together with what he knew. That I'd lost it in Afghanistan because I'd seen Joel on the Skype feed from Alex's room. That my overreaction had ended up costing Roberts his life.

Sherman knew it all now, and I didn't want to look at him, because if I did I might fucking break down.

I'd told him most of the story, anyway. We'd emailed back and forth several times while I was in the hospital, and he was still out there in Afghanistan. He'd said several times that none of the guys blamed me for what happened. But I knew that was bullshit. It was my fault. Of course they blamed me. I blamed myself.

Carrie was sitting next to Sherman, close. She leaned forward and said to me, "You know, I don't have to say this. But I want you to be careful with my sister. She's... she's fallen really hard for you."

"I wouldn't hurt her for the world," I said.

Speaking of which, where was she? She'd left to go get water like five or ten minutes before, and hadn't come back. "Where did she go, anyway?"

"She was in the kitchen a few minutes ago," Sherman said.

Kelly suddenly went stiff, her eyes wide. "I thought I saw Randy Brewer headed that way."

"Who?" I asked.

"That's the guy who—" She cut herself off, I guess not knowing whether Carrie or I knew. But I knew. Randy Brewer was the son of a bitch who'd tried to rape her last spring.

That's when I heard the cry, clear across the building, barely above the music. It her voice, screaming, "Let go of me! Help! *Dylan!*"

I was on my feet running before the scream finished.

He was protecting me (Alex)

"Woah," Randy said as he grabbed my arms. "Be careful!"

I'd lost my balance, and when he grabbed my arms I still didn't have my feet under me. He shoved me against a wall, hard, then pressed himself against me.

"God I want you so bad," he said, putting his lips against the side of my face. I tried to push him away, but he was a lot stronger than I was. As I squirmed, I screamed, as loud as I could, "Let go of me! Help! *Dylan!*"

"Oh, shut up," he said. He pushed his right hand against my mouth, and with his left he stuck his hand under my skirt, his disgusting hand reaching between my legs. I fought, as hard as I could, struggling against him, against the need to vomit and scream and cry out at the same time.

Suddenly there was a huge muscled arm around his neck. He was yanked off of me, and I heard a guttural shout. "Get your hands off of her!"

I fell to the floor. Dylan was dragging Randy away from me, his face murder.

Randy struggled against him, pulled away, and then Dylan grabbed him by the shoulders and slammed him against the wall.

"I'll kill you, you motherfucker!" Dylan screamed. Then, with his right fist still encased in the cast, he punched Randy in the face. I heard bone crunch, and Randy's face just collapsed, blood spurting out of his nose. It was a nightmare.

Randy fell backwards to the floor, and Dylan rushed forward, straddling him. He was like nothing I'd ever seen. Savage, his face twisted in rage, the muscles in his shoulders and arms bunched and tense. He threw a punch, then another, screaming in Randy's face the entire time. Then he grabbed Randy by the shoulders and lifted his upper body and slammed it on the floor, twice, hard. Randy's head bounced off the floor with a loud crack.

The music had stopped, and there were screams as some of the other guests saw what was happening. Dylan raised his fist to punch Randy again, and suddenly Sherman was behind him, grabbing Dylan behind the elbows.

"He's down," Sherman shouted in Dylan's ear. "That's enough!"

Dylan struggled in his rage, trying to get away, to get back to Randy.

Sherman shouted, "It's enough! Go check on Alex!"

At my name, Dylan stopped struggling. He turned, suddenly, toward me. I could see spatters of Randy's blood on his face.

I burst into tears as someone called out, "Somebody call 911!"

The next moment, Dylan's arms were around me, and I was sobbing. I was sobbing because of the attempted rape, because of my fear, because of Randy's attempt to attack me a second time. But I was also sobbing for Dylan, for the man I loved, who had been in such a murderous rage. I was sobbing for what might happen to him, because Randy was unconscious and looked as if Dylan had hit him hard enough to kill him.

I was sobbing because I was terrified that I was going to lose him.

The next twenty minutes were a blur as the paramedics and police arrived. The paramedics went to work on Randy, and soon carried him out on a gurney, a brace around his neck, bandages on the back of his head. Then the police went to work, questioning people. Then they came to us.

They had to pull us apart, because I wouldn't let go of him. His arms were calm, down by his sides, but I kept mine around his waist as they pulled us apart and placed the handcuffs on him. I sank to the floor as they took him away.

As they hauled him away, one officer on each side, hands gripping his upper arms, he turned his head and looked back at me, his eyes wide. I couldn't tell what he was trying to tell me.

A female police officer approached me, and said, "You're Alex? I'm Officer Perez. You can call me Christina."

I nodded, unable to stop the tears, sobbing uncontrollably.

"I need to take your statement now, while it's fresh, okay?"

I tried to control myself, and it just got worse. "Is he going to be okay?"

"Well, it's too soon to tell. They're taking him to the hospital now; there may be a head injury."

"I don't mean *him!* He's a rapist! I want to know about Dylan."

Her eyes widened, then she said, "Wait. Let's back up, and please tell me the whole story."

And so I did. Starting with the first date I had with Randy last spring, then when he tried to rape me and his roommates intervened. About how I was too ashamed to report it. And how he had cornered me in the kitchen, backed me into that dark hallway, and then stuck his hand up my skirt while holding me against the wall.

"He was going to rape me," I whispered. "Dylan stopped him. He was protecting me."

All the time I was telling the story, Carrie and Sherman were standing at the other end of the kitchen. Carrie's eyes were huge and sad. When the questioning was over, without a word, she walked over and put her arms around me. I began sobbing again, breaking down this time completely. I cried like I was never going to be able to stop. I cried for the boy I loved, who had grown not just into a man, but a man filled with rage.

A man who might be capable of murder.

A man who had just been led away, his arms locked behind his back in handcuffs.

CHAPTER TEN

Right where I belonged (Dylan)

Oh, fuck, I thought, as the police started to lead me out of the apartment. I looked over my shoulder, saw her still standing there against the wall, a cop next to her. She was sobbing, and met my eyes with a look of longing mixed with fear. I would have done anything to erase the fear. But there was no going back. She'd seen what I was capable of. *I'd* seen what I was capable of.

Randy, or whatever the hell is name was, had already been carried out by the paramedics before they arrested me. But I couldn't clear my head of the vision of him, slamming her up against a wall, one hand over her mouth and the other up her skirt as she struggled.

I didn't care if I went to prison. I hoped the son of a bitch was dead.

As they shoved me into the back of a patrol car, a wave of exhaustion and nausea swept over me. Was it really only three hours ago that she whispered, *I'm losing my virginity tonight.* God, I wanted to cry. I wanted to scream. I wanted to kick my way out of the back of the car, run back to her and throw my arms around her, protect her, love her, take care of her forever.

But, I'd screwed that up, too.

So, instead of doing any of that exciting, dramatic, powerful stuff that I'd have liked to do, I sat there in the back of the car for what seemed an eternity while the police continued to do whatever it is that police do. Onlookers on the street walked by, glancing in the back of the car, where I was Exhibit A for the guy you do not want your daughter to fall in love with.

Fuck. Fuck. Fuck.

I was there for maybe thirty minutes before the police car finally pulled out. Two officers were in the front, a male and a female. Neither of them said a word to me at first, until we got stuck in traffic. Finally, the male officer, sitting behind the wheel, said, "If you care, dispatcher says it looks like the guy you beat up is going to live."

My hands, still wrapped behind my back, were hurting like hell, especially the one in the cast. I suspected I'd done more damage to my hand. *Worth it.*

I shrugged in response to the officer's comment.

"Why'd you do it?" he asked.

I looked up at him. Conventional wisdom said I should have stayed quiet until I saw a lawyer. But what difference did it really make? I wasn't going to fucking lie to anyone. Yes, I'd gone way too far. But the fact was, I was protecting her. If I had to go to jail for that, so be it.

I finally answered. "He sexually assaulted my girlfriend. I intervened."

The female officer winced.

"I call bullshit," said the male. "I'm guessing she was getting a little on the side, and you got pissed off."

I had to swallow the surge of rage I felt. *Do not respond. Don't do it.*

I finally said, "I don't think I want to talk to you any more."

The officer burst into laughter and slapped the steering wheel. "You hear that, Perez? He doesn't want to talk to me any more. Fucking college kid punk. I tell you what, he ought to be in the fucking Marines learning some discipline, instead of fucking around at penthouse parties on the Upper West Side. You hear that?" he shouted at me. "I fucking hate rich kids. All of you. Think you can do anything, get away with anything. I bet your dad's lawyer will be pounding on the front door of the police station before we even get there."

Perez, the female officer, leaned over and whispered something urgently, to her partner. Whatever. I shook my head, turned to stare out the window. He could think what he wanted, it didn't make any difference to me.

The abuse continued for a little while, but I tuned it out, concentrating instead on the growing bloom of pain in my right hand.

The problem was simple.

I was no good for Alex. I wasn't even any good for myself. Yeah, I'd protected her. But what about next time? What if the next person who pissed me off and I lost control was Alex?

Hopefully, after tonight, she recognized that. But what if she didn't? What if she had some misguided belief that she could somehow heal me? There wasn't any healing. What happened in Afghanistan was part of who I was now, and if I thought about it honestly, something like tonight was bound to happen again.

I'd kill myself before I ever laid a hand on her. But I'd seen what happened to couples over the long term. I'm sure, once upon a time, my parents had had that bloom of love and happiness. But too much alcohol, and too much stress and anger and hate finally turned them into a perfect caricature of the abusive couple. It wasn't until my Mom got clean—and kicked his ass out—before she finally got her life together.

No way in hell was I going to put Alex through that. And it would happen. It would happen sure as the sun was going to rise in the morning.

I blinked back tears. Because I was going to have to figure out a way to let her down easy, to say goodbye, and disappear into my own world, this time permanently. Like I should have done in February, when the bomb meant for me killed my best friend instead.

At the jailhouse, they booked me in, which took forever. Fingerprints. Search. It was humiliating.

That was the point where my escort, the cop from the car, finally muttered something when he got a look at the mess of my leg.

"What the fuck happened to you?"

"Got blown up in Afghanistan," I answered.

He grunted. I guess that was all the apology I was going to get.

They confiscated my wallet and everything else, and into the jail cell I went. Right where I belonged.

The holding cell was packed, and then some, with about ten guys in a tiny little space. I took up a station near the door, and eased into a sitting position. No one looked at me or said anything and that was fine with me.

The cell itself was small, maybe ten feet long, with long benches down each side which might have once served as beds of a sort, but now each seated four or five guys, most of them slumped over trying to approximate sleep.

Closest to me was someone who stood out: a man in a suit and coat, though his tie and shoelaces were missing. He looked more like a banker than a hardened criminal. He also looked terrified, and huddled on the end of the bench as if his life depended on holding onto it. It was dark, the only light coming in through a narrow grate in the door, and the floor was damp. At the opposite end of the cell from the door was a toilet with no seat. It stank of piss and shit and unwashed bodies.

This hole wouldn't have looked out of place in Afghanistan. In fact, some of the accommodations we provided prisoners over there looked considerably more humane than this.

Where was Alex? I wondered if they'd taken her to the hospital for an examination, or had the police questioned her? I didn't want her to have to go through any more trauma than she'd already had to deal with tonight.

Except, I thought, I was going to be the one to deal the final blow.

For a moment, I had second thoughts. We loved each other. There was no doubt. Could that survive all of this? Could we overcome whatever challenges we had? Could love heal the fucked up state of my heart and mind and soul?

Yeah, right. Not likely.

Hopefully I wouldn't be in here long. Crazy as it sounds, I had about thirty thousand dollars left in the bank. A year of tax-free hazardous duty pay, plus my infantry-signing bonus, all my paychecks for a year, had been sitting in the bank, pretty much untouched. I didn't need anything in Afghanistan, didn't need anything in the hospital. When I moved home, my mother insisted I hold on to the money, not spend it on anything at all, though I'd been sorely tempted to buy a car. Not that I could use one here anyway. So the money sat and earned interest, and now I was going to end up using it to bail myself out of jail. If they let me make bail. If there was any way for me to access the money.

The sad thing was, if they ever gave me the phone call rumor said I was supposed to get from jail, I didn't have anyone I could call. Sherman, I suppose, but I didn't have a clue how to reach him. And if I called him, he'd probably be with Carrie and Alex. And I didn't want to drag them into this. Not any more than I already had.

My eyes pricked with tears, and I turned away from the other men in the cell.

Tears because I was going to miss her. Tears because even though I knew I was doing the right thing, it was breaking my heart all over again. And I knew it would do the same to her.

It would have been better if Roberts had lived. It should have been me.

I closed my eyes, and pictured her long, lush brown hair, her deep green eyes, the tilt of her lips, her cheeks and neck, her beautiful spirit and her loud, free laugh. And I thought that if I had to live without her, I didn't want to live at all.

Now it's my turn (Alex)

"We're going with her," Carrie told the police. "She is not going alone with you to the hospital. I'm her sister, and Kelly's her best friend."

The police officer looked uncomfortable, but finally agreed.

Carrie turned to Sherman.

"Ray, you take Joel, and go down to the police station, and see what you can find out about Dylan. Call me as soon as you know anything?"

Sherman nodded, took out his phone. "Let me get your number," he said.

She gave it to him, and Sherman came over and squeezed my arm.

"We'll talk later, okay. I know you're shaken up, but remember, he loves you. We all do... we're sort of family now, okay?"

My eyes teared up again. I'd not even known Sherman a day, and he was being incredibly kind. Impulsively, I reached out and hugged him.

Then I said, "Take care of Dylan, okay? Let us know, as soon as you know anything."

"I will," he said, patting my back.

Joel reached over and squeezed my shoulder, then kissed Kelly on the cheek. The two of them turned and left the building.

Half an hour later I was at the hospital. Carrie held my hand while the doctors did the examination. The *rape kit*. I'd made it clear that he hadn't succeeded, but the police were insistent. While the doctor was doing the exam, I stared off at the wall, tears running down my face. It was hideously uncomfortable, and more so, it was humiliating, to a degree I'd never imagined.

But that was nothing to the police interview.

It happened in a borrowed office in the hospital, and because they were both considered witnesses, neither Carrie nor Kelly were allowed to stay with me during the questioning. In fact, both of them were being questioned, too.

The office was cramped, and I was sitting, exhausted, with a cup of stale, burnt-tasting coffee in my hand.

"Have a seat, Miss Thompson," said one of the officers, a somewhat florid, overweight man who introduced himself as Sergeant Campbell.

"We're trying to sort out this mess, and we'd like you tell us, in as much detail as possible, exactly what happened tonight."

I did, starting with the two dates I'd had with Randy last spring. The whole time I was talking, Campbell was taking notes, and didn't interrupt me. I fought to stay composed. I was still in shock, and frustrated, and angry. Especially angry that for the second time, Randy had used physical force against me and I'd done nothing to stop it. Nothing to turn him away. Dylan shouldn't have had to come to my rescue like that. And if I'd been able to handle it on my own, he wouldn't have needed to.

"Okay, I've got some questions," Campbell said. "Starting with... You say he assaulted you once before. Why didn't you report it then?"

I could feel my face flush. I stared down at the floor, and kind of shrugged, and said, "I guess I was ashamed. I'd been drinking, and I thought I knew him better than that, and... I don't know exactly why. I just wanted it to be over. And I thought it was, until a few weeks ago."

"What happened a few weeks ago to change your mind?"

"Randy showed up at the 1020 Bar and started to harass me. When he wouldn't let go of me, Kelly pepper-sprayed him and the bouncer threw him out."

Campbell frowned, then said, "That's twice now you've told me you were drinking. Underage."

I nodded, looking away.

"What about tonight? Were you drinking?"

"No."

"Why not? You were drinking with him last spring, and again at the 1020 Bar, why not last night?"

"My boyfriend doesn't drink. I didn't want to make him uncomfortable."

"I see. That would be Dylan Paris."

I nodded.

"So Dylan doesn't drink. How long have the two of you been dating?"

That was a complicated question. I answered the best I could. "We met on a foreign exchange program three years ago, and were together after that. But we split up last February, while he was in Afghanistan. Then just recently got back together."

"How long ago?"

"A few weeks."

"Did Randy Brewer have any reason to believe the two of you were together?"

I shook my head, violently. "I made it very clear I wanted nothing to do with him."

"Tell me how you ended up alone with him. You're in a dark hallway all alone with the guy you claim tried to rape you previously. In a short skirt. How did that happen?"

In a short skirt? What the fuck?

"I went to get some water. I didn't even know Randy was at the party, but he showed up in the kitchen while I was in there, and backed me into the hallway. I was trying to get away from him."

"So you went off on your own and led him into the hallway."

"No! Why are you treating me like this is my fault?"

"Miss Thomas, I'm just trying to get to the bottom of what happened. A young man is in the hospital with a possible fractured skull. I need to know if you were playing any games. Maybe trying to make your boyfriend jealous? I mean, I'd be jealous if I came along and found a girl like you in a dark hall with some guy's hand up your skirt."

I couldn't help it. I started to cry, in disgust and rage.

"You are so wrong. You have no idea what you're talking about."

"Then help me understand."

"I've already told you. I was trying to get away from him. He threw me up against the wall and I screamed, so he put his hand over my mouth. I was struggling." My voice rose to a shout. "Do you want to see the fucking bruises?"

"I don't think that will be necessary, Miss, I know the hospital personnel took photos. All right, let's go through this again. Last spring, you and Brewer were dating."

"We dated exactly twice."

"Right. While your boyfriend was off in the Army."

"*After* we broke up!"

"So you went out with him, drinking underage, and started to have sex and wanted to stop?"

"No! He pushed me down! If his roommates hadn't come in when they did I don't know what would have happened!"

"Gotcha. His roommates come in, interrupt, and you... what? Call the police? Report him? Run away?"

I stared at the floor. "Yes, I ran away. And I tried to forget about it."

"So he comes back tonight, at some upscale party in a penthouse apartment, and sexually assaults you, and ends up with a fractured skull. It just doesn't add up to me. If you'd reported it last spring, it'd be one thing. You say Dylan doesn't drink. Did you know he does drugs?"

"What?"

"Oh, you didn't. Yeah, his system was completely loaded. Opiates, among other things."

I shook my head. "Did *you* know that his right leg was pretty much shredded by a roadside bomb in Afghanistan nine months ago? The painkillers are prescription."

"What happened to his hand? Why's it in a cast?"

I swallowed, and whispered, "We were having an argument, and he ... he punched a wall."

"Jesus Christ," Campbell said. His face twisted, one side of his mouth lower than the other, and shook his head just slightly. "He punched a wall hard enough to fracture his own hand?"

I nodded. "It's not how it sounds."

"You better be glad he didn't punch you, kid."

"Dylan would never do that."

"Look, Miss Thompson. I get it. I served in Iraq myself. But let me tell you, when someone is fucked up on drugs, and angry, sometimes they can't distinguish between the wall they're punching and the girlfriend they're punching. You need to stop trying to defend him and worry about yourself for a change."

"I don't want to talk to you any more."

"I didn't ask what you wanted, Miss Thompson."

"If you have anything else to say to me, you can speak to my lawyer. This discussion is over."

I stood, and stared at them, then said, slowly and quietly. "What I don't understand is this. Just about every question you've asked me seems designed to blame me—the victim—or Dylan, who protected me. Why aren't you asking questions about Randy Brewer? Why aren't you interested in him? He's the *rapist!*" My voice rose to a scream as I finished the sentence.

I turned, opened the door and walked out of the office.

"We're leaving," I said to Kelly and Carrie. "Has Sherman called?"

Carrie nodded. "He said no contact. Dylan will have to go to an arraignment hearing on Monday sometime, and they'll set his bail, or not, then."

Monday. Christ, two nights in jail. God only knew what was happening to him in there. This was so unfair.

I swallowed, hard. There was nothing I could do about it, other than try my best to help him when the time came.

"Let's get some sleep, then. Would you guys mind if we got together in the morning—all of us—to figure out if and how we can help him?"

Carrie and Kelly both stared at me, open-mouthed.

"I don't know what we can do," Kelly said.

"That's what we have to figure out. What I know is, he's all alone in there because he protected me. Now it's my turn to protect him, and I'll do the best I can, with your help or without it."

#

Everyone looked pretty rough when we met at the big round table in the back of Tom's the next morning. Carrie's eyes were swollen and red, and she'd pulled on jeans and a pullover. She looked as relaxed as I'd ever seen her, but also exhausted. She sat next to Ray Sherman, something I'd have been incredibly tickled about if it had been any other time. Sherman was the only one at the table looking reasonably normal. Wide awake, stuffing away about a thousand pounds of food. The two of them had arrived together, and I had the funny feeling they'd been together all night.

Kelly and Joel were slumped together, picking at their breakfast. Joel had ended up staying over with us, but out of courtesy to me, and probably exhaustion, they'd done nothing more than sleep. He had snored, sounding something like a rhinoceros running away from a freight train, and even if I hadn't had trouble sleeping anyway, that would have kept me up.

I'd lain in my bed, staring up at the ceiling, listening to his snores, Kelly's soft breathing, and thinking that if there had been any justice in the world, I'd have been spending the night in Dylan's bed, definitely not sleeping.

"My brother-in-law is a criminal defense lawyer," Joel said. "I can't guarantee he'll take the case, but it's worth asking. He's expensive, though."

Sherman spoke up. "Dylan's got cash, or he should. If not, I can spring for it."

I tilted my head. "You don't have to do that."

He leaned forward, and said, "Yes, I do. Dylan's closer to me than my own brother. I'd pay every last penny. Clear? Don't argue with me on this."

I nodded, blinking back my watering eyes. Carrie put her hand on Sherman's and whispered something to him, I don't know what. Then she said something that almost made me fall over dead. "I can help with that, too. Dad gave me forty-thousand at the beginning of the school year."

My mouth dropped open. First at the idea that our father had just *given* her that kind of money, and second that she'd be willing to give it up for this.

"Dad will have a fit," I said.

"It'll be good for him," she responded, her eyes dancing.

"I have to fly back tonight, but I'll get you as much of the money as I can before I go, okay? If you don't use it, fine, send it back."

"And I'll come to the hearing with you," Kelly said. Joel nodded. "We'll all go. You in, Ray?"

Sherman nodded.

I didn't know what I did to deserve friends like this.

Joel stepped outside to make his phone call to his brother-in-law.

Sherman said, "Alex, before we all split up, we need to talk for a few minutes. Alone."

Carrie and Kelly both raised their eyebrows in curiosity.

"Okay," I said hesitantly.

"Let's take a quick walk, this won't take long."

I nodded, and found myself standing, my limbs feeling numb. What did Sherman need to talk about? Something to do with Dylan, obviously. And it made me afraid. Very afraid. And I didn't even know why.

Outside, we walked about half a block away, and he turned around and leaned against a wall.

"Listen," he said. "I told you last night... Dylan...he's like a little brother to me."

I nodded.

"Well... I'm a little worried. Honestly, I'm a lot worried. About how he's going to react to all of this. Being thrown in jail, the fight, everything."

I bit my lip, staring at the ground. "I am, too," I whispered.

"That guy's got a martyr streak a mile wide. You need to understand... I doubt he ever told you the details, at least in the right time sequence. But after you guys broke up, and he shot up his laptop, our squad got mixed up in the patrol rotation as part of the punishment."

I nodded. "I know."

"That was the patrol when they got hit by the roadside bomb, Alex. When Roberts died."

I shook my head in confusion. "He told me it was several days later."

Sherman shook his head, sadly. "No. Now listen, Alex... nobody blamed him. Nobody said it was his fault. It could have happened any time. We were getting hit all the time. But Dylan blamed himself. He and I emailed back and forth about it a lot when he was in the hospital. I tried to get him to see it, but ... well... guilt is pretty ugly stuff. And he's convinced that if he'd just kept his shit together, Roberts would be alive."

"Okay. So... what does this have to do with now?"

He looked at me, closely. "Think about it, Alex. What else happened to someone he loved after that?"

I felt my stomach cramp. "Oh, no."

He nodded. "Yeah. I'd bet a million dollars he's got the idea that it's somehow his fault that asshole tried to rape you."

I shook my head violently. "No. It was not his fault. It wasn't my fault. That was all Randy."

"Yeah, well... just be careful. Be prepared. Because I think Dylan's going to be blaming himself, and I don't know what he's going to do about it."

"You don't think he's going to break up with me, do you?"

"He might."

A tear rolled down my face. He reached out and touched my chin, and said, "You and me... it's our job to try to bring him back, okay? I don't know if we can, but... well... I love that guy. And I'm not going to let him go off the edge if I can help it."

"I won't either," I whispered.

CHAPTER ELEVEN

Just stay quiet (Dylan)

When I was escorted into the courtroom, my hands were still cuffed, in front of me now, and a police officer had me by the left arm.

I was not in the best of shape. My cast had cracked, and most of it had simply fallen off. My fingers were curled, and I wasn't able to do anything about it. They hurt like hell. My entire hand had the sickly grey pallor I associated with zombie movies. My shirt stank of vomit, though I'd done my best to clean myself in the sink before they took me out for the arraignment.

The vomit happened when I'd had a seizure.

From a clinical perspective, the seizures were minor. The doctors said I might have them for a year, or five, or maybe never again. There was no way to know. I'm careful to take my anti-seizure meds on a daily basis. But obviously I didn't take any that Saturday or Sunday night, and sometime around four a.m. on Monday, I felt it coming. My whole body tensed, a blinding headache descended on me, and the next thing I knew, I was shaking, tiny rapid shakes that were so jarring I couldn't move at all. I don't think anyone would have noticed anything at all, except that I aspirated some of the vomit and started choking.

I didn't know what to expect walking into the courtroom, but this wasn't it. I'd never been in a courtroom, and I guess I expected some old crumbly building, something like the old Night Court reruns my Mom used to watch. Instead, I walked into a clean, carpeted, well-lit room with lots of lush wood paneling. The police pushed me into a pen with the various other criminals and told me to sit and wait.

That's when I saw them. Not just Alex, but also Sherman, Joel, Kelly. They sat together, in a group around Alex, as if to support her. And she was staring at me.

I had to close my eyes. I couldn't do this. I couldn't hurt her. I couldn't break her heart all over again. But I don't know what choice I had. I could hurt her in the short term, like tearing off a band-aid, or I could hurt her permanently, in the long term, by involving her in my fucked-up life.

The hearings went on forever. One right after the other, with the judge basically handing out decisions rapid-fire. So I was a surprised when they called my case.

The officer leaned over to me and said, "Come this way," then led me to a table at the front. A man in a suit came up the center aisle and sat at the table next to me.

I stared at him. "Who the hell are you?"

He leaned close. "I'm Ben Cross. I'll be representing you. For this morning just stay quiet; I'm familiar with the details of the case. We're going to get you out of here as quickly as possible."

"Who hired you?"

He jerked a thumb toward the back of the room. "They did. Your friends. Joel's my brother-in-law."

Oh, no. They were mixed up in this even worse than I realized. "I didn't ask for that."

"Be glad you don't have a public defender."

"I don't want you here."

He shook his head. "Do you *want* to go to prison? Look, we can settle the details after the arraignment. For now, can we do it my way?"

"Whatever."

I turned and looked away. I didn't mean to be ungrateful. But what the hell? They went out and hired a lawyer for me? Who the hell could afford that? And why? Jesus Christ.

So Ben Cross went to work for me. Before I knew it, bail had been set, and I was back in the holding cell, waiting. An hour later, the cops came for me again, and led me out to the lobby of the jail.

I was dreading what was coming next.

Let him smell your socks (Alex)

I knew Dylan was going to look rough when he came in to the hearing room. He'd been in a holding cell all weekend. But it hit me, hard, when I saw just how rough he looked. He was obviously exhausted. Dark circles framed his eyes, and after three days without a shave, dark stubble covered his chin. The black T-shirt I had and drooled over looked torn, and a stain ran down the front.

His hand. The cast was off, and he held his right hand in his left, as if protecting it. It was washed out, pale, and the fingers were curled up and unmoving. His face had a similar pallor. It was obvious he was in a lot of pain.

But the worst part was his eyes. They looked... faded. Dull. Dead. I grabbed Kelly's hand when he looked over at me, met my eyes for a moment, the looked away, almost as if he didn't recognize me. I had to stifle tears. Again.

No. I was not going to sit here and cry. I was going to be strong, because right now, he needed me.

Even if he didn't know it.

The hearing was over quickly. Joel's brother-in-law was obviously experienced and knew what he was doing, and quickly ran through what had happened the night of the party. He argued persuasively that Dylan was exactly what he was... a wounded soldier who had been protecting someone he loved from a sexual assault. That he should be given a medal, not a trail. The judge told him to get on with it, and the lawyer made a motion that the case be dismissed.

At that point the prosecutor stood up and said, "Your honor, the defendant put a twenty-one-year-old Columbia student in the hospital with multiple skull fractures and possible permanent brain damage. He's dangerous, and we request that he be denied bail."

I held my breath.

The judge set his bail at twenty thousand dollars. When the words came out, Sherman grinned, then turned to me. "We've got enough," he whispered.

"He looks awful," I said, as I watched the bailiffs lead him away.

Ben, Joel's brother-in-law and now Dylan's lawyer, approached us. He already had the money in his briefcase.

"Okay, I'm gonna go bail him out. You guys can wait in the lobby; it might be an hour or two before we finally get him loose."

"Thank you," I said, and hugged him impulsively.

"I got to tell you," he said, looking mostly at me. "Dylan is … not exactly cooperative. He as much as told me to go to hell."

I sighed.

"I had a bad feeling," Sherman said. "We'll talk him around. He's pretty screwed up right now."

Would we be able to talk him around? What was he going to say when he came out of that holding cell? What was he going to say to me? About us?

I was terrified. I walked out of the courtroom feeling numb, and found myself pacing in the lobby of the courthouse. I thought of all the things we could have done differently, to arrive at a different place. If we hadn't gone to the party. If we hadn't met again in September. If I hadn't called him, drunk, from my room last February. If he hadn't freaked out, and been sent out on that patrol. If we hadn't met and fallen in love in the first place.

It was too much. There were too many paths that could have been taken, and no way to know what would have led here and now. What I knew was, I loved Dylan Paris. And I was going to fight for him.

I sighed. Pacing around wasn't doing any good. And I was probably driving the others crazy. I walked over to the bench where they sat, between Sherman and Kelly.

"So, Sherman… What are your plans? I know you came to visit Dylan, and that's not exactly turned out how you expected."

He yawned, looked up at the ceiling.

"Not sure yet," he replied. "I spent a couple weeks with my mom and dad when I got home, but we were driving each other crazy. So I floated down here, thinking to hang out with Dylan, check out Columbia. But… I'm going to finish college. Somewhere."

He gave me a speculative look, then said, "I was thinking about Texas, maybe."

"Oh really?" I asked.

"Yeah. Rice seems like a good university. And I met a PhD candidate there who worked really hard to sell me on the place."

I grinned. "You two really hit it off."

"I wasn't expecting it," he said.

I let out a short laugh. "I'm sure she wasn't, either."

He chuckled. "Carrie says the guys in her graduate program are terrified of her."

"I'm not surprised," I answered. "I always have been."

He gave me a puzzled look, eyebrows kind of scrunched together. "Why?"

I shrugged. "I don't know. She's always so… together. School, life, clothing. Carrie's always been bigger than life. I'm a little more down to earth."

"Well, you can't go through life thinking people are better than you. Look at Dylan—"

He cut himself off.

"What do you mean, look at Dylan?"

He frowned, then said, "Look, I shouldn't say anything about all of this. He'd kill me. But you've got to realize, he's never felt like he was good enough for you."

What? No. "That's not true."

He nodded. "Yes, it is true. God, you have no idea how much he talked about you over in Afghanistan. *Constantly.* No offense, but it was pretty damn tiresome. But he's always said, since the moment that you met, you were way out of his league. And he'd tick off the reasons. You're rich, he's dirt poor. You come from some kind of crazy successful family. Your father's an ambassador or something, right?"

I nodded.

"That's the kind of thing he'd talk about. His dad's a drunk, and he was always half afraid he'd end up just like his Dad. So he puts all this together, and concludes that he's not good enough for you. He's *always* believed that. And Afghanistan only made it worse."

I shook my head. "It's not true. I mean... yeah, so our families are different. But that doesn't mean anything. It's not about who your parents are, or how much money you have. It's about what you do with who you are."

"Well, try convincing him of that. I never could."

"I will, if he gives me a chance."

Kelly said dryly, "Let him smell your socks. Then he'll get it."

Joel suppressed a laugh, and ended up giving an unconvincing coughing instead.

"Thank you guys for coming today," I said, very quietly.

"Don't start that," Kelly said. "This is what friends do."

I smiled at her. She could talk all day about what friends do, but where I grew up, that wasn't true. I didn't have friends who would

go to court for me. Or jail. Or anything else. I was only then starting to realize just how special the bonds I'd formed here were.

Without a word I reached out and took the hands of my friends.
There really weren't any words for what I felt.

That's what war is (Dylan)

etting out of jail was kind of a reversed process of going in. They didn't search me on the way out, but otherwise, it was scarily similar. I signed paperwork, collected my phone and wallet and keys, and then I was free to leave.

I walked out slowly, because I was dreading it. They were probably out there. Sherman, and Alex, and her friends. And they'd seen how savage I'd been.

I'd done the right thing. I'd protected her. But... I couldn't stop. I let the rage and anger take over me to the point where if Sherman hadn't stopped me, I would have killed Randy.

I would have killed him. No question.

It's not that I hadn't killed before. I had. Three times, that I know of for sure. Others are a little hazier, where I'd fired in the direction of buildings or insurgents under cover, but for those three, I knew for sure.

Killing was easy. Living with it was difficult.

When the police finally let me out, they directed me to the elevators, and I was done. Two minutes later I stood in the lobby.

Alex sat across from me, surrounded by our friends.

I took a step or two forward, and the full weight of what I was planning to do sank in. My heart started pounding like crazy, and my stomach was turning, and I wanted to turn and run away. I was having second thoughts again—very real ones. Maybe I should just stop now. And try to figure out a way to make it work. There had to be a way to make it work.

Then she looked up at me, and I caught my breath, and I could see the same happened to her. Her eyes went wide, and she stood and strode toward me. As she did, her face started to twist, and she started to cry, and I couldn't let her just cry, so I put my arms around her.

I took a deep, slow breath through my nose as I held her, inhaling the scent of her hair, her body. She was wrapped into me, her arms thrown over my shoulders.

Then she kissed me, and the feeling of her lips on mine made we want to scream in grief and terror. Was I really willing to hurt her? Was I really willing to give her up? To give this up?

Our friends approached.

"You okay, man?" Sherman asked. I carefully lowered my arms from Alex, the pain in my right hand excruciating, but she held on, shifting around to my side.

"Yeah, I guess," I said. "Thanks for, um… everything. I don't know who paid my bail, but I'll pay you back. I've got the money in the bank."

Sherman shrugged. "We can deal with that later. Important thing is getting you out of here."

I went along with them, because I didn't have the courage to do anything else. We rode back to the Columbia campus in silence, with Alex resting her head on my shoulder. It was as awkward and uncomfortable a moment as I'd ever experienced in my life. And it was only going to get worse.

Knowing that it was a matter of minutes before I was going to lose her forever, I tried to memorize Alex's voice, her hair, her scent, everything about her. One day she was going to have a wonderful, amazing fucking life. And while I might not be a part of it, I was going to remember. I'd remember every second we had together, and never, ever let it go.

Sherman looked at me, and gave me a curious look. Almost as if he knew what I was thinking. For all I knew, maybe he did. He's a sharp guy, and he'd been the other half of a long email exchange about me and Roberts and Alex, and I may have even mentioned suicide once or twice.

We dropped off Kelly and Joel, then continued to my apartment.

After getting out of the cab, I said, "I really need to wash up."

God, I was such a coward. I couldn't just spit it out.

But why? Why was I afraid? I was going to lose her anyway.

So Sherman and Alex sat on the couch, and I carefully took a shower, trying not to injure my hand any further. Afterward, I slipped into my room, and changed into clean clothes. Just as I was pulling my shirt into place, there was a knock at the door.

I opened it. It was Sherman. Before I could say a word, he said, "Before you do what I think you're about to do, you need to listen to me."

I closed my eyes. "Sherman, this isn't your business."

"Yeah," he said, sounding exhausted. "Yeah, it is. Because you're my friend. And because she's my friend. Just hear me the fuck out, all right?"

"Jesus Christ," I said.

He paced for a minute, turned toward me and looked like he was going to say something, then turned away.

"Oh, for fuck's sake, spit it out."

He turned back and pointed his finger at me. "I warned her."

"What?"

"I warned her yesterday. I warned her that your fucking overblown victim mentality was going to twist things up and make you break up with her."

"What the hell?"

He shook his head. "Tell me you haven't been screwing yourself up to do it the whole ride home. Tell me I'm wrong, Paris."

This time, I was the one who looked away.

He pointed, out the door and down the hall. "She's out there, waiting. With her hands on her lap. Her back straight. Trying to hold it all in. Trying to stay brave, even though she knows you're about to fucking blow her heart into a million pieces. For *the second time.* We both know you as well as you know yourself, asshole. And let me tell you, you aren't saving her from anything by doing this. You're just going to break her heart, and your own, and fuck everything up that's good in your life."

I frowned, and said, "You don't know what the hell you're talking about, Sherman."

"Bullshit, I don't. I was *there*, Paris. I was there when Kowalski threw himself on that grenade. And I was there when Roberts died. And I'm telling you, you need to stop killing yourself over that shit. You didn't kill either one of them. It wasn't your fault, it wasn't mine. It wasn't anybody's except the fucking terrorists who killed them."

"What does that have to do with anything?"

"Just tell me what you were going to say to Alex."

"Why? Why in God's name do you care?"

"Because we're brothers, man. We've been through shit no one else knows about. We've been through shit they don't *want* to know about. And I don't want to see you fuck your life up. And, I care about Alex and her sister, and I don't want to see you fuck her up, either!"

I shouted back. "Don't you understand, I'm no good for her! I'm no different than my father was! What if it was her I hit? Instead of that fucking wall? What then? It'll happen some day! Some day I'm going to lose control of myself and end up hurting her! And I'd rather die! I'll kill myself before I do that to her, Sherman. I mean it."

He shook his head. "That's a fucking cop-out, Paris. You're you, not your father."

The door opened. And she was standing there. Crying. And I couldn't fucking take it any more. Because she was crying because of me. She was crying *for* me.

"Oh, God, Alex, I'm so sorry. I can't do this."

She looked at me, tears running down her face, and said, "You don't have to."

I turned away from them, put my uninjured arm against the wall, and slowly, slowly, leaned my head against it. "Alex," I said, "You're... you're so much better than me. I was always a fuckup. Don't you get it? I don't want to drag you down with me."

She approached me, and touched my arm, then slowly wrapped her arms around it.

"Dylan," she whispered. "You bring out the best in me. You always have."

I whispered, "But I fucked up, Alex. If I hadn't lost it the way I did, the way *my father* always did, we would never have been sent out on that patrol. And Roberts wouldn't have died."

"Fuck," Sherman said, throwing himself on the bed. "Maybe you're fucking right. If we hadn't been sent out that day, it would have been a different patrol. And you know what? Then they would have caught the shit instead. If it had been second platoon, if they'd gone out there as scheduled, and gotten fucked up like we did, would you be sitting here feeling guilty about it? Jesus Christ, Dylan. What about later on, after you left? Weber bought it three weeks later. Taking a piss, and a sniper got him. He died with his fucking dick hanging out. Is that your fucking fault too? That's what war is."

I looked at him, feeling as lost as I've ever been in my life. I didn't know that. *Jesus Christ.* Weber died taking a piss?

I took a long, careful look at Alex. At her tears and grief. And then I thought how much worse it would be if I dragged her into my world. A world where people died taking a piss, a world where drunken husbands beat their wives half to death, a world where her boyfriend was going to be on trial for assault, or maybe attempted murder.

I couldn't do that to her.

I shook my head, in sudden negation, and said, my voice at a broken near whisper, "I'm sorry, Alex. I can't do this to you. It's too big a risk. It's over. I'm so sorry."

Her expression didn't change, except to slightly stiffen. She stood up a little straighter maybe. But I could see in her eyes that I'd dealt a blow, one that she'd likely never forgive me for. She blinked to clear her eyes, then said, "I am too, Dylan. You have no idea how much. But let me tell you just one thing."

She stepped even closer than she already was, until we were face to face, no more than two inches apart.

In a clear, strong voice, she said, "You don't get to decide what's too big a risk for me. You don't decide what's good for me and what isn't. That's my decision, Dylan. If you care about me so much, then how dare you do this all by yourself? I choose not to destroy my present because of the risk of a future that might or might not happen. You should think about that."

Then she turned and walked out.

Sherman stood there, looking at me, then muttered a curse. He shook his head, and then said, "I never thought I'd say this to you, Dylan. But you're a fucking idiot. I'm not staying around to watch this train wreck."

My eyes darted to him, and I said, my voice cold, "I didn't ask you to."

He sighed, and his shoulders slumped. He looked defeated, his face and eyes turned to the floor. For a second, it looked like he was going to say something else, but he stopped. Then he turned and left.

And just like that, I was all alone again.

CHAPTER TWELVE

I'm sorry I got your kid killed (Alex)

Sherman caught up with me about two blocks away from Dylan's apartment. I heard him calling, but kept walking. I was too caught up, too angry to stop.

He finally reached my side and matched my pace. He didn't say anything at first.

It was a chill afternoon, a little dark, and a few leaves were scattered here and there. It matched my dark mood perfectly.

I finally came to a full stop. Sherman took two more steps before he could halt his momentum, then spun around and said, "You're taking this well."

"I could kill him," I said.

"Anger is good," he replied.

"I can't do any more crying, all right? He's made his stupid decision."

"You want to talk?"

"Not really."

"Humor me."

I took a deep breath, and closed my eyes. I couldn't zero in on my emotions. There was an empty hole there. That scared me, more than anything else I'd experienced. How did Dylan have the power to just... take away a part of me like that? I knew it was a matter of time before the pain came. And when it did, I didn't know what I was going to do. Maybe just fall apart entirely.

I gave a firm nod. "All right."

So we turned, and walked to the coffee shop.

"Let's sit outside," I said.

He nodded, and we went in and got our coffee, then sat down in the seats closest to the street. He ostentatiously slapped a pack of cigarettes against his hand several times, then ripped off the cellophane and lit up a cigarette.

I said, "Can I have one?"

He blinked, then passed a cigarette over. "I didn't think you smoked."

"I don't. Let me have a light."

He shook his head. "Seems like everyone I know is making stupid decisions today."

"Fuck off," I answered, then took his lighter and made an attempt at lighting the cigarette. I took a long drag from it, feeling it burn down my throat, then coughed.

"Didn't Bloomberg ban outdoor smoking, too?"

"Fuck him, too," I said. "God, that's nasty."

"Yeah, well..."

I took another drag. God, I was getting lightheaded.

"Look, Alex... would it help if I said this is probably temporary?"

I looked at him, and said, "No, not really."

He frowned, then slumped in his seat.

"It won't help, because it's not temporary. He might change his mind tomorrow or the next day or next week, but he'll still have the same issue. Thinking he's not good enough. Hating himself."

He sighed, and I took another drag off the cigarette. Now I was really buzzed. "Do you always get buzzed when you smoke?"

He shook his head. "No... that's only for people who are smoking for the first time, or who only rarely do it."

I think I grunted. That was disappointing. What was the point in smoking, then?

"What are you going to do?" he asked.

I shook my head. "I don't know."

He nodded, and took a sip of his coffee. He was slumped in his chair, staring at the traffic. "I hope it isn't selfish to say, I hope you won't give up on him. Dylan's a good guy. He's just ... a little fucked up right now."

I nodded, then stamped out my cigarette.

"I don't know why you smoke those things," I said, putting my head in my hands. "I feel woozy."

We were silent for a little while, the traffic just passing by. I was calm. Steady. Unnaturally so. I was relatively sure that once I sat down and let myself actually feel something, that would be the end. I wasn't ready to fall apart. Not yet.

I looked up at the sky. "No, I won't give up on him. But I won't... I won't be fooled, either. I love him. I really love him, Sherman. I don't even know what to think anymore. How can he be so damn stubborn? What if he comes back around tomorrow? Do I take him back, and just get hurt again next time he's down on himself?"

"God, I need a drink," Sherman said.

I nodded. "Me, too. But I missed all my classes today. I'm going to need to keep it together tomorrow."

He nodded, then said, "If it helps any... Ah, shit. Dylan will not appreciate this. But fuck him. I'm sending you some emails. From last March, when he first got to Walter Reed. I think you need to read them. If nothing else, it will give you some insight into the crazy shit going on in his head."

He took out his phone, and I could see him paging through it. "All right," he said. "What's your email address?"

"Um... AlexLovesStrawberries, all one word, at yahoo.com."

He grinned. "That's hilarious. Okay. Just... delete these or something, okay? I shouldn't be sending them to you at all. But... look. He's my friend. And it's killing me seeing him do this to himself."

My phone chimed a second later. I checked, and there were the emails from Sherman.

"Thank you," I said.

"You going to be okay?" he asked.

I shrugged. "What's okay, when your heart is breaking apart? I'm not going to go kill myself, if that's what you're asking. But no. I'm not okay." For the first time since the talk with Dylan, my voice broke. "I'm not okay at all."

There wasn't anything else to say. I asked him how long he was staying in town.

"Couple weeks. At least that was the plan. I don't know if Dylan's going to want me around, but all my crap's at his place. We'll see what happens, okay? I'll keep you in the loop. If nothing else, I need to try to keep him out of jail."

I swallowed, then said, my voice very quiet, "Thank you."

We stood, and he gave me an awkward hug, and I began to trudge back to my dorm. I could see Dylan in my mind: lean, exhausted, pale, leaning his head against the wall. Telling me that he had to protect me from *him*, that he was ending it, because he wasn't good enough. The heartache and pain in his eyes as he pushed away from me.

If I had any doubts whether or not he loved me, they were gone. But maybe love just wasn't enough.

I didn't realize it when I started crying. Not until the guy who ran the flower shop at the corner of of West 109th and Broadway saw me. He stared, then pulled a single rose out, and said, "Hey, girl. This is for you. Whatever is making you sad... I hope this makes it better."

I stopped, stunned, and took the rose.

"Thank you," I said, and started crying harder. "I really appreciate it," I said, wiping my face and feeling like a complete idiot.

He literally bowed, then backed into his shop. I walked on, arriving at my dorm five minutes later. But I wasn't ready to go in and face Kelly, so I kept going, turned right on 103rd and walked down to Riverside Park. It had been quite a while, but I used to sit on the benches here—sometimes alone, sometimes with Kelly—and watch the river.

In fact, Kelly and I used to picnic over here on the weekends last year, sometimes with Joel. We hadn't this year, and not only did I wonder why not, but I also wondered why, when Dylan asked me about my favorite thing to do in New York, I never included our times down here.

Of course, the answer was simple. I spent most of last year pining for him. Worrying about him, knowing he was in danger every day in Afghanistan. Then, not knowing anything at all, except that his name had failed to appear on the lists of soldiers killed-in-action—which I checked every day—but that he'd disappeared all the same.

My whole life was wound up in his.

So I sat by the river, and I thought, and I remembered.

I remembered the first time we kissed, halfway around the world from here.

I remembered sitting with him the night before we left Israel. He was wearing his black trench coat, both of us on a wide balcony, facing each other.

I'd asked him what he wanted. Did we want to commit to each other? Was it over when we returned to our respective homes? Would we stay together, even with the distance? What did he want?

He couldn't answer.

I remember slapping him on the chest, and crying out, "Why won't you tell me how you feel?"

He couldn't. "I don't know how to answer that," he said. "I think we just need to see what happens."

So we made no plans at all. It was all muddled, no commitment, but we still loved each other. Both of us broke it off with the people we'd been dating back home within days of our return, but even so, it was still just so unclear.

To think that less than nine months after that, he told his drill sergeant that he intended to marry me. *Why the hell couldn't he tell me that?*

"Hey baby, why you crying?" asked a guy on his bike, stopping in front of me. "You need some comfort?"

"Oh, fuck off," I replied.

"Bitch," he said, then rode off.

I took a deep breath. I was a mess. I rooted around in my purse, found a not-terribly clean napkin, and wiped my face. Then I took out my phone, and started to read.

At first the messages didn't make sense. Then I realized the newest ones were on top, of course. So I scrolled way down to the bottom, and started reading up. And tried to keep from falling apart.

MARCH 24, 2012
TO: <RAY.M.SHERMAN@HOTMAIL.COM>
FROM: <DYLANPARIS81@GMAIL.COM>
SUBJECT: WASSUP?

Weed,
I'm at Walter Reed. They say I might get to keep the leg, but it doesn't work worth a shit. What's up with you? How's everybody?
I miss you guys more than you know.
Dylan Paris

MARCH 25, 2012
TO: <DYLANPARIS81@GMAIL.COM>
FROM: <RAY.M.SHERMAN@HOTMAIL.COM>
SUBJECT: RE: WASSUP?

Holy shit, it's alive! You get your laptop replaced? How's Walter Reed? I'm sure the hospital sucks, but is the food at least better than here? We're doing okay, mostly. Weber got whacked by some fucking hajis a couple weeks ago, and Sergeant Colton got hit. Colton's back on duty already, and raising hell because we got caught with a fifth of gin in the tent. Bet he took it to drink himself.

I miss you too, dude. For one thing, there's no one here worth talking to. Bogey keeps going on about his fucking conquests with girls, all day and all night long. The only conquest he's ever really had is with his hand. Which, we caught him doing, on patrol. I mean, come on, in your sleeping bag at the FOB, sure, but out in the field? Give me a fucking break. You ever hear from Alex?

Write me back and soon, motherfucker. If they don't extend us, I'll be out of here in six more months. Or so. Whenever. I hate this fucking place.

Ray

I couldn't help but laugh at the tone of the emails, even though my heart gave a twinge at the sentence, *You ever hear from Alex?* They sounded just like the way Dylan and Sherman talked with each other. I continued to read, slowly scrolling up after each email.

MARCH 25, 2012
TO: <RAY.M.SHERMAN@HOTMAIL.COM>
FROM: <DYLANPARIS81@GMAIL.COM>

Weed,

Sorry to hear about Weber. Wow, I wish I'd had a chance to say goodbye. Or something. I've been thinking about going to see Robert's parents when I get out of the hospital. But I don't know, maybe I should stay away. How do you tell someone's mom,

"I'm sorry I got your kid killed?"

As far as Alex goes, we're done. I'm pretty sure she staged the whole fucking thing anyway. But seriously,

I never had any business falling for her. She's way out of my league. I hate it, but that's life.

Tell Sergeant Colton I had two liters of vodka in my bags, and I want that shit back. I know he took it before they shipped my stuff here.

Dylan

APRIL 1, 2012
TO: <DYLANPARIS81@GMAIL.COM>
FROM: <RAY.M.SHERMAN@HOTMAIL.COM>

Stop calling me Weed, Mr. Studmaster.
On that topic: You need to sit back and take a good look at the pictures you have of you and Alex together. Yeah, she probably got over you. But if I were you, I'd be chasing that down. Seriously.

With regards to Roberts: don't be an asshole. You didn't get him killed, the hajis did. Not your fault, dude. If we hadn't been out on that patrol, someone else would have. And they'd be just as dead.

So, seriously, don't take this the wrong way. But go see a shrink. Like tomorrow. You got knocked on the head pretty hard, and the things you're writing worry me.
Your friend,
Ray

P.S. Sorry it took me so long to write back. Been out on a fucking 5-day patrol. They're saying Lieutenant Eggers volunteered us for it, the shit.

And bullshit on the vodka. Since when do you drink?

APRIL 1, 2012

TO: <RAY.M.SHERMAN@HOTMAIL.COM>

FROM: <DYLANPARIS81@GMAIL.COM>

Ray,

Listen, dude. We're friends. But please don't write to me about Alex. I'd just ruin her life. We're too different. Sometimes I think I'm going to end up like my dad. Until my Mom got wise and kicked his ass out, he used to knock her around whenever he got drunk. Which, my friend, is why I don't drink.

I gotta tell you, being in this hospital, it makes me think I do need a shrink. Except for my mom, who comes to visit pretty much every day, it's very quiet here. Nurses and docs come and go. I get tests done. And I watch TV and read. That's about it. Lots of time to think. And think. And think. Dude, I'm gonna write some stuff here I gotta think about and talk about, and you're elected to listen. Because there isn't anyone else.

Alex sent me a bunch of emails. Right after I blew my laptop up, and again the next day, and the day after that. Every day for a couple weeks, then about once a week. Then they stopped.

I haven't read them. Every time I open my email, there they are. 16 unread emails. I'm sure she hates me now.

I'm also sure it's better that way. You say I should take a second look. But I already know. I loved her more than my own life, Sherman. But she's smart, and beautiful, and going to a great college, and has her whole life ahead of her.

I did get an email from her Dad. He's a real sweet-heart. Former Ambassador, likes to keep his tentacles in everything. Back when I went to visit her in San Francisco, a couple years ago, he took me aside at one point to tell me what a worthless piece of shit I was. That I wasn't nearly good enough for his daughter. Would you believe he had run a background check on me? And my parents. I'm sure he dug up some good stuff on Dad. He told me to stay the hell away from her in his email. "Let her believe you are dead. It's better for both of you."

The thing is though, he's right. She's got a chance for a beautiful life. I, on the other hand, am a disabled vet who gets seizures, and blackouts, and flashbacks. Sometimes I wake up at night screaming. Because I keep having the same dream over and over again. We're headed down that fucking dirt road, and I can see the bomb, it's right out there in the open. And I can't stop it. We're headed right for it, and we're go-ing to run over it, and I grab the wheel, and it's too late. Boom. Roberts is vaporized, about two gallons of his fucking blood all over me, and then, eyes open, I'm awake and screaming my fucking head off. They come and give me sedatives, and I'm out again. Until the next night.

I'm never going to be worth a shit after this. She doesn't deserve that. She doesn't need me in her life, dragging her down, ruining everything for her.

Ray, I love Alex, like nothing you can imagine. And because I love her, I'm going to leave her alone, and let her move on. Anything else would be hurting her. And I would kill myself before I harm one hair on her head. And that's not an idle threat.

So, no more fucking talk about Alex, all right? The subject is closed.

Dylan

APRIL 1, 2012
TO: <DYLANPARIS81@GMAIL.COM>
FROM: <RAY.M.SHERMAN@HOTMAIL.COM>
Dude,

Your email made me cry like a fucking baby.

All right. I won't bring up Alex again. But you better fucking promise to get better. Do you hear me? I don't give a shit how bad you feel. Get better. Man up. Do whatever it takes to get it through your head that a) you're a good guy, and b) you deserve better than the shit you're writing about, and c) You are NOT fucking responsible for Roberts' death.

Dude, get some help.

Fuck the Army,

Ray

Oh, God. I missed Dylan. I loved him. But I didn't know how to help him. I don't know that anyone could. Not unless he was willing to help himself. And this about my father, I had no idea. Dad and I would be having a discussion when I went home for the holidays.

I did some googling. "How to Help a friend with PTSD." And it wasn't much help, to be honest. It was all generic, useless stuff. Don't take his behavior personally. Have good boundaries. Yeah, *right*. Don't judge. Love them.

Love them.

Oh, God. I couldn't stop loving him. But I couldn't help him either.

The sun was setting, on what was possibly one of the longest and saddest days of my life. I stood up, put my phone away, picked up my rose, and began walking back towards my room.

How can you be so casual about it (Dylan)

When the alarm went off the next morning, I got up as usual. Really, I didn't know what else to do. Keep going. Go to class. Go to court. Whatever.

It was dark, quiet, and bitter cold. An icy wind blew off the Hudson River, turning the green in front of the library into a wind tunnel. I hoped it wasn't going to snow any time soon. In the meantime, I wore my army sweats, kept my hood on, and got out there and started to stretch.

I'd gotten pretty adept at doing pushups with just my left hand, but I hoped my right would be back into shape soon. Needed to go see a doctor, and soon, about that. I'd missed my Monday appointment at the VA, because of jail, but I'd be down there Wednesday. Maybe they'd put it in another cast.

I was doing pushups when I heard footsteps. I kept doing what I was doing, but my eyes darted up.

It was Alex. She was in sweats and running shoes, and started stretching. Just like it was any normal morning.

Jesus Christ.

I kept doing my pushups until I got to one hundred, then rolled over and started stretching my legs.

She didn't say a word.

I didn't say a word.

I don't know what she thought. That I was just going to change my mind? She didn't understand. It's not that I didn't want her. God, I wanted her more than anything else in the world. Except to let her have a decent life. And that wasn't going to happen with me.

Finally, I stood, ready to run. I said, "I don't really need a spotter any more."

She looked me in the eye, and said, "I'm not here for you. I'm here for me."

I shook my head and started running. She started out beside me, in her normal long lope, keeping pace with me. I gritted my teeth. Why did she have to make it so hard? Why couldn't she just accept that it was over? She could have such a wonderful life.

By the time I hit 101st Street, I was going fast, and picking up the pace. She stayed right beside me as I turned onto 101st and started heading for Central Park. Traffic was just starting to pick up, taxis and commuters from Connecticut and God only knows where else. Who the hell drives into New York City, anyway? Crazy.

I stopped at a red light, diagonally across from the park, and ran in place until the light changed.

Even though I was getting winded, I started to talk, half to myself.

"I was six the first time he came home drunk and hit her. I don't know what it was about... I think he'd lost his job or something. They were both fucking lushes, and that probably led to him getting fired. But I do remember sitting there, about a week after first grade started. We were making brownies in the kitchen of this shitty little apartment in Chamblee, just outside Atlanta."

Breathe. I paused in my monologue, not sure if she was listening. "Anyway. They had all these pictures, of the two of them. Happy and stuff. They went to high school together, believe it or not. Dated, then got married. Anyway, that day he came home, and he was angry. I could sense it, and I got real quiet. But I wanted to show him what we'd been making. So I picked up a big spoon, and dipped it in the brownie mix, and carried it into the living room shouting something. I don't know what. 'Dad, see what we did?' Or something like that. And the fucking brownie mix... there was too much of it on the spoon, and it fell on the carpet."

We were almost halfway down the length of Central Park now, and though not quite at a full out sprint, we were going really fast. I glanced over and saw her face was bright red. Well, I didn't ask her to come.

"Anyway," I continued, slower now, taking long pauses to breathe in between sentences. "My dad... he stands up and starts shouting. About how I fucked up the carpet, and we were going to have to pay for it. And she went to defend me. It's all muddled in my head, but the next thing I knew, he hit her, in the jaw. She went down, hard. And I held on to my mom, and yelled back at him, told him to leave my mommy alone."

I grimaced, realizing a tear was falling down my face. I wiped it quickly. "Point is... people who love each other don't always stay that way. Sometimes they hurt each other, too."

She snorted, then said, "Yeah, I know something about that."

Fuck.

I picked up the pace. I was running flat out now, as fast as I could go, and she was still keeping up. I took the left turn around the south edge of the park at a dead sprint with Alex beside me, and a crowd of birds launched into the sky as we ran through them.

This was my normal route for running, but I never ran it at this pace. I was getting blown out, sucking air into my lungs, and it was starting to really hurt. After the next turn, I stumbled, got back to my feet and kept running, now going north along the east side of the park, up Fifth Avenue.

As the reservoir came into sight, I knew I wasn't going to make it any further. I slowed to a walk, blowing out my lungs in big gasps, my chest shuddering, legs feeling like rubber.

Alex slowed her pace, running in place beside me.

"Too much?" she asked.

I shook my head, suddenly angry. She knew how I felt about her. It was like she was torturing me. Staying in sight, knowing that I had made the decision I had to protect her.

"What do you want from me, Alex?" I cried out.

She stopped running, dropping into a walk at my side. She looked serious, so I was blindsided by what she said.

"I want you to teach me hand-to-hand combat. Self defense."

"*What?*" I asked, my voice incredulous.

"I'm serious. I've faced two sexual assaults in my year and a half in college. Next time anyone touches me, they're going to regret it."

I shook my head, flabbergasted. "Are you for real?"

She nodded. "Yeah. And since it looks like I'll eventually be dating again, well... my history with that isn't so hot."

I winced, feeling a stabbing pain. I turned my eyes away. The thought of her dating someone else, anyone else, made me want to howl.

"Well, for God's sake, Dylan, don't look so upset."

I stopped in place, turned to face her. "How can you be so casual about it?"

She shook her head, her face a mix of anger and disappointment. "I'm casual about exactly nothing, Dylan. But you didn't give me a choice. You didn't talk about it with me. You decided to make all the decisions on your own. Well, suck it up. I won't go through another year of crying in my room over you. I'm done with that."

She was right, and I deserved whatever she was throwing at me anyway. But it hurt. It hurt to see her so angry. It hurt to know she was prepared to move on just like that, even if that's what I kept telling myself I wanted.

I didn't know what I wanted.

"All right," I said, my mouth once again going into gear before my brain engaged.

"What?"

"I said, all right. I'll teach you what I know."

She looked at me speculatively, then nodded once.

"When?" I asked.

She looked at me, then said, "I'm busy on Tuesday, Thursday and Saturday mornings. That's when I go running. How about Monday, Wednesday, Friday?"

That's when *she* goes running? *Oh, for God's sake.* She was going to drive me insane.

"You're nuts," I said.

"Look, if you don't want to teach me, I'll get somebody else. I'm sure I can get a class or something."

I shook my head. "No. I'll do it. Wednesday morning. Six a.m. Don't be late."

She nodded, her face still dead serious, and said, "I'll be there."

Then she turned and took off running. I watched her go, admiring her audacity, her courage. As I watched her recede down the sidewalk, all I could think was how I'd do anything for her. Anything at all. And I wanted to run after her, and tell her I was wrong, and beg her to take me back. But it was too late for that. Love meant a lot. It meant everything, and it meant nothing.

CHAPTER THIRTEEN

Your brain is the real weapon (Alex)

"Okay," Dylan said. "Let's try that again."

I'd asked for these lessons, but I hadn't bargained for how intense they would be. The first couple days, I'd worked with Dylan alone. But his hand was a mess, and for some of the rougher stuff he'd asked Sherman to come along as well.

This was our sixth lesson. For almost two weeks, we'd been at a sort of... truce, really. We still saw each other six days a week, three of them running together, three of them working together on this. Plus the time spent together working for Doctor Forrester.

We barely spoke to each other, except about whatever it was we were actually doing at that time. Businesslike. It was sad beyond belief, and I'm not sure why I was putting myself through this. Except that it allowed me to keep track of him; it allowed me to know that he hadn't started drinking himself senseless, or skipped town. But it also kept the tension between us alive and well, and that tension was nowhere more at the fore than when he was training me.

"Look," he said. "You're not exactly very big. You're never going to be able to use pure strength to push an attacker off balance. You've got to use speed... and most especially your brain. Your brain is the real weapon."

Sherman nodded. "He's right. You're still trying to fight using strength. What you've got to do is use his strength and weight against him."

I nodded, biting my lower lip. "Okay. I'm ready to try again."

Dylan came at me, without warning, grabbing me around the neck and waist. For a second, as always, I smelled him, and the sensory memory of us embracing was almost too much to bear. His cast was finally off, for good this time, though his hand hadn't fully healed. He wore heavy layers of padded clothing that he and Sherman had picked up at a sports store. Our practice had become rough more than once. But I needed that. Among other things, Randy Brewer was out of the hospital, and the police didn't seem to be interested in pursuing charges against him.

Dylan had his right arm around my waist, left arm around my neck, and he started pulling me back. I relaxed for just a second, then kicked straight back, in the same direction he'd been pulling.

For just a fraction of a second, he teetered, losing his balance. I kicked straight back at his knee, and we went down, Dylan losing his grip and crying out.

I was free! I scrambled away, out of reach.

"Great!" Sherman shouted.

Dylan lay on the ground, eyes shut in pain. Then he opened them, and looked at me, and a huge smile grew on his face.

"You did it," he said.

I shifted on my feet, then smiled back. "I did, didn't I. Are you okay?"

"Yeah, I'll be fine," he said. "Trust me, it's not nearly as bad as the other day."

I flushed a little, looking away, and said again, "Sorry about that."

I'd kicked him between the legs the other day, hard enough that he hadn't been able to move the rest of our session. That had prompted the purchase of the padding.

Dylan laughed. "It's okay. What we're here for." He paused for a breath, then said, "I bet you've been wanting to do that for a while anyway."

I raised an eyebrow and shook my head, then let out a low chuckle. "Maybe you're right at that."

I dropped to the ice-cold ground, and said, "No practice or running for the next two weeks. I'm going home for the holidays."

Dylan nodded, and Sherman said, "Yeah, vacation's over for me too. Headed back home Sunday. I might be able to drop in and visit around Christmas, though. And Dylan... let me know when it goes to trial. I'll be there. Understand? You call me."

Dylan nodded. "Yeah, I will, man. Thanks."

I looked at him. We'd not talked, not even once, about the events at the party that night. My knowledge of it extended to several interviews with the police, and a deposition with Dylan's lawyer. They'd listed me as a witness for the defense, but outside of that, I didn't know anything at this point.

"What's going on with that?"

Dylan shrugged. "The lawyer says I've got a strong chance of going free. The law is pretty clear; you can use deadly force to prevent rape or sexual assault."

He looked at the ground, and I could see the difficulty he was having, the shame he felt. "The problem is that I kept hitting him after he was down."

I nodded. There wasn't much to say to that, because it was true. Even though simple facts didn't capture everything.

Quietly, he said, "He says they're probably going to offer some kind of plea bargain. I accept a conviction for assault or something, and they drop the charges otherwise. I don't know if I'm willing to accept that. I don't like the idea of having a felony conviction. I'd lose my VA benefits... I'd have to drop out of school. I'd lose... everything."

I looked at him, sitting there, obviously miserable, and I wanted to take his hand. I wanted to put my arms around him. But I couldn't.

Sherman spoke up. "Dude, we'll support you, whatever you decide. Put me on the stand; I saw most of it. Yeah, you went too far, I'll agree. But you also rescued her. Don't forget that and go wallowing in guilt."

Dylan nodded. He looked deeply unhappy, and it was driving me crazy that I couldn't do anything about it. I leaned forward and spoke. "Can we try one more?"

"Yeah," Dylan said.

"I got this one," Sherman said. "You're getting beat up enough."

So we stood, and Dylan coached. Sherman was harder than Dylan. I think Dylan was holding back. The emotional connection between us, the history, made it impossible for him to go after me aggressively. Sherman had no such compunctions, and he came in blindingly fast, grabbing me around the waist and knocking me to the cold ground.

I kept rolling with the momentum, and managed to roll most of his weight off of me, but he recovered quickly, grabbing my right arm and twisting it up behind my back. I cried out, and froze.

"Crap," Sherman said, letting go, then rolling off of me.

"We've got to work on that one," I said.

"Yeah."

Dylan came forward, reached out and gave me a hand up. "We'll work on that when you get back from San Francisco. You've got to practice using your attackers weight against him. Roll, rather than push."

I nodded. I was still winded. "You going to be up for it? I can get pretty mean."

He smiled. "I'm looking forward to it," he said.

I looked at him and said, "Why don't we all go grab some breakfast. It's been a while."

Doubt clouded his face. "I don't know if that's a good idea."

Sherman shook his head. "Come on, Dylan. It's only breakfast. Let's go."

He sighed. "All right."

So, wet and dirty as we were, we walked the five blocks to Tom's. Sitting down, we all ordered coffee, and I pulled my legs up under me in the seat.

"You looking forward to going home?" Dylan asked.

I shook my head. "No, not really. Anxious. My parents can be just a little over-controlling. And I've not been very, um, communicative this fall. To tell the truth, I've barely spoken with them. It's going to be one long, tense week. And all my sisters are coming into town, which will mean chaos."

"Speaking of sisters," Sherman said. "I guess I should break the news. I'm going to Texas the week after Thanksgiving. You know, for a campus visit."

"Oh, my God," I said. "Does Carrie know?"

He nodded. "Yeah. I've applied at Rice. Don't know if I can get in; my grades aren't as fantastic as my looks, you know. But close."

I laughed. "Good luck," I said, smiling.

"So, you know her better than I do. What's a good gift to take?"

"Condoms," I replied.

They both burst into laughter, and Sherman gave Dylan a high five. I blushed.

"Sorry. Sometimes I forget to consult my brain before I speak."

"In all seriousness, though... you know, Carrie's hardly dated at all. She's always been so career-focused. Not to mention that a lot of guys are intimidated by her height, and her looks. She mostly gets complete assholes chasing after her. You're a nice change, Ray."

He grinned, then said, "I've been practicing my nice-guy exterior. But I'm pretty much an asshole underneath."

"Whatever. Just get her something nice. Something... unusual. She's got a ton of clothes and jewelry... my Dad gives her lots of money. He treats her like she's a model. But something thoughtful, and different, would be perfect."

He nodded seriously, then said, "Oh, shit, look at the time. I gotta go—see you guys later!"

I couldn't help but notice that he hadn't actually looked at the time before he said it. Instead, he dropped a twenty on the table and practically ran out.

"See you guys later," he called as he went for the front door.

"Jesus," Dylan said. "That was a setup."

"You think so?" I asked.

"Yeah. He wanted to dump us alone with each other."

"I wonder why?"

He looked at me, and swallowed. Then he took a deep breath, and said, "Probably because I told him last night that I've been having second thoughts."

I looked away from him, suddenly numb in my fingers and toes, feeling as if I had stuck my head in a refrigerator. "Second thoughts about what?"

He sighed, then said, "About... me and you. Us. About my decision to walk away."

I stared at the black and white checks of the wall near us, trying to maintain control of myself. I didn't answer. I didn't look at him. I couldn't. Because this hurt. This really hurt. I'd done this to myself, knowing that if I kept hanging around, he'd eventually start to waver. And now he had. It was what I wanted. But not exactly.

When I didn't answer, he continued awkwardly, his voice sounding very, very sad.

"Look," he said. "I know I hurt you. I know I screwed up. And... maybe I'm hoping you'll give me a second chance."

I still couldn't answer. My mind was running visions of us at a thousand miles a second. Running together around Central Park in the darkness before sunrise. Huddled together in his room or mine. The night we held each other in a breathless, awkward, yet wonderful make-out session in Golden Gate Park.

I closed my eyes. I could see those things, but I had to remember other things. Being curled up in my bed, not knowing if he was alive or dead. And him not having enough respect for me to tell me to my face why he wouldn't have anything more to do with me.

"Will you consider it?" he asked.

Dylan rarely opened up so much, rarely made himself vulnerable like this. It was legitimate: I could see it in his eyes. I could see it in the very slight, almost invisible shaking in his hands. He was asking me to take him back, and it was laying him open, vulnerable to being hurt as bad as he'd hurt me.

That's why it was really tough to do what I knew I had to do.

I shook my head. "No," I said, very quietly.

He nearly collapsed into his seat. I kept my eyes away from him.

"I can't live with that. With you... deciding it's over, then just as quickly deciding you want me back. You don't get to make those decisions all by yourself."

I cut my eyes away from the wall, and back to him. He sat, looking glum, staring at the table. Then he said, his voice rough, "I was afraid of that."

I leaned forward, and said, "Damn it, Dylan. This is twice. Twice you've broken my heart. Twice you've made me feel like I was... like I was *worthless*. If you want me, you damn well have to convince me. If you want me, you have to finally, after all this time, start telling me what you are thinking and feeling. No more bullshit, no more hiding, no more long silences. If you want me, you need to make a commitment and work for it."

I stood up, knowing I was going to start crying if I didn't get out of there right this instant. Looking down at him, I struggled to maintain my composure as I said, "I love you, Dylan Paris. But sometimes love by itself... it's just not enough."

I threw some money on the table and walked away, my back straight, trying to hide the tears starting to leak from my eyes.

That's not much of a plan (Dylan)

I walked back to my apartment in a fog. I was a damned fool.

I've never been much of one for waterworks, so there wasn't much of that. Instead, I just felt dead inside. I'd give a lot to be able to break down and cry, which is what I suspected she was going to go do.

If you want me, you damn well have to convince me.

I didn't have a clue how to go about doing that. Not a fucking clue. What I knew was what I'd been coming to realize in the last couple weeks, as we were going through her farcical self-defense training. Did she think I didn't know the university offered self-defense training for free? This was about pulling us together. This was about her keeping an eye on me, about giving us an opportunity to come back together. And maybe I ... maybe I relished that safety a little bit. Maybe I took her for granted, and assumed that if I changed my stupid mind, she'd be waiting for me.

I was wrong.

Her face when she said it firm, direct, and very clear. The answer was no. She wasn't having me back. Not unless I made some changes. But I didn't know what kind of changes she was looking for.

When I walked back into my apartment, Sherman was sitting there, packing his bag, preparing to go home. He looked up as I entered, and when I closed the door behind me he said, "Where's Alex? She didn't come back with you?"

I shook my head.

"Shit," he said. "You didn't ask her? If she'd take you back?"

I stood there, then nodded. "I did."

"Oh. Oh crap," he said. "She shot you down."

I nodded, then told him what she'd said. He listened carefully. Then he sat, considering for what seemed like an eternity. I collapsed on the couch.

Ron, my elusive roommate from the chemical engineering department, came out of his room then. He nodded to me, walked to the kitchen and grabbed a beer. Then he waved, and disappeared back into his room. That was my fucking life.

"Dude, you fucked up, bad. You know that, right?"

I sighed. That was damned helpful. "Yeah. I know."

"So... what are going to do?"

"Convince her," I replied.

"How?"

"Not a fucking clue."

He frowned. "That's not much of a plan. Tell me what she said again."

I went through it again. Commitment. Telling her how I felt, as if I knew the answer to that. *Convince me.*

He frowned, and then said, "Look, dude, I've got to get to the airport or I'll miss my flight. But it seems to me like she gave you the plan already. She told you what you have to do. Now it's up to you. Listen, I'll call you next week. Keep me updated on the plans for the trial, all right?"

I nodded. We clasped hands, and then he grabbed me in a bear hug and growled, then headed out the door.

I went back to my room and collapsed on the bed, staring at the picture of her I kept on my nightstand.

Don't freak out (Alex)

I love flying west. It's quirky, I know, but the nice thing about it is, you can leave in the morning and actually arrive still in the morning if you're on a non-stop flight. Going east, across the United States, isn't nearly as much fun. Going against the sun, a four-hour flight turns into an all-day ordeal: leave in the morning, don't arrive until late at night.

Actually, I'm lying, just trying to stay positive.

The fact is, I hate flying. Being cooped up in a tin can with two hundred other people at nearly the speed of sound, thousands of feet above the surface of the earth? I get the shakes on takeoff and landing. The only tolerable flight I've ever had in my life was the one home from Tel Aviv to New York three years ago. I spent that entire flight in Dylan's arms, and didn't notice the fear. He held my hand on takeoff, and I was asleep when we landed.

I was already regretting what I said to him. Even if it was the right thing to say, the right thing to do. I'd gambled, and it was a big one. But I'd also done what I needed to protect myself. I loved Dylan, but I wasn't going to take him without conditions. I wasn't going to take him without being able to trust that he'd be there tomorrow.

So this flight I mostly spent crying. God, sometimes I'm pathetic. Is that a definition of strength? Doing what you have to do even when it's horrible, when it tears your heart out, when it feels like a huge mistake? If so, I guess this counted. I felt strong. I felt self-affirmed, empowered. I felt miserable.

To make things worse, I spent the entire ride going through my album. I was updating it, adding the very few pictures we'd taken in New York. Together. Every picture I saw of us together made me feel like crying just a little more.

The flight attendant stopped by twice to ask if I was okay. The second time, I answered forcefully, "Do I look okay? Please, just leave me alone."

She did.

Before the flight landed, I went back to the bathroom and carefully washed my face, then re-did my mascara and makeup. One thing I was not going to do was give any indication to my family that I'd been crying on this flight. This fell under the category of things my mother did not need to know.

At the end of the flight, as I was packing away my carry-on bag, the poor guy who'd been sitting next to me during the flight said, "He's a lucky guy, I guess, to have you love him so much."

I grinned. "Maybe. If he only knew it."

"Good luck," he said.

I guess I depend on the kindness of strangers. Because I'd put the rose in, as well. The rose given to me by the florist around the corner from the dorms, just two weeks ago.

So, bag slung under my shoulder, a fake smile plastered on my face, I walked through the security gates and greeted my family.

My dad wasn't at the airport, of course. He'd be sitting at home, waiting to greet me in some formal way when I arrived in his domain. But my mom was, and the twins, Jessica and Sarah. Expecting the same sort of giant, chaotic family bear hug I'd been greeted with when I got home for the summer, I was a little surprised (and disappointed) when my mother hugged me first, then each sister separately. They'd arrayed themselves on either side of my mother, Jessica dressed in a white dress, Sarah in black jeans and a grey T-shirt.

"Welcome home, darling," my mother said.

"Hey," Jessica said.

Sarah didn't say a word.

My mother leaned close and whispered, "The twins aren't speaking with each other at the moment. Sorry about that, it's made things terribly awkward."

She wasn't kidding. I had to sit in the middle seat of the minivan with Jessica, because Sarah and Jessica, both sixteen, refused to sit in the middle row together, and the back row had been taken out, the space filled with boxes of God only knew what. Sarah sat up front, staring out the window, refusing to acknowledge anyone.

Jessica looked at Sarah, then crossed her arms, pouted, and stared out the window.

Oh, boy. This was going to be a fun vacation.

"So, uh, Mom, what have you been up to?"

"Oh, not much. Mostly worrying about you girls, and waiting hand and foot on your father while he writes his memoirs."

"He's still working on them?"

She met my eyes in the rearview mirror for just a second, then said, "Yes, he's still working on them." She didn't sigh, or roll her eyes or anything else, but it seemed like she wanted to. "How is school? We hardly ever hear from you, Alexandra."

I shrugged. "I've been really busy; lots of commitments this year. I'm sorry I haven't been in touch more. I'll try to do better."

"Your father and I would appreciate that."

Jessica blurted out, "Carrie's home. And she has a new boyfriend."

Sarah turned around in her seat and glared at Jessica, then muttered, *"God!"* and turned back around.

I raised my eyebrows. "Carrie has a boyfriend?"

My mother interjected, "It seems so. But she's being very mysterious about it. She's been home two days, and she's constantly texting, or giggling on the phone, or locked in her room talking on her computer. It's really undignified for a woman her age."

I grinned, suddenly happy for the first time in days. "That's great, Mom!"

"Well, of course you would think so," she said, putting me neatly in my place.

I guess I wasn't in the mood, though, because I replied instantly, "What's that supposed to mean, Mom?"

She sniffed. "You know we've not always approved of your choice of boyfriends."

I shook my head, keeping a smile plastered on my face, and looked out the window. "Yes, Mom. I know that."

"Well, let's not get into all of that, it's all over now anyway."

I took a deep breath. If she only knew.

For the first time since I'd seen her, Sarah spoke. "What happened to Dylan, anyway? I thought he was cute."

"Sarah!" my mom said, in an injured voice.

"Well, it's true, he was cute. Didn't he join the Army or something?"

I replied, my voice calm, trying desperately to not reveal anything. "Yes. He was badly wounded in Afghanistan."

"Oh dear," my mother said, her voice low.

I looked at her, trying to discern from her expression what she knew. My dad emailed Dylan when he was in the hospital. *He* knew. He saw how miserable I was last year, and he knew, and didn't tell me.

"Did you know about that, Mom?" I asked.

She shook her head. "No, I'm so sorry. I hope it wasn't serious. Even though we didn't really approve of him, he's a nice boy."

"It *was* serious," I answered, still trying to gauge her reaction. We were sitting at a red light, and she met my eyes in the rear-view mirror. "He nearly lost his leg. And his best friend was killed."

She went pale, then whispered, "I'm so sorry, Alexandra. I know you cared for him."

I exhaled and sat back in my seat. My mother was, as usual, inscrutable. She could have made millions as a poker player, though I suppose being the wife of a diplomat was much the same thing.

This drive was excruciating. I took my phone out and turned it on. I knew it was too much to hope for, but maybe there was a message from Dylan. Or an email. A text. Something. Some clue that he'd really heard what I was trying to say. Anything.

As soon as the phone turned on, text messages started coming in. None from Dylan, but one from Kelly, and two more from Sherman, then one from Carrie.

Kelly's message was short and to the point:

Call me the moment u land. Urgent.

Sherman wrote:

Alex, do not turn on the news. Call me or Carrie ASAP.

Carrie's was far less cryptic, but but no more helpful.

If mom wants to stop for lunch or something, pretend you are sick. Tell her u need to come home. Now. Call soon. Luv u.

Oh, God. What was wrong? Did something happen to Dylan? What was wrong? I blinked back tears, trying to erase them before my mother saw.

"Your phone sounds like a car alarm, dear, what's wrong?"

"Oh, nothing," I replied, trying to keep my voice from shaking. "It's just Kelly, I'm going to give her a call real quick, okay?"

"Alexandra..." my mom started to interject, but I was already dialing. Jessica gave me an odd look, eyes falling to my hands, which were shaking, but I brushed it off.

Carrie answered on the second ring.

"Alex?"

"Hey, Kelly," I said a fake cheery voice. "I got your text messages. What's this about a paper?"

Carrie immediately understood what I was up to. She asked, "Are you in the car with Mom?"

"I am! On my way home right now, we'll be there soon."

Mom looked over her shoulder at me as I said that and said, "I thought we'd stop for lunch."

I frowned. "Hold on, Kelly." I said to my mom, "Mom, do you mind if we skip lunch? I don't really feel well; the flight and all."

Sarah shook her head and muttered something, then crossed her arms over her chest.

"Oh, hon, your sisters were so looking forward to it!"

Oh, God, why wouldn't they all just *shut up and go away!*

"Please, Mom? I think I need to lay down for a while."

"Of course, dear."

"Thanks," I said, then put the phone back to my ear. "Sorry. What was that you were saying?"

Carrie's voice came through loud and clear. "Alex, don't freak out. All right? Whatever you do, I want you to stay calm."

"Of course," I said, the fake smile still plastered on my face. My cheeks were starting to hurt.

"Okay. Listen... this morning, Randy Brewer was arrested."

I closed my eyes, and felt my knees draw up involuntarily. I didn't want to hear it. I didn't want to hear what she was going to say next.

"He followed a girl home from a bar last night and raped her."

I gasped, and my hand flew to my mouth.

"Alexandra, are you all right?"

"I think I'm going to be sick," I whispered. My stomach was cramping, hard, and I couldn't stop the tears that started to run down my face.

"Alexandra, put down the phone. What did you eat on the plane, do you have food poisoning?"

"Kelly," I whispered to my sister. "I'll send you that email. So sorry, I gotta run, not feeling well."

She replied right away. "I'll be here waiting for you, Alex. I'm so sorry."

I hung up the phone and laid it on seat next to me. I leaned forward in my seat, arms crossed over my chest, trying to hold in the emotions that were threatening to overpower me.

"Alexandra, do you need to go to the doctor? I think we need to take you to the doctor."

"No!" I shouted.

The silence following my shout was deafening.

My mother screeched to a stop a second later, after almost missing a red light. She looked up at me, her mouth open, eyes wide. I'd never yelled at her before.

"I'm sorry," I whispered. "I just... need to lay down for a little while, okay? Please?"

I pulled my legs up in my seat and lay my face against them, wrapping my arms around my legs and trying to shut everything out.

All I could think about was those minutes last spring, when I'd been unable to get up, unable to defend myself, as he ripped my shirt, before his roommates intervened. And then it happened again, only this time it was Dylan who'd protected me.

I hadn't been able to protect myself. What Randy had done made me feel worthless. Less than worthless. Like a piece of meat, to be touched and poked and prodded, pushed into position. The more I thought about it, the more I wanted to vomit.

Because if I had reported it last spring, he'd have been in jail a long time ago. That girl wouldn't have been raped. Dylan wouldn't have been arrested.

It was my fault.

After a couple minutes of dead silence in the car, I felt a poke in my left side. I looked up, and it was Jessica, one eyebrow raised, looking suspicious.

She was holding my iPhone, with the call history displayed. The last call, of course, was to Carrie's cell phone. When I'd been pretending to be talking to Kelly. A couple of calls to Kelly below that, and fourth on the list in my call history: Dylan. The contact picture next to his name was a picture taken two weeks ago, of the two of us.

CHAPTER FOURTEEN

Mistakes happen (Dylan)

I was sitting in my room, writing, when the knock on the door came. I was in limbo: going to trial for aggravated assault in a few weeks, unsure where my future was going, rejected by Alex. For hours, I'd been sitting here in the dark, listening to quiet music, occasionally writing thoughts in a new journal.

I was trying to make sense of my life. Trying to make sense of what had happened with Alex. Trying to make sense of *us.*

The only conclusion I could come to was this: Alex was absolutely right. I'd spent three years avoiding telling her how I really felt. I'd spent three years not opening up, not telling her I loved her, not telling her that I wanted to spend my life with her.

No wonder she wasn't willing to take me back.

I was so deep in thought that at first I didn't hear the knocking. I had a pen in the corner of my mouth, chewing on it, a habit I'd tried to break for years, but came back when I was tense.

The knock came again, and I looked up, focusing outside myself for the first time in hours.

I stood up, shouted, "Coming!" and padded across the carpet in my bare feet.

When I opened the front door, I sighed in frustration.

It was two police officers, the same two officers who had arrested me.

"Can we come in?" Alvarez said.

Funny... looking at her now, I realized she was kind of pretty, even in the severe uniform.

"Of course," I said. As if I could stop them.

I led them into the living room, and said, "What can I do for you? Am I being arrested again? Do I need to call my lawyer?"

Both of them shook their heads, and Alvarez looked a little sheepish. She got to the point pretty quickly.

"Last night, Randy Brewer followed a girl home from the 1020. A neighborhood girl, not a student. He broke into her apartment and raped her. Her roommate—a cop—walked in on the scene."

I closed my eyes, and muttered, "Jesus Christ. Is she okay?"

"No one is okay after a sexual assault," Alvarez replied. "How is your girlfriend?"

"We broke up. But I'm giving her hand-to-hand combat lessons."

Alvarez grinned. "I'm sorry to hear you broke up, but good for her."

I nodded.

"Look," Alvarez said. "For what it's worth, we just wanted to say... we're sorry. The DA's dropping all charges against you, in light of what happened. I imagine your lawyer will be in touch. They'll have to have a hearing, and you should be clear."

I nodded. "Thank you," I said.

"We were just doing our job," said the other cop. The one who had harangued me about rich kids the night of my arrest.

"I get it. I was a soldier. Mistakes happen."

They stood up, and I shook their hands, and they walked out of my life, hopefully forever. Wow. For the first time in years, I found myself wanting a drink, badly.

Screw that. Instead, I changed into sweats, and walked out into the early evening to go for a run.

I took the same route Alex and I always took. But I had to admit, it lost its charm without her.

Before I reached the end of Central Park, I cut west across West 72nd to Riverside Drive, then started back up the Hudson River Greenway. Something about the crowded evergreens, even in the icy cold night, was calming.

I was a soldier. Mistakes happen.

It was interesting how easy it was to forgive the cops for arresting me instead of Randy, but I couldn't forgive myself. How many times had I blamed myself for Roberts's death? How many times had I blamed myself for all of the blood and pain and shit that came down on my life after the day I lost my temper and shot up my laptop?

God, was I that fucking neurotic? It wasn't just that: I'd blamed myself for a lot more. After all, I was the kid who blamed himself for dropping the brownie mix that resulted in his mother getting a beating.

But see, it wasn't my fault. It was *his*. I didn't hit her. My son of a bitch fucking father did that, over and over again, and in the end it didn't really matter what I did or didn't do. All I did was my best to protect myself. To protect myself from the hurt. To protect myself from parents who were at best unreliable. And let's face it... the fact that my mother finally kicked him out, joined Alcoholics

Anonymous and cleaned up her life during my freshman year in high school? It meant a lot. But it didn't change what had happened to me. It didn't change the defenses I'd set up for myself.

In the end, Alex suffered because of that.

Our last night in Israel, she'd pushed me to tell her what I wanted. Were we going to commit? Were we going to stay with each other, despite the distance, despite the pain of separation? Or would we go home, go back to dating other people, slowly forget each other, slowly forget our first loves, and that would be the end? Maybe think of each other every few years, or run into each other somewhere ten years later and reminisce for a few minutes?

What she needed from me three years ago was a clear declaration of what I felt. And I knew exactly what I wanted. I wanted *her.* Nothing else. But to say that would make me vulnerable, in a way I'd long since learned wasn't safe. The one thing I wasn't about to do was risk losing myself in another person.

And that's the reason I lost her. Simple as that. We let it drag on, not one thing and not the other.

Why can't you tell me how you feel? she'd cried out.

Because you might hurt me, was the only answer.

It was time to jettison that fear. I might not be the perfect guy for her. I was a little crazy; I was a disabled vet with some serious mental problems, a little brain damage and plenty of other issues. But I also loved her. And even if it killed me, even if she shot me down so hard I never approached another human being again in my life, I was going to do whatever it took to let her know exactly how I felt.

One can always hope (Alex)

*S*omehow we made it to the house without me completely falling apart. Jessica handed me the phone, silently, and I wiped my call history on the spot. But I knew that before very long, she'd be coming to me with questions.

Questions I didn't really have answers for. My parents were going to be insufferable enough this trip. They always were. They wanted to control every aspect of my life, from the classes I chose to the boys I dated, and they'd never liked Dylan. Worse, for much of high school, they'd unsubtly pushed me toward a series of stuck-up boys from families they knew: rich boys, boys with futures. Randy Brewer was one of those boys, and when we ended up going to Columbia together, they'd hinted more than once that Randy would be a good choice for my future.

If they only knew. I was certain that Randy's parents, two of the most arrogant, stuck-up people I've ever met in my life, would do everything they could to bury the charges, to avoid publicity, to scrub their son's life clean. *Oh God.* My stomach cramped again.

Dylan was strong. He was brave. But was this going to be too much for him? Would it be one last thing that would finally push him over the edge?

And I had just rejected him yesterday!

I didn't think it would be possible to hate myself more than I did at that moment.

Of course, just getting into the house was a production. Jessica and Sarah finally spoke to each other as we got out of the car. They started bickering over some nonsense, and my mother got flustered trying to get them to stop.

Our house was a four-story townhouse, two blocks from Golden Gate Park, overlooking San Francisco. Our garage was on the ground floor, then the living room, kitchen and dining room just above. My bedroom was on the fourth floor. Getting up there meant stopping in the library first to greet my father, who was sitting in front of his computer when I walked in. He was a tall man, with a gaunt face accentuated by a neatly trimmed beard. Even here at home, he dressed formally, in a tie and sweater.

He stood, held his hands out and hugged me.

Jessica had paused at the door when I walked in, and said, "Alex isn't feeling well today."

"Oh no," he said. "Do you need to go to the doctor?"

I shook my head. "Just something I ate. I'm going to go lay down for a bit; I'll be fine."

"Well then. Go get some rest, and we'll see you at dinner."

"Thanks, Dad."

I escaped with no further questioning, then dragged my bags up to the fourth floor.

Thirty seconds after I entered my room, Carrie joined me, closing the door behind her.

"Tell me what happened," I said.

She sat down on the bed, facing me.

"Kelly called me. She saw a news report about Randy... apparently last night he met a girl at the 1020, and followed her home. And raped her. "

"Oh, God," I whispered. "It's my fault. If I'd reported it last spring..."

"Alex, stop that. Randy Brewer is to blame. Not you."

I put my arms around myself and leaned forward, breathing slowly and carefully, trying to keep myself together.

Then I blurted out, "Dylan talked to me yesterday. Told me he'd had second thoughts, and asked me to take him back. Just yesterday."

She put her arms around my shoulder, and I whispered, "I told him no, Carrie. I told him he'd have to... somehow prove himself. Prove that he's serious, and won't leave again."

I began to shake with great wrenching muscle spasms, gasping for air as I sobbed on her shoulder.

"Oh God, I screwed up, Carrie. I told him no, right when he needed me the most."

She whispered, "There's no way you could have known this was going to happen, Alex."

"It doesn't matter what I knew or didn't know. What matters is he's all alone, and I'm *stuck!* I should be there with him, and instead I'm stuck in San Francisco for ten days."

She whispered, "You've got friends who care about you. We can get a message to him through Kelly or Joel, okay? Just keep it together. You're going to have a tough enough time with all this, without Mom and Dad getting on your case."

"Screw them," I said.

Just then my bedroom door opened. No knock. Nothing.

It was Jessica.

"You can stop whispering," she said. "I heard everything."

Carrie sat up straight, shock on her face. "How dare you?" she demanded, sounding at that moment exactly like my mother.

"I knew she was lying to us in the car. And then I saw her call history. She was calling you instead of Kelly."

"So you just come and eavesdrop? Is that why you and Sarah have been at each other's throats? Because you've lost all sense of decency?"

"Jessica," I gasped. "You *can't* say anything to Mom and Dad about this."

She closed the door, and pulled the chair out from my desk and sat down. "I won't. Of course I won't. I can't speak for Sarah, of course. But I want to know what happened. You and Dylan are back together? And Randy Brewer raped someone? What have you been *doing* in college, Alex?"

I started to laugh and cry at the same time, uncontrollably, and then, before I knew it, I spilled the entire story.

All three of us heard the creak of the stairs at the same moment. Quickly I wiped my face, then dived under my covers. Carrie and Jessica were still arranging themselves when there was a knock on the door, and then it opened.

It was my mom.

"Alex, I brought you some soup... *oh!*" she said, surprised to find my sisters with me. She recovered quickly, and set the soup on my desk. "This might help you feel a little better. I see your sisters are taking care of you?"

She phrased it like a question, but what she meant was, *I see you and your sisters are gossiping?* or something similar.

Carrie stood, straightened her blouse, and said, "We've got her all taken care of, mother. You don't need to worry about anything."

"Well, then," my mother said, looking a little nonplussed. "I'm so glad to see at least some of you are getting along. Do you think you'll be up for dinner tonight, Alexandra? Your sister Julia and her horrid boyfriend won't be in town until tomorrow night, so it's just the six of us. I can't imagine why they aren't staying here, we have plenty of room."

Carrie gave our mother a level look. "He's her *husband*, mother."

Mom gave a quick, insincere smile, as if to dismiss Carrie, and said, "One can always hope."

Carrie responded with a sniff, and said, "You're right, Mother. I can't possibly imagine why they wouldn't want to stay here with us."

My mother stiffened her back and looked at Carrie imperiously. "You are impertinent. If you're going to take that tone with me, I'll just go downstairs. Perhaps Sarah would like some company."

Jessica rolled her eyes and said, "Like *that* will happen. Good luck with her, Mom."

My mother left in a huff.

Carrie took a deep breath, as if shaking off something, after mom left. Then she turned to Jessica and said, "All right, spill it. What's going on between you and Sarah? You two are usually inseparable."

Jessica frowned. "She's gone bipolar I think. Or schizophrenic. Wearing black always, like some goth girl. And … God, I hate her! She kissed Mark Wilson, when she *knew* I wanted to go out with him. I heard she let him feel her up. At *school!* I could kill her."

Carrie's jaw dropped. "When did all this happen?"

"She's been like this since school started."

"Wow. I bet it's been pretty tense around here, with you two at each other's throats."

"It's not *my* fault."

"Well, whatever is going on with you and Sarah, you can't say a word about Alex and Dylan to anyone. You understand? This is serious."

Jessica turned to me.

"Do you love him? Dylan?"

I nodded. "Of course. I… I always have."

She looked serious. "Then I'll do whatever I can to help. It might not be much, but I promise."

I smiled at her, and said, "Thank you."

What Happens Next? (Dylan)

"*S*o what happens next?" I asked.

Ben Cross, my lawyer, said, "Well, we go in there. The DA will tell the judge they're dropping the charges and why. Then the judge will dismiss the case."

"And that's the end? I get my bail money back and we're done?"

"It'll probably take a couple of days to get the money back."

"And no more travel restrictions?"

"No more anything, Dylan. Look... it was one thing for them to prosecute you for assault when there were no other witnesses to the sexual assault on Alex. But after this? The DA knows exactly what will happen to him if they proceed to try a wounded combat vet who stopped a rape, when the police let the rapist go. I mean, seriously. This was as bad a case of negligence as I think I've ever seen. They looked at you... with your build, your angry face, your scars, and they looked at Randy Brewer, spoiled rich kid, and they jumped to absolutely the wrong conclusion."

I shook my head. "All right. I don't really care about all of that. I just want to make sure I'm free to travel, and that Alex is safe. Nothing else matters."

Ben nodded. "For what it's worth, Dylan... even though the circumstances are horrible, I'm glad they got the guy."

The hearing was an anti-climax, taking all of fifteen minutes. Unfortunately, it looked like it was going to take a couple days to free up my bail money. Whatever. I had places to go, and people to see, and still a few thousand dollars in the bank. Time to spend some of it.

CHAPTER FIFTEEN

It's about me (Alex)

When the alarm on my phone went off at 5:45 a.m., I quickly rolled over in bed and silenced it. I didn't want to disturb the rest of my family. With any luck I could be out and back before anybody else woke up.

I slipped into sweats, and, perversely, put on Dylan's grey Army T-shirt, which hung like a tent on me. I'd appropriated it from him a couple weeks ago. Something about having it here was comforting.

Then I tied on my running shoes, put my hair in a messy and quick pony tail, and slowly made my way down the five flights of stairs to the front door, trying desperately to avoid waking anyone.

It was dark and quiet outside, but not the bitter cold I'd grown accustomed to running in. For a second, as I stared out at the darkened street, I felt a tinge of fear. I was used to running in the dark with Dylan. I didn't realize until now how much safety that afforded me. Safety to run through a city park before the sunrise.

Safety to feel free, not afraid of a random mugger or rapist or other dangers in the dark.

As I stretched on the sidewalk in front of our house, I pondered the fact that I'd never felt that kind of fear before. And the irony was, it wasn't a random stranger who had attacked me. It was someone I'd known since middle school. That's what the statistics say, of course. The person most likely to rape a woman is always someone she knows.

But the reality was far different from the statistics. The reality was confusing, frightening. It was being too drunk, feeling almost sick, and having someone hold you down while they stuck their hand up your shirt. It was feeling hot, unwelcome breath against my neck. It was the stink of alcohol on his breath as he said, "You know you want it, why are you struggling?"

I didn't want it. Not from him. Not then, not ever.

I set out, running first up 23rd Avenue to Fulton Street, then along the edge of Golden Gate Park. There was little traffic this early in the morning, especially during a holiday week.

I worked myself up to a good pace, keeping an eye out for dark corners, places people could hide. Because like it or not, Randy Brewer had changed the way I looked at things. I was making a lot of progress, learning self-defense from Dylan, but I still had a long ways to go. I was going to get there, though. With him or without him.

One thing I knew for sure. I was done being a victim. Never again would anyone hold me against my will, not if there was anything I could do about it.

As I reached the end of Fulton Street, I ran toward the beach, then down the sand to the water. The waves were coming in, loud, and I turned and ran along the sand. I'd never run at home before.

There was something freeing about it, something that made me feel bigger than I'd ever been before.

It was in Dylan's hands now. I loved him. I knew what I wanted: to spend my life with him. I wanted us to move forward, together, into a life that we could have together. But I needed to know that he was ready to do that. Something in him always pulled back. And all I could do was hope and pray that he'd move past that.

If he didn't, though, I was ready to accept it. I'd always love him. I'd alway care for him. But if I had to say goodbye, I was strong enough to do it now.

I ran for an hour and a half that morning, only finally slowing down a dozen blocks from my parents' house, coming to a walk two blocks away. I was drenched in sweat, my hair running wet down my back, and I felt absolutely fantastic.

Quietly, I unlocked the front door and went up the stairs.

As my foot touched the landing, I heard my mother's voice. So much for an unobtrusive entry.

I sighed, then walked into the kitchen and said, "Good morning." I walked over and kissed her on the cheek.

Carrie was sitting at the kitchen table, a cup of coffee in front of her. It was so rare that I saw her disheveled that the sight of her now, in a bathrobe, her hair a mess, made me smile. I walked over and kissed her on the cheek, too, then poured myself a giant glass of water and began drinking.

"Good God, you haven't been out running, have you?" Carrie asked.

My mother looked stunned.

"Alexandra Charlotte Thompson, the sun is barely up, and you've been out running in the dark? What's gotten into you? Don't you know it's dangerous to run alone at night in the city? Strange men and rapists and God only knows what are out there."

I finished off my water, then quietly replied, "It's not the strangers you have to worry about, Mom, it's the people you know."

Carrie gave a little gasp, then took a sip of coffee to cover herself.

My mother, her face screwed up in consternation, changed the subject. "Where did you get that T-shirt? It's ... truly ugly."

I smiled. "I feel much better this morning. Thanks for asking, mother. I've been out getting my exercise, and I think it's going to be a fantastic day, don't you?"

"Oh, dear," she said. "Of all the children I raised, I never expected to find one of them turning into an athlete, and a morning person at that."

Carrie burst into laughter. "You can't control everything, Mom. And personally, I think it's nice to see Alex happy."

I was getting my coffee when my mother conceded. "I suppose that's true. You *were* rather miserable to be around last summer. I suppose you're finally over that Dylan person."

I looked at my mother, and said, "It's not really about him, Mom. It's about me."

Mystified, she said, "Well, drink your coffee then. And... it's nice to see you smiling."

I sat down and took a sip of my coffee, and my mother wandered off.

Carrie gave me a sideways look and said, "Nice T-shirt. Know where I can get one?"

I knocked her in the shoulder, and said, "Get your own. I'm sure you can find a soldier who'll leave one lying around somewhere or other."

She smiled, then said, "Ray's coming to Houston next week."

I grinned. "I know."

She smiled back. "I don't know how serious we are. But... well, he's a nice change from the guys Mom and Dad are always pushing on me. And the guys in my PhD program?" She mocked a shudder. "Hopeless."

I whispered, "Can you imagine Mom and Dad's reaction if we both got serious with former soldiers? Dad would finally keel over from a heart attack."

"Maybe it would be good for him. You know he's warming to Crank."

I shook my head. "Not possible."

"Anything is possible, Alex."

I shrugged. "Let's hope so. I... I just wish I knew what Dylan is thinking."

She said, "He's going to have to figure it out on his own, I think."

"I know. I'm just afraid... I'm afraid that he'll pull back. That this is really the end."

She put her hand on top of mine, and squeezed gently. "What will you do if it is?"

A wave of sadness swept over me.

"I'll grieve," I said. "And then I'll move on with my life. I'm not going to let him tear me up again like that. If he wants me... he's going to have to go the distance this time."

Go get her (Dylan)

"Come on, Sherman, answer the damn phone," I grumbled. On the fifth ring, he picked up.

"The fuck?" he said as greeting, his voice thick with sleep. "It's not even noon yet. This better be good, Paris."

"Sherman, I need your help."

He sighed. I could hear it on the other end of the line. *Paris needs help* again.

"What is it, man?"

"Is Carrie in San Francisco? Do you know how to get in touch with her?"

"Yeah, she's there, hanging with the family. Why?"

"Okay," I said, breathing a sigh of relief. "I need you to do me a favor. Talk to her. Ask her to make sure Alex doesn't go out anywhere tonight."

There was silence at the other end of the line for a moment as he processed that, then he said, "Dude, where are you?"

"I'm at JFK airport."

"Gotcha. You're gonna make a run for it?"

"Yeah."

"Good luck."

"I'm going to need it."

"Yeah, you aren't kidding. Go get her. I'll call Carrie, and we'll make sure Alex is home. What time's your flight get in?"

"Seven p.m. And then I gotta catch a cab across the city... it'll be eight or nine before I get to her place, probably."

"You know where you're going?" he asked.

"Yeah, I've been there."

"Dylan. That was two years ago."

I shrugged, even though he couldn't see it. "Some things you never forget, Sherman."

"Jesus, you are such a girl, Paris. Whipped."

"I am," I said.

"Seriously, man. Good luck. Maybe Carrie can help lay some groundwork. I know she's hoping for you, too."

"Thanks, man."

"What are friends for? Go get your flight."

We hung up, and I looked up impatiently at the information board. Twenty minutes before my flight woud begin boarding.

I'd been to her parents' house before, of course. The summer after senior year of high school. That time, I'd taken Greyhound, a three-and-a-half-day bus trip all the way across the continent. It was a strange, strange, trip. Seven days on a bus, to spend only four days with her.

The thing was, even after taking that trip across the country to see her? Even then, I'd still not gone the final distance. I'd not said what I really wanted to say, which was, "Why don't we go to the same college? Why don't we think about maybe getting married some day?"

Of course we were too young. And I was too scared. And I never imagined the twists and turns that my life would take.

When the flight started boarding, I was nearly first in line.

A nice young man (Alex)

This was going to be the dinner from hell, I thought.

I was sitting on the couch, reading the New York Times on my phone. I should have known better. The headline in the metro section told it all: *Columbia University Student arrested for rape.* The picture beneath the headline showed Randy Brewer, in a mug shot. His eyes were wide, startled almost, in the photo. Somehow the combination of the circumstances of the photo, his unshaved face and unkempt hair, and the wide eyes made him look crazy.

Julia and her husband Crank (yes, that's really his name) were running late, eliciting a spate of critical comments from both of my parents while we waited.

Carrie and I sat together in the living room while; she was busy texting Ray Sherman. Carrie wore a stark and attractive pair of black pants and a rose-red blouse with ruffles. I wore a sleeveless white dress with a light sweater embroidered with roses, and Jessica sat with us, also reading messages on her phone, wearing a nice print dress. We made the very picture of a happy family, all absorbed in our separate electronic devices.

Sarah, on the other hand, was wearing torn black jeans, a ripped T-shirt sporting the album cover Beyond Redemption by what I think was a death metal band, *The Forsaken*. Or maybe it was the other way around? Not my normal choice of music, so I wasn't sure. The picture on the shirt was guaranteed to spark a reaction from my parents: what appeared to be a screaming, bloody skull. She glared at anyone who came close.

My father hadn't come out of his office yet, but my mother had passed back and forth between the kitchen and the office several times, each time stopping to tell Sarah to change her clothes before dinner. The response was sullen silence, and no action.

I'd have been happy to go into the kitchen to help out: my mom looked stressed, and I knew she was crazy busy putting together a dinner for eight. But if one of us were to go into her private preserve, she would completely blow her lid. That's my mom: a complete martyr, angry at the lack of help, but refusing it when offered.

The doorbell rang, and the tension snapped. I put away my phone, feeling reprieved.

"I'll get it!" shouted both Jessica and Sarah.

They glared at each other for just a second, then Jessica sat down again, crossing her arms across her chest in a mirror of the look Sarah had worn only moments before. Sarah thumped loudly down the stairs in her combat boots.

Two minutes later, she trailed my sister Julia and her husband Crank back up the stairs.

Before you think that Julia was adopted, or kidnapped by aliens as a child, I should tell you that she graduated as Valedictorian of her class at Harvard. Up until the age of twenty-two, she followed the same script the rest of us: the script written by my father and directed by my mother, the script that we rarely deviated from. Carrie was following it by going for her PhD. I was following it by majoring in pre-law at Columbia. Undoubtedly the twins would follow, though time would tell if Sarah's sudden rebellion was a permanent fixture. If it was, the Thomas household was not going to be a happy place for the next couple of years.

The day after Julia graduated from Harvard, she announced that she wasn't going to graduate school, and had decided to go to work as manager for her boyfriend's band, Morbid Obesity. True to form, she'd been quite successful in her chosen career. Between Crank's guitar licks and over-the-top lyrics, and her business acumen, the band had become a phenomenon in the alt-rock scene. They weren't particularly hurting financially, but I know for a fact that my parents absolutely hated the direction Julia had taken with her life. And I admired her, very much, for her independent spirit.

Julia came in wearing what was, for her, formal dress: a pair of tight black jeans, heels and a sweater. Crank was... well, Crank. His jeans were faded and torn, his T-shirt looked like it was old before I was born, and his hair was spiked and multi-colored. Crank was a perfect example of why admiration and desire are two very different emotions. How my sister managed sex with her husband without injuring herself was a complete mystery.

That said, I loved them both and was delighted to see them.

As they came up the stairs, my sisters and I crowded around them, exchanging hugs.

Julia, who is ten years older than me, smiled when she saw me, then engulfed me in a lingering hug. "Oh, Alex, it's great to see you."

"You too, Julia. I've missed you so much!"

Crank came over and gave me a hug, and I was careful to avoid puncturing myself. He turned to Sarah and said, "The Forsaken? Awesome. How you been, punk?"

I was fascinated to see Sarah blush a bright red. "Oh, I've been great, Crank, you?"

He shrugged. "Ehh, you know, just playing my guitar and hanging. Your big sister keeps me in line."

Sarah stumbled over her response as Julia looked on, amused. She was fourteen when the twins were born, so had missed much of their growing up. It was painfully obvious that Sarah had a huge crush on her husband.

At that point my father came out of the office.

"Julia, it's delightful to see you," he said, and hugged her. Then he turned, as always a little disconcerted, and held his hand out.

"Crank," he said, his tone reserved.

"Hey, Dad," Crank said, grinning, and engulfed my father in a huge bear hug. Carrie and I exchanged wide-eyed glances as Julia snickered a little.

As they parted, my father's eyes landed on Sarah. I waited for the explosion.

"Sarah," he said, "Please go upstairs and change before dinner."

Defiance immediately flared in her eyes. "But Crank isn't wearing anything formal! I don't want to wear a dress," she said.

"If Crank were wearing a dress, I might ask him to change. But what Crank does is immaterial, young lady: Crank is a professional, who supports himself, and can choose to dress as inappropriately as he chooses. You, on the other hand, are still a junior in high school. And I'm paying for your food and housing for at least the next few years. Therefore, if I tell you to go change, you will go change. I will say nothing more on the matter."

She threw a glare at my father, muttered, *God!*" then stomped upstairs, her combat boots shaking the entire house.

"Well, then," my father said, in the same oddly formal tone and language he always used. "Let's move ourselves into the dining room, and perhaps Sarah might join us later."

He led the way into the dining room, with Julia and Crank behind them, and me and Jessica trailing. The dining room was set with my mother's best china, which my father purchased for her during the two years we lived in Beijing, just before I started high school.

My mother entered from the other direction. She'd set the table, brought the food in, then stepped out to "freshen up" as she liked to say. Now she hovered over us, providing unfortunate stage directions.

Normally, my father would be at the head of the table and my mom at the foot. Crank and Julia would be closest to Dad, facing each other. Carrie and I would take the center two seats, and the twins would be relegated to the foot of the table with our mother.

Unfortunately, it seemed that the war raging between the twins was throwing a twist in things. To minimize conflict, Sarah sat to my left next to Dad, and Carrie to my right. Across from us, Jessica was next to Mom at the far end of the table from her twin, and Crank and Julia were next to each other.

Julia met my eyes as we sat and gave me a warm smile. Crank, sitting across from the blank seat where Sarah would be, grinned and launched into a conversation with my dad about *foreign policy* of all things. If he'd opened up a conversation with a brain surgeon by talking about the complex anatomy of the brain, I wouldn't have been more surprised.

What happened next surprised me more. My dad answered, not only in a calm and reasonable tone, but actually seemed to warm to the gesture. Within minutes, the two were buried in a discussion of Chinese economic policy, which was my father's specialization.

"Well," my mother said to Carrie. "Isn't this nice? We'll give Sarah another minute or so, then go ahead and serve."

Rather than add a third conversation to the table, Julia and I both stayed relatively quiet.

Then Sarah walked in.

She'd changed into a dress, as my father had asked. But I didn't think this was what he had in mind. First of all, she'd also put on makeup. Thick black eyeliner, black eyeshadow, and black lipstick. She was wearing the black lace dress she'd worn to Uncle Rafael's funeral two years ago, and which decidedly didn't fit her now. Her breasts were practically spilling out of the dress, and it was quite obvious she was wearing a black lace bra underneath. She still wore her scuffed combat boots.

I caught my breath, waiting for the inevitable explosion. My father gave her a cutting glance, but said nothing, instead choosing to return to his conversation with Crank, who brought up the problem the band was having: massive quantities of counterfeit memorabilia being manufactured in China and sold worldwide. The problem had really taken off after the band's second album went gold.

"I understand a little piracy, you know?" Crank was saying. "I've been dirt poor. But this isn't like a couple of bootleg albums— it's whole factories turning out stuff that looks just like ours. And that's a big part of how we make our living."

My dad nodded. "Really, this was one of the biggest issues I worked on during my last few years with the Foreign Service. It's part of the reason I was appointed to the ambassador slot. But I have to tell you, the Chinese government really isn't interested in cooperating."

Sarah was crushed. It was clear enough that she'd expected— even wanted—the explosion. Instead, both my father and mother ignored her. As she walked into the room and made her way to her seat, Jessica sneered at her.

Sarah shot Jessica a dirty look and took her seat to my left. But Crank fixed it with one simple and easy motion. He gave Sarah a big, obvious wink, and a smile. She instantly brightened, much to my parents' displeasure.

"Well then," my father said. "Let's eat. Adelina, will you say grace?"

We took each other's hands, and my mother said a short prayer. All of us said, or mouthed "Amen" at the end.

My father began to serve the meal. I leaned toward Carrie and whispered, "Dad and Crank seem to be almost… chummy?"

She whispered back, "I think Julia gave Dad a look at Crank's bank account since the latest album."

I snickered, and my mother said, "Girls, I realize you've been away in college, but you must remember your manners."

I nodded an apology. Carrie was 26 years old, a PhD candidate at a major university, with a significant amount of published research already under her own name. I was certain that she was never referred to as a *"girl"* except here at this table.

Somehow it didn't sting much to be included under the same umbrella as Carrie.

"Adelina, I heard the most disturbing news this morning. The Brewer's son Randall has been arrested."

I froze in place, and underneath the table, Carrie gripped my thigh. Across from Carrie, Jessica's eyes widened.

"Good lord!" my mom said. "What happened?"

"It seems he's been accused of rape. I'm sure it's not true… it's probably one of those situations where they had too much to drink, and she regretted it after."

I froze, unable to think, unable to breath.

"It's terrible," my father said. "After dinner, I think it would be appropriate for us all to go visit the Brewers. It's been a long time since we've seen them, and it would be good to pay our respects, and offer what help we can."

"No." The word escaped from my mouth.

Carrie gripped my thigh tighter, and Jessica's mouth dropped open. Julia and Crank stared at me, and my father did a double take. It was my mother, however, who responded.

"Alexandra, I realize that despite our efforts, you never liked Randy. But you will behave courteously at this table. And you will go with us, as your father has suggested. He's a nice young man. I'm sure this accusation is nothing more than scurrilous."

I leaned forward in my seat, my stomach cramping, and found myself grinding my teeth, trying to hold back a rage I'd never before experienced. I could feel it sweeping down my body, and for a second I wanted to smash something, anything.

"Your mother is right," my Dad said. "If it were up to me, you would have abandoned your puppy love for that soldier years ago, and married Randy."

I was paralyzed. I couldn't say anything, because if I started, I was never going to be able to stop. I reached out, tried to pick up my wine glass, and ended up spilling it instead. Now everyone in my family was staring in shock at my strange behavior, or, in the case of Jessica and Carrie, just plain horror.

My mother jumped to her feet, running to grab several napkins, which we used to sop up the spilled wine. As we finished, my father said, "I trust this conversation is over."

I shook my head.

"Excuse me?"

I looked at him, no longer able to hold it all back. A tear streamed down my face.

"I don't go anywhere near his parents. Or his house. Don't even say his name to me. Do you understand me?" The bitterness and rage in my tone surprised even me.

"I don't understand," my mother interjected. "Whatever has gotten into you, Alexandra? Randy Brewer is a perfectly nice young man—"

"Oh, for Christ's sake!" Carrie cried out. "Can't you see what you're doing to her? When did you two become so clueless?"

"Well, I don't..." my mother started to say, then trailed off.

My father's tone was ice. "How dare you speak to us in that manner, young lady?"

Carrie turned on him, rage in her eyes. "How dare you continue hurting your own daughter like that?" she shouted. "Can't you see it? Even if you don't know the details, can't you see the pain you're causing her? For God's sake, that *poor nice young man* you're talking about sexually assaulted your daughter twice!"

Oh, God. Carrie, why did you blurt that out at the dinner table? I stared in horror, meeting first Julia's eyes, then, for just a second, my father's. Then I buried my face in my hands.

"I'm sorry, Alex, I know I told you I wouldn't tell them anything. But if you won't, I will. I won't have them torturing you."

My mother, in shock, said, "Carrie, we would never hurt her...."

"You don't know what you're talking about, mother! Until you find out, can you kindly *shut up!*"

Utter silence descended on the dinner table.

Carrie turned to me, and in a faint, gentle voice said, "Alex, I know you're afraid. But we're your family. Let me tell them."

I buried my face in my hands and began sobbing. Sarah moved over and put her arms around me, burying her face and hair in my shoulder, and Carrie put her hand on the other shoulder and said, in a very quiet voice, "Randy tried to rape her in his room last spring. But his roommates intervened. She didn't file a complaint, or tell anyone. But a couple weeks ago, it happened again. He assaulted her at a party. Dylan Paris pulled Randy off her, and they fought, and... Dylan beat up Randy. He ended up being charged with assault. But you need to hear me, father. I know you don't like Dylan. I know you never have. But he saved your daughter. So you better swallow your dislike. You better just keep it to yourself. Because when the police charged Dylan with assault, they just let

Randy Brewer go. And so he went, and followed a girl home, and raped *her.*"

I started crying harder.

"I didn't know," my father said.

I clenched my fists and looked up at him, rage rushing through me. "*You didn't know?* You knew Dylan was injured last spring! You knew the reason he didn't write me was because he couldn't, because he was so badly hurt! You knew! And you didn't tell me!"

My mother gasped. "Alexandra, you don't know that."

"Yes, I do! Dad wrote him. He told Dylan to stay away from me, that he wasn't good enough for me." I turned on my father. "When the man I loved was in the hospital near death, about to lose his leg, you kicked him while he was down! And you lied to me about it! Don't talk to me about what you knew or didn't know, Dad. Don't *ever* talk about what you knew."

Dad's face had gone completely pale. Julie looked at him, disgusted, and said, "Is this true?"

Dad closed his eyes, then nodded once. After a long time, he muttered, "Perhaps I was wrong."

Carrie took my hand, and said, "You can be sorry all you want, Dad. But right now, this family has a problem. Because Dylan and Alex love each other. And you've got a choice, dad. You can keep up your pretense, keep trying to script all of our lives right down to who we love. Or you can get behind your family and support them. Alex, let's go upstairs. You don't need this right now."

She pulled me up and I followed her, still in shock.

"Stop," my father said. Carrie's back went straight, and I turned, facing him.

He looked different. Smaller somehow. Less sure of himself. I took a deep breath, ready to shout a denial in his face, when he said, "It's true? Dylan... he... intervened and stopped Randy from assaulting you?"

I nodded, slowly.

He returned my nod, then said, "Well. It seems I've misjudged your young man. And... Alexandra... I'm sorry. I'm not going to ask for your forgiveness. Not now. But... I will ask you to allow me a chance. To make up for it."

My lower lip started trembling uncontrollably, and he blurred in my vision. I looked at my dad, and nodded. That was all he needed to hear. He came around the table and took me in his arms. Then I felt my sisters surround me, even Jessica and Sarah, as they all put their arms around me in a huge hug. I felt the muscles in my body go limp as my family held me up, enfolding me, somehow making the pain smaller, more manageable.

What seemed like a long time passed before we broke up, then resumed our seats at the table. My mother had tears in her eyes, as I did.

Crank smiled at me, then playfully said, "That's what I love about family dinners. There's never a dull moment."

That's when the doorbell rang.

My mother muttered, "Dear God, who can that be? Dinner will be ice cold before anyone gets more than a bite."

"I'll get it," Sarah said, just as Jessica stood up. They looked at each other, the first look I'd seen between them in two days that wasn't a glare. Then, wordlessly, they both left the dining room.

Two minutes later, I heard Sarah call from the front door. "Alexandra! You need to come to the door!"

CHAPTER SIXTEEN

On index cards? (Dylan)

"This is it," I told the cab driver.

The meter said forty-five dollars. *Christ on a crutch.* I passed the driver the money, then opened the door and slid out. I only had a small backpack on me. Leaving New York, I figured a change or two of clothes would be more than enough. This might be a very short trip, after all. And even if it wasn't, I could always figure out something for clothes. Waiting for an hour to get luggage when I could be here instead? That was something else entirely.

I stared at the house in front of me. Jesus, how it had intimidated me when I visited her two years ago. Working-class me, growing up in crappy apartments with drunk parents. How did I dare to chase after the rich daughter of an ambassador with a five-story house in the heart of the most expensive city in America? I was nuts.

Not nuts enough, not then. I'd let her life, her father, my past, all of it, intimidate me.

I took a deep breath, then stepped forward and firmly rang the doorbell.

Jesus, I hoped Sherman had pulled it off and kept Alex here. It would not go well for me if her father answered while she was out at the movies or something.

I heard the pounding of footsteps, and then the door opened suddenly, and I was faced with two open-mouthed sixteen year olds.

"Hey," I said uncomfortably. "You must be Sarah and Jessica... I don't know if you remember me, I'm Dylan."

The darker one, who wore a tight black dress that would make a nun blush, put her hands over her face in shock. The other one, in a white dress, said, "I remember you. And yes, I'm Jessica."

Her twin, Sarah, turned around and shouted up the stairs. "Alex! You need to come to the door!"

I grinned. "Awesome. Um... I don't know if I'll see you again, because I don't know if Alex is going to tell me to go to hell. If she does... well, it was great to see you."

Jessica leaned forward and whispered, "Are you here to try to get her back?"

I nodded, and she said, still quietly, "She still loves you."

I closed my eyes and said, "Thank you."

Then I saw her, slowly descending the steps. I felt tension grab me by the throat. She was wearing a white sleeveless dress, embroidered with roses. Around her neck was a heart pendant necklace that I'd given her two years before. That was possibly a hopeful sign. Her mouth was slightly open as she approached the door. I could see she was cautious. She was afraid of me. Afraid I'd hurt her again.

I took a deep breath, drinking in the sight of her, then said, "I um... I was hoping we could talk, so I thought I'd drop by."

Her mouth quirked up in a half smile on the right side. "You thought you'd drop by? From four thousand miles away?"

"Distance wasn't really a factor in my mind."

She looked at me, and whispered, "I can't do this if you're going to hurt me again, Dylan."

Oh, God. I swallowed, then said, "Will you just... hear me out? Please? If I'm wrong, and you tell me to go away, then I'll go, and you'll never have to hear from me again if you don't want to. But I'm begging you, Alex. Give me a chance. Just hear me out."

"Okay," she said in a small voice. She looked at her twins and said, "Can you tell Mom and Dad to continue dinner without me? And not to come down here under any circumstances?"

The twins nodded simultaneously, and Alex stepped outside, with me, and shut the door behind her. She took a seat on the front stoop, carefully sweeping her dress under her.

"Sit down," she said, indicating the space next to her on the stoop. I nodded. My heart was thumping. I couldn't remember the last time I'd felt like this, unless it was the night I first asked her out an eternity ago. Christ, I was terrified. What if she said no? What if she told me to go to hell, to get out of her life? Or worse, what if she said yes, and then we ended up hating each other later?

Damn it, I thought. *Stop that. Just do it. Go for it. For once in your life, step the hell out of yourself and say what you mean.*

"Okay," I said. "Look, I've been doing a lot of thinking, a lot of writing. About what you said. About... me, and who I am. About you. About us."

She nodded.

"I'm not very good at this, Alex. But... it's something I have to do, okay. I've got some things to say, and I'm asking you to hear me out, without interruption, all the way through."

"Without interruption?"

I nodded. "I don't want to lose my train of thought, all right? Please? When I get to the end, you can ask me questions, or tell me go take a hike, or whatever, all right?"

She gave me a sardonic smile, and said, "Okay. You set the rules. No interruptions."

"Thank you," I said.

I took a deep breath, then felt in my pocket, filled with index cards. I took them out.

"Wait," she said, grinning, her eyes bright. "You wrote this down? On index cards?"

"I don't want to forget anything," I said. "I told you, I'm not very good at this. So I wrote some notes to keep me focused, okay?"

"Wow," she said. She had a half smile on her face.

"You're interrupting."

"You haven't started yet."

I rolled my eyes up at the dark sky and muttered, "Oh, boy. All right." I glanced at the first card. It said, *Jaffa*.

"Do you remember the night we were in Jaffa? In the Old City?" She nodded.

"Okay," I said. "That's the night I realized that I really wanted to get to know you. I saw you before that, at Hunter College before we flew to Tel Aviv. But you were so far out of my league, I didn't even know where to start. And the flight over was awesome, and well, I mean, we flirted. And that was awesome. I was very attracted to you. But when we were walking back to the Youth Hostel, and I saw that really old house. It looked like it might have been a thousand years old."

"Abandoned," she said. "I remember."

"Yeah. The thing was, I wanted to explore. And you came with me. The others were all worried. We might be trespassing or something. I don't remember what they were worried about, to tell the truth. But that was when I realized how brave you were. And... wow, I admire courage. I think that night was when I started to fall for you."

She took a deep breath, and I could tell she was just as caught in that memory as I was. She'd taken my hand as we walked through the old house. It was just for a moment, but it was a moment that still burned in my memory.

"See, courage can come in a lot of ways. It can be on a battle-field, and I've dealt with a little of that. It can be... something like you getting up every day, even after what Randy did to you, and still going back to school, going on with your life even though I know it hurt like hell. Alex, you need to know that I admire that about you. The night we left Israel, you wanted me to tell you how I felt. I didn't know how to do it, then. I didn't have the courage to do it, then. But I'm telling you now. Okay?"

She crossed her arms over her chest, and stared at me, her eyes huge, intoxicating. She nodded and bit her lower lip.

I set the card down next to me. The next one said, *En Gedi.*

I looked at her. Was she hearing me? I thought so, but that didn't mean I'd won her over yet.

"So, anyway. I know I shouldn't say this as part of what I'm say-ing, because it's going to be all sexist and objectifying and all that stuff. But I'm trying to tell you how I feel. So here's the thing... Alex, you're so beautiful, sometimes just looking in your eyes makes my heart stop. Even if I never see you again after today... even if I get to be ninety-nine years old, and have a life that goes on without you... I will never, ever forget our first kiss."

She blushed, her color going deep red, and I whispered, "You make me feel alive, Alex. We fit together in ways that I didn't imag-ine were possible. I know I'm not the most articulate of guys, so it's hard for me to say this and have it make any sense at all. But over the last few years, I'd been with a few girls. And you're ... something different entirely. Holding you in my arms... touching you... it's like plugging me into an electric socket. It's hard for me to be around you and not touch you, you're intoxicating—sometimes I'm desperate just to reach out and touch one little hair on your head."

I took a deep breath, looking her in the eyes. "If you send me on my way today," I whispered, "If you tell me to get the hell out of your life and never come back... I'll accept it. But it will be the one and only permanent regret of my life: that we never made love. That we lost our future together."

She began to tremble, and opened her mouth to speak, and gently, I placed an upright finger over her lips.

"You promised," I said quietly. "No interruptions. Let me get this out before you send me away. I'm begging you."

A tear rolled down her cheek. I don't know if she was sad, or angry, or happy, or what. So I moved on quickly to the next card, hoping desperately that she was going to allow me to continue until I was completely finished. When I set the card with the words *En Gedi* down, she picked both of them up, and held them in her hands.

The next card said, *The Rules.* As I opened my mouth to speak, she snatched it out of my hands.

I blinked, surprised, as she read the card, and her eyes immediately watered. What was she thinking of, when she saw that card? Her silly rules, her perfect rules, that had allowed us to tolerate each other long enough to fall for each other all over again?

"Alex, I love the fact that you're ... you're creative as hell. You're smart. Even after I broke your heart, you figured out a way for us to be around each other. It might have been flawed, it might have been a little crazy, but it worked. I love the games we played. I loved when we asked each other questions and took turns, and I hope we never ever stop doing that. When I'm ninety, I want you to tell me that it's my turn to ask you a question, and if that miracle happens, then my question is going to be, 'Do you still love me?' and I hope the answer will still be yes."

Tears were running down her face now.

The next card had one word on it: *Dad.*

She took that one from me too, as soon as I read it. I took a deep breath and closed my eyes, and said, "My dad used to blame me for all kinds of crazy stuff. Like the first time he hit my mom. I told you about that. And I think I blamed myself, too. I thought... if I could just be better, then maybe they wouldn't drink so much. If I didn't screw up so much in school, maybe they wouldn't be stressed out so much, and drink so much, and then maybe they'd realize that parents are supposed to remember to buy groceries."

I took a deep breath, and said, "So... when we met, I guess part of me still blamed myself for things that weren't my fault. And it made me... so cautious. So afraid. So I held myself back. I never let you know exactly how I felt, because that's part of how I control situations, it's part of how I keep myself safe."

Oh God, I thought, taking a deep breath. This was hard. I looked her in the eyes, and my eyes were watering too. "Alex, I don't need to keep myself safe from you. I don't want to keep myself safe from you. You mean too much to me. I'd rather have a lifetime of heartache, from you breaking my heart, than even imagine my life without you. Because a life without you wouldn't be a life at all."

She was huddled over, her arms wrapped around her shoulders, looking as if at any moment she was going to burst into tears. I looked at the next card, and it said *Running*. She reached out, and took it from me.

I whispered, "Alex, you make me want to push myself harder. You're right... the thing is, I never believed I was good enough for you. I never believed I measured up. But here's the thing: you believed in me. No one has ever done that before in my life. And being around you, it makes me want to push myself to be better. It makes me want to be the best person I can. It makes me want to work, to deserve to have you in my life. You don't just complete me. You make me a better person. When I'm with you, every single moment, I want to work to become someone you look up to, someone you admire, someone you can love. And I want to do the same for you. I want to protect you, and make you feel safe. I want to support you, whether you continue on to law school like your parents have pushed you, or if you decide to do something else entirely. If you took on a life of running a roadside concession stand, I'd want to be right there beside you, supporting you, no matter what you chose. I want to protect you, but I don't *just* want to protect you... I want to help you learn to protect yourself. I saw the pride and happiness in your eyes when you threw me on the ground during our self-defense practice the other day, and I think that may have been one of the happiest moments of my life."

She took a deep breath, as if she was going to say something else, and I said, "Wait... one more." My voice dropped to a whisper. "Just one more, okay? I have to get this out, because it scares the hell out of me."

She nodded, and I took up the last card. It said, *The Ring*.

I swallowed, my throat suddenly dry as hell. She reached out and put her hand on the card, hesitated, then took it from me. When she saw the words on it, she started to shake uncontrollably.

I couldn't talk any louder than a whisper.

"The night we left Tel Aviv, you were right to yell at me, because I couldn't tell you how I felt. I was too afraid. And then I came out here to San Francisco, and I thought I was ready, but I wasn't. We had a wonderful time, but it was tense, it was scary, and in the end, I went away and didn't say it. And then I was in the Army, and you were in your senior year of high school, then at Columbia, and the time never seemed right. And then ... well... we both know what happened."

I took a breath, and then said, "So, I'm going to tell you what I wanted to say that night in Tel Aviv, what I wanted to say here in San Francisco. What I've wanted to say every day since, but couldn't."

My heart was thumping in fear. Where did she get the power to do this to me, I wondered, to make me terrified that she would break my heart, to make me so damn afraid that I'd lose her?

I'd rather take the risk and lose her forever than not say it at all.

"Alex, that night in Tel Aviv, what I wanted to say was this: Let's pick the same college. Despite the challenges in our life, and the distance, and everything else, let's make a choice. A choice to be together. I can imagine a life without you, but it seems impossibly dreary, imperfect, unhappy."

I took a deep breath, then whispered, "Alex, I don't want to date you. I don't want you to be my girlfriend. I don't want us to be together for just a little while. I want you forever. I want us to look at each other, and say we love each other, and decide to be together forever. Alex.... I want to spend our lives together. If we ever decided we want to have kids, I want it to be me and you."

I was trembling as I reached in my pocket. This time I didn't take out a card. I took out a tiny jewelry box. She gasped, and tears began running down her face freely. Her hands flew up to her face, covering her mouth, as I spoke again.

"Alex... you are what makes my life worth living. Will you... will you consider becoming my wife? Will you let me commit my life to you? Please?"

She stared at me, eyes wide. I think she was in shock, and I half expected her to run. I was shaking from tension and fear.

Instead, she took the box from me, and slowly, ever so slowly opened it. Then she looked at me; she looked me in the eyes, and she whispered, "You're crazy, Dylan. Oh, my God, you proposed marriage with index cards? No one else in the world would do that. Yes. Yes, yes! If you ask me a thousand times, then every single time I'll say yes."

Both of us moved, quickly, and I was holding her in my arms, and looking her in the eyes. I took a deep breath, then slowly, gently leaned forward and kissed her. Her lips tasted like salt, salt from her tears, and then our kiss turned passionate, hungry, and I pulled her to me as her arms went around my neck, and at that moment, I'd have done anything to stay right there, like we were, forever.

Asking them not to bite (Alex)

When Dylan's lips touched mine, it was as if the sun had just risen. My entire body responded to his, melting into him. If we hadn't been sitting on my parents's front steps, I might have ripped his shirt off right there. As it was, we kissed for what seemed a thousand years, his lips pressing hard against mine, and my mouth opened, at first just a tiny bit, then I sucked in a breath as his tongue gently, playfully touched mine.

Then the front door opened.

Dylan and I broke our lips away from each other, but I wasn't letting go of him, no matter who it was.

Jessica had opened the door a crack, and was blushing to the roots of her hair. I looked at her, a huge stupid grin on my face, and she returned it.

"Um, sorry to interrupt, but mom and dad want to know if you are planning to come back up."

"We'll be right there," I said. "Give us just a minute."

"Okay," she said. "See you."

She shut the door.

"How much does she know?" Dylan asked.

"All of it," she said. "Jessica and Carrie. I'm afraid your timing ... well...let's just say we had a huge blowout at dinner. My parents know about Randy."

He nodded. "And... their reaction?"

"We got it worked out. In fact... my father apologized. Sort of."

His mouth jerked up in a half smile. "Hard to imagine. Your dad is ... formidable."

"Are you ready for this?"

"Yes," he said. He took a deep breath, then said, "Alex, with you by my side, I'm ready for anything."

"Then... let's go upstairs."

Hand in hand, we entered my parents' house and went up the stairs.

My family was still arranged around the dinner table, the food mostly finished, having after-dinner coffee.

The room went silent when I entered with Dylan.

I took a deep breath, then said, "Mom, Dad... you remember Dylan Paris."

My father did something at that moment that stunned me. Something so out of character that I wouldn't have believed it if I hadn't seen it.

He stood up, and walked around the table, approaching Dylan, and held out his right hand to shake.

"Dylan... it is good to see you. And... as my daughter put to me in the strongest terms earlier... I owe both of you an apology. Thank you for protecting her."

I could see Dylan was just as shocked as I was. He took my father's hand, and said, "Thank you," quietly.

"We've got something to tell you," I said, very quietly. Carrie's eyes were as round as saucers, and I could see they were focused on my left hand. Where I wore the ring Dylan had just given me.

"Mr. Thompson... Mrs. Thompson," Dylan said. "I think you know that Alex and I... we love each other very much. I flew out here today because... well... I've asked Alex to marry me. And... she's said yes. I'd like to ask you for your blessing."

Oh. My. God. What was he thinking? Asking my parents for their blessing was insane. It was like jumping into a pit of snakes and asking them not to bite.

But once again, I was surprised. My father smiled, but it was my mother whose reaction really shocked me. Tears began running down her face, and she stood up, and walked to Dylan.

She put her hands on his shoulders and said, "Of course you have our blessing. And... I hope I can be the first to say, welcome to our family."

Oh, God. I was going to start crying again. Jesus, bring on the waterworks. My sisters started crying out, crowding around us, hugging me and Dylan. My sisters of course had to see the ring, and I felt my hand yanked up into the light, and I couldn't stop smiling. My cheeks were starting to ache, but this time it was a real smile, and I didn't mind.

Then my father broke down, and hugged Dylan, too.

Carrie whispered in my ear, "You've given me hope. They've accepted a punk rocker and a former soldier. Who knows who might be next?"

I grinned, and I knew then that things were going to be okay.

CHAPTER SEVENTEEN

You're not finished yet (Alex)

Six days later, we were home.

I say home because, as much as I love San Francisco, and the house where I grew up with my parents, New York City is my home now. With Dylan.

For those six days, my parents made Dylan welcome, letting him stay in the guest room on the fourth floor. The two of us spent our early mornings together, running, or him teaching me hand-to-hand combat techniques. Sarah actually joined us for that, and I could tell she thoroughly enjoyed it. I quietly mentioned to my Dad that she might enjoy enrolling in self-defense classes. Both of the twins would benefit from it.

The day after thanksgiving, Crank and Julia left for New Zealand, to return to the band, which was on tour. Carrie flew out two hours later for Houston, where Ray Sherman was going to meet her for a week-long visit.

The twins, of course, had another year of high school, but hopefully that year would be tolerable for my parents. Jessica and Sarah were inseparable again.

I got to take Dylan out to dinner with Kelly and Joel, and show off my ring. We'd set the date for July, and the wedding would take place here in New York. Our families would have to come to us.

That night, I went with Dylan back to his apartment. When we got back, we sat on the bed in his room and I said, "I want to play a game."

He looked at me, a wry grin on his face, and said, "What?"

"Okay. You get to go first. Ask any question, but we don't ask about the past. Ask questions about the future."

Dylan looked at me, then said, "Okay. The future." He took a deep breath, then said, "Where do you see yourself five years from now?"

I thought for a moment, then said, "Here in New York. I've finished law school, and I'm working for a nonprofit organization, I think. Maybe working with rape victims? And you're here. We've got a gorgeous apartment, with high ceilings, and huge windows, but not much space, because working for a nonprofit, I wouldn't be making much money probably."

He chuckled, then said, "I like it. Your turn."

"Same question," I said.

"Well... to be honest, I've been thinking about changing my major. I love writing, but I'm not sure it makes sense to study literature. It makes more sense to study life. I see myself working as a counselor, for the VA. Social worker. Trying to help vets who get screwed up in the head like me."

"You're not screwed up."

He nodded. "Oh, I still am, Alex. I'm working on it, but it's not going to go away overnight. Or even this year, or next. I still have nightmares about when we got bombed. I still... see it sometimes. I just don't like to talk about it."

I pulled my arm underneath me, resting my head on it, and said, "You'd better get used to talking, Dylan. You're not putting me through that again. I expect both of us to be ready to talk about what's going on inside."

He closed his eyes, and whispered, "Alex, I'm sorry. I don't know what I was thinking."

"Yes, you do," I replied.

"Okay... well yeah, I guess I do. I thought I was protecting you."

"There's such a thing as over protecting. There's such a thing as ruining your present because of worries about the future. You understand what I'm saying?"

He nodded.

"What is it you're really afraid of?"

"Turning into my father."

I sighed. "Tell me more about him. You almost never talk about your father."

He grunted. "Like I said, there's things I don't like talking about."

"Oh, I figured that out a long time ago, Dylan." I put my arm down, and rested my head on his shoulder. He was warm.

"Dylan," I said, screwing up my courage. "Listen to me. And listen closely. I love you. With all my heart. I'm willing to spend my life with you."

I could feel his heart beating as my hand rested on his chest, right next to his hand. Then he said, his voice a low growl, "I'd rather die than lose you again."

I closed my eyes, and tried to focus. "Then you have to talk to me. You have to tell me what you're thinking and feeling. You don't decide for me what the best way to protect me is, Dylan. Don't you dare. You ask me, you don't decide for me. Am I clear?"

He looked at me, and I could see I was getting through. He smiled, actually.

"I'm serious, Dylan. I'm a big girl. I can take whatever you throw my way. But I damned well better be informed."

"You have no idea how much you're turning me on right now."

I burst into laughter and slapped him lightly on the shoulder.

"What? I told you how I felt!"

"Will you promise me?"

He nodded.

"Not good enough. I want to hear it."

He took a deep breath, then looked into my eyes, and said, "Alex, I promise. I'll tell you what I'm thinking, and feeling, no matter how fucked up it is. I won't... I won't try to protect you from me. Not without talking about it."

His voice caught, and we looked in each other's eyes. Those beautiful blue eyes that caught me from across the room three years ago and never let me go.

"Please forgive me," he whispered.

"I do," I replied. Then I leaned forward and kissed him, very softly, on the lips.

He closed his eyes, and I could feel his body tensing, hungrily, and I found myself biting his lower lip. He moaned softly, and for me, that led the floodgates loose. I pushed myself closer, pressing my body against his, and lowered my lips to his neck. He was clean-shaven after his shower, and I could taste the faint tang of his aftershave.

I was breathing heavily, suddenly so wound up with desire I wanted to rip his clothes off on the spot. I looked up at him, met his eyes, and whispered, "Something very important was interrupted Saturday night a few weeks ago."

He smiled, and our eyes met, and he sat up, then leaned close to me and very slowly kissed my neck, my chin, below my ear. Each kiss sent a small shudder through my body. As his tongue and lips worked their way down to the top button of my shirt, my hands moved of their own accord, underneath his T-shirt, running up his strongly muscled ribs and around his back.

He began to unbutton my shirt. As he stopped at each button he kissed the skin he revealed. I lay back, arching my back as his lips slowly worked their way down my chest, then my stomach. Each pause was excruciating, and I let out a loud moan as he lightly breathed against the underside of my ribcage.

"You have no idea how beautiful you are," he murmured.

"Tell me," I whispered.

He slid his hands up to my shoulders, and I slightly lifted myself off the mattress as he slid my shirt off. He kissed my shoulder and said, "You're like looking at a sunset on the beach," then began working his way across to my other shoulder, stopping at the base of my neck.

"Hmmm..." I said.

"Sometimes you're so beautiful I have to shade my eyes just to look at you," he murmured.

At that, he slid his left hand behind my back and awkwardly undid the hooks in my bra. I slid the bra down my arms, and he brought his mouth to my right breast and kissed first the underside, then slowly worked his way to the nipple. I almost screamed at the sensation, as he quietly said, "You were so beautiful when we met I was terrified to talk with you."

I closed my eyes and shuddered as his lips worked their magic, now moving toward the button on my jeans. He paused there, and said, suddenly and soberly, "Alex, stop, I have to tell you how I feel right now."

My eyes popped open.

"*What?*" I said.

"Just kidding."

I growled at him, and he carefully undid the zipper and I slid my jeans down my hips and kicked them off onto the floor.

I heard him gasp. Meeting his eyes, he whispered, "I've been waiting three years to see you like this. I just want to look at you, drink the sight of you in."

I stretched, then said, "You're not finished yet."

He chuckled in a low voice, and said, "No. Not yet."

Then he brought his lips to my navel and began kissing again, working his way down. He slid my panties down around my hips, kissing me everywhere, his hand gently caressing the side of my hip, down to my calf.

I was absolutely alive with sensation, every nerve ending in my body crying out for relief as he slowly kissed and licked all the way down one leg to the calf and my feet, then began working his way back up the other leg.

Oh. My. God. I was going to scream with pleasure or frustration or both, and then suddenly his mouth touched me *there*, and I really did think I was going to scream. I'd never experienced such intense sensation and pleasure, and I felt my hands grip the blanket, bunching it up in my fists as I gasped.

"Oh, God," I cried out, leaning my head back, my eyes rolling up. I almost started to cry at the intense pleasure of it, and didn't even realize that even as he was doing it, he was working his own clothes off of his body, until he suddenly stopped. I wanted to cry out, *Don't stop!* until I realized he was working his way back up, kissing my navel, the undersides of my breasts, my ribs, my neck, then my mouth.

"Are you sure you're ready for this?" he whispered.

I couldn't talk anymore. I just nodded, frantically, and put my arms around his waist and pulled him to me, and suddenly he was inside me. I let out an involuntary cry, because it *hurt*, and he paused, watching me, waiting.

I bit my lip and nodded at him, wanting to say *go* but I couldn't say anything at all. Then he moved again, and the pain of our separation, the heartache, the arguments and questions and complications—everything was washed away in that moment of intense pleasure that was so amazing it hurt.

I wrapped my legs around him, crossing my feet behind his back, and dug into his back with my nails, and at first he moved so slowly that I wanted to cry out in frustration. When I thought I couldn't go on anymore he would stop, and smile, looking at me. He was drawing it out, stopping himself so we didn't have to stop.

I didn't ever want to stop, but I didn't want to go slowly any more. I pushed at his chest, rolled him over, and straddled him, our chests together, and brought my lips to his as my hips pushed against him. Then we both cried out, one right after the other, and I felt my whole body shaking and shuddering. I grabbed his shoulders, then collapsed against his chest, my pulse thumping in my chest.

We were silent, just breathing in and out slowly. We twined our fingers together, and I lay against his chest, listening to his heartbeat.

Slowly I slid off of him, and curled up at his side, then rested my head on his shoulder. He turned his face toward me, and I could see his eyes were watering.

"What's wrong, Dylan?" I asked.

"Nothing. Nothing at all. It's just that... if you had asked me, three years ago, what my single, secret, biggest dream was... well... this is it. You and me, Alex. You've managed to make it all come true."

I slowly kissed him, then we lay there, talking long into the night, about our shared dreams for our future. And I drifted off to sleep, knowing that after all this time, all the complications and pain and separation, that somehow we'd managed to work our way through it, and that together, we'd face our future, and our dreams, with smiles on our faces and courage in our hearts.

THE END

Playlist for Just Remember to Breathe

Beautiful, Christina Aguilera

Green Eyes Make Me Blue, Dead Cool Dropouts

Playing for Keeps, Dead Cool Dropouts

Keep Holding On, Avril Lavigne

Linger, The Cranberries

Fifteen, Taylor Swift

Fully Alive, Flyleaf

I'm Sorry, Flyleaf

What Doesn't Kill You (Stronger), Kelly Clarkson

Love the Way You Lie, Eminem feat. Rihanna

Bleeding Love, Leona Lewis

Love is a Beautiful Thing, Group 1 Crew

Did Ya Think, The Veronicas

Lolita, The Veronicas

Give Your Heart a Break, Demi Lovato

Together (feat. Jason Derulo), Demi Lovato

Don't Speak, No Doubt

It's My Life, No Doubt

Sign Your Name, Terance Trent Darby

Long Live, Taylor Swift

Angels, Moon Dust

Breath (2 AM) (Acoustic Version), Anna Nalick

Breaking the Girl, Anna Nalick

Innocence, Avril Lavinge

Coin-Operated Boy, The Dresden Dolls

Feedback

Thanks for reading Just Remember to Breathe. If you'd like to contact me with feedback, or want to find out when the next book will be released, please feel free to get in touch by visiting my website www.sheehanmiles.com. I'm also on twitter at @CSheehan-Miles and on Facebook:

www.sheehanmiles.com
www.facebook.com/CharlesSheehanMiles

I'd like to encourage readers to post a review on Amazon.com—whether or not you liked the book. Word of mouth is what makes the publishing world go 'round, and for independently published authors all the more so. When you post a review, it makes a huge difference both for me and for other readers.

Thanks so much!

Charles Sheehan-Miles